THE ALCHEMIST OF MONSTERS AND MAYHEM

AN ACCIDENTAL ALCHEMIST MYSTERY
BOOK SEVEN

GIGI PANDIAN

GARGOYLE GIRL PRODUCTIONS

ACKNOWLEDGMENTS

I'm so thankful for you, my readers. You're the reason the Accidental Alchemist Mysteries are such fun to keep writing. (Well, you and Dorian; that gargoyle refuses to adhere to an outline, which keeps things interesting.) I appreciate your enthusiasm, your letters, your reviews, and the fact that so many of you put *The Accidental Alchemist* into the hands of skeptical friends and tell them to read it. And special thanks to reader Amy Solko for giving me the brilliant title of this new book!

Thanks to the writers who helped me brainstorm and gave me notes on *The Alchemist of Monsters and Mayhem*: Nancy Adams, Ellen Byron, Lisa Q. Mathews, Sue Parman (aka my mom!), and Diane Vallere. And my dad, who brings me copious snacks when I'm visiting my parents in Oregon on writing retreats.

I think of myself as a storyteller more than a writer, which means my writing itself is messy in many ways early in the process, so this book wouldn't have come together without my editorial team of Amy Glaser and Trish Long.

Many of you are listening to *The Alchemist of Monsters and Mayhem* as an audiobook. For the fantastic production of my audiobooks, big thanks to my audiobook team at Audible, especially narrator Julia Motyka who brings the Accidental Alchemist characters to life so wonderfully.

And my biggest thank you goes to my husband James, who takes care of so many things while I disappear into my writing cave for long chunks of time and supports my creative endeavors in so many ways, not least of which is building me extra bookcases to support my book-buying compulsion.

I'm very lucky to have you all in my life.

CHAPTER 1

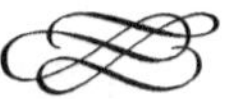

The Alchemy of Tea wouldn't be opening until tomorrow, but that didn't stop the man from peering into the window and shaking the storefront's door handle.

The "closed" sign hung prominently in the window, but so did a "Summer Solstice Grand Opening!" sign. Perhaps the man wasn't sure of the date. I had suggested to Max that he might want to be more precise with the sign, but since it was a shop selling tea and goods related to tea, he liked the seasonal theme more than a date.

"The grand opening is tomorrow," I said.

At the sound of my voice from behind him, the man gave a start and stumbled away from the door of Max's new shop. As he turned, I caught a glimpse of his profile. Tall, dark haired, handsome, and, most importantly, *familiar*.

Maybe. There was definitely something familiar about him, yet I couldn't place him.

He held a takeaway cup of tea from Blue Sky Teas next door, and was dressed somewhat formally, in a marginally rumpled brown suit but no tie. I guessed he was in his sixties. Perhaps I'd known him years ago, but without context, I couldn't place him now.

"It'll be open tomorrow morning at eight o'clock," I added.

"Not if I can help it," the man muttered.

I was too shocked to reply. He gave one last glance at the decorated front window of the shop, then hurried down the street. A splash of tea fell from his cup. I'm sensitive to herbal scents, so I recognized it immediately. Oolong. One of Blue's newest tea offerings.

A strange impulse made me consider going after him, but what would I say? He clearly liked tea, so why was he upset about Max's shop opening next door? It was a perfect fit. Blue Sky Teas, with its weeping fig tree growing in the center of the cozy café that served both herbal and traditional teas, and the empty storefront next door now filled with Max's dried tea leaves, tea accoutrements, and books about tea.

I'd been drawn to Max as soon as I'd met him right after moving to Portland, but we hadn't met under the best circumstances—he was the detective investigating the dead body found on my front porch. But now? I was ready to shout from the rooftops that I loved Max Liu.

I wondered for a moment if the angry man worked for the city in the zoning division, but I knew Max had spent months obtaining the proper permits and licenses for his new venture. He did everything by the book, which is why the shop was opening much later than he'd initially hoped.

I pushed open the door of Blue Sky Teas, my original destination. It was a few minutes before closing time, and a line of two people were waiting at the counter. About half the tree ring circle tables were filled with people. Blue would undoubtedly let them stay for a while after she flipped the sign to "closed" in ten minutes, while she cleaned up the counter area. When she'd given up her old life practicing law to open the tea shop, she stopped wearing power suits and straightening and dyeing her hair, and no longer measured every minute by the metric of billable hours. The formal hours of her café were loose guidelines at best.

Blue greeted me with a smile as I reached the counter. "Lovely to see you, Zoe. You're a perfect last customer of the day. Dorian's pastries sold out hours ago, but I'm only out of a couple of teas."

"Golden milk." The warm drink made with turmeric and other spices would keep me going for the evening I had ahead of me. It wasn't technically tea, but "Tasty and Healthy Beverages" didn't have the same ring to it as Blue Sky Teas.

"Nice choice. I've got just enough fresh almond milk to make you an extra-large cup, and I'll use that big hand-thrown mug I know you love."

"I don't have time to stay," I said as I paid, "so I'll need it to go. I'm running—"

"Nonsense. I won't make it too hot, so you can relax for ten minutes before whatever it is that's so important."

I consented. She was right. I'm almost three hundred years older than Blue, so I should have been the wiser woman. But like anyone else, sometimes I get caught up in what's going on around me and forget to be present in the moment.

I'm Zoe Faust, plant alchemist, herbalist, and proprietor of the online antiques store Elixir. I wasn't joking when I said I'm nearly three hundred years older than Blue. I was born in Salem Village, Massachusetts, in 1676. Ever since accidentally discovering alchemy, I've never been able to stay in one place for too long, but I've been based in Portland, Oregon, for the last couple of years. Here, I built a found family that made it worth the risk of staying for a while. The love and friendships I'd fallen into by both accident and design were far more than I ever imagined possible for someone who'd long since given up on finding those things ever again.

So yes, Blue was right. I could enjoy a warm and energizing drink, sitting at a tree ring table underneath a weeping fig tree, for a few minutes. Or at least, I could let myself enjoy the moment if I first figured out what was going on with that strange encounter moments before entering the café.

I leaned closer to Blue, not wanting to be overheard. "Do you remember a nervous man who ordered a large oolong tea a few minutes ago?"

"The good-looking fella about my age? Sure." Blue turned away from the counter to begin making the drink, but since it was a cozy little café, that only meant taking two steps. "He knew his tea and exactly what he wanted. Now that I've added a bunch more black and green teas to the menu, most people go for the splashier names, like gunpowder green. Why are you asking about oolong guy?"

"I saw him outside, and he was really interested in The Alchemy of Tea, but not in a good way. He's upset that it's opening."

"Seems strange for a tea lover. He was incredibly appreciative of the tea I brewed for him. He said I got the water temperature and timing exactly right."

I grinned, my apprehension melting away.

"What?" Blue blushed as she grinned back at me.

"You have an admirer. *That's* why he doesn't like it that Max's tea shop is opening next door."

"But we're not in competition with each other! I brew all sorts of herbal blends for people and provide a meeting spot, and Max will be teaching people about tea and selling dried tea and all sorts of books and merchandise so they can brew it at home and enjoy it on a deeper level. It's a perfect combination that will help us both."

"I don't think your admirer sees the distinction."

She blushed again, but tried to hide it behind her poof of gray curls as she poured my golden milk into a mug.

I headed to a tiny tree-ring table, feeling much better from both the drink and Blue's words. My gaze fell to the new window that was now in place next to the front door. A vandal had smashed the window earlier this week, and it had been boarded up neatly for a few days before the replacement was installed, good as new. I closed my eyes, felt the warmth of the solid clay mug in my hands, and breathed in the scents of the spices.

Through my closed eyes, I sensed someone close to me. I opened my eyes and saw that my respite was over. Blue stood above me, her cell phone in her outstretched hand and her worry creased into her forehead.

"You weren't answering your phone." Blue handed me hers. "Dorian called mine to reach you. There's an emergency."

CHAPTER 2

I reached home ten minutes later with the missing ingredient that had constituted the "emergency." Coconut milk from the corner market. Dorian had run out, and he claimed it was of the utmost importance to have more.

It's not like he could have run out to the store on his own to buy it. Still, he didn't have to be so dramatic about it. With the murderous plots we'd encountered lately, I didn't appreciate the word emergency being employed to describe a missing ingredient.

Dorian was running late with his baking. He and I were supposed to leave for Max's dinner party shortly, but Dorian insisted on bringing the world's best cake to accompany tea, to celebrate the occasion of Max's grand opening.

"The cake must be perfect!" Dorian cried from where he stood on a stepping stool at the kitchen counter, lifting the whisk of a stand mixer and tasting his homemade coconut cream frosting. "How can I arrive with a *gateau* with less than the proper ratio of cake to frosting?" Tonight was the night that Dorian would be meeting Max for the first time.

"You already baked a cake earlier today," I pointed out. "I saw it. It was beautiful."

"Beauty is only one aspect of food, Zoe. Surely you realize this."

He clicked his tongue. In his agitated state, his French accent was even thicker than usual. "Layers of my new cake are cooling, but it lacks frosting."

"What did you do with the old cake?"

Dorian gave a dismissive wave of his hand. "I was not paying close enough attention the first time. The proportions were not quite right. It tasted more like a fruitcake than a cake that simply contained fruits and nuts. By using both fresh strawberries and dried berries, the flavors were overwhelming, not subtle. Max would think me a monster."

I couldn't argue with Dorian on this point. It was a real danger. Not because Max was a cake snob, though. Because of Dorian himself.

I've been completely honest with Max about the fact that I'm an alchemist. It took me a while to convince him that I'm almost three hundred fifty years old, but he understood now. Dorian is an alchemist as well, which is how I met him. He sought me out because his life force was tied to an ancient book of alchemy that was slowly turning him to stone. Max would have accepted Dorian in a heartbeat if alchemy was his only secret. But it's not. Dorian happens to be a gargoyle.

Not many people know that my gargoyle housemate exists, or that his life began as a stone grotesque carved for the cathedral of Notre Dame in Paris. But Dorian now had a high enough opinion of Max's character, and knew how serious my relationship was with Max, so we couldn't put off introducing the two of them in person any longer.

Max and most of my friends, including Blue, thought Dorian was a French friend of mine who had been disfigured in an accident and was shy about meeting new people in person. He spoke with people on the phone, and in the dead of night, he baked pastries for Blue Sky Teas, making sure to return home before dawn. I've tried explaining Dorian's unusual state of being to Max in the past, but he hasn't known what to think. Was I joking, or perhaps suffering mental distress? It was time for them to meet.

"You understand how important it is for me to make a good

impression." Dorian opened his black eyes wide and wriggled his horns, making himself appear far more innocent than he was.

Dorian's gray form very much resembles the *Thinker* gargoyle that stands at Notre Dame Cathedral in Paris, except that Dorian is only three-and-a-half feet tall. But on the stepping stool he used in the kitchen, he stood eye level to me. Before he was brought to life through alchemy, he was a stone prototype for the cathedral, but proved too small. It was a good thing, too, because if he'd been any larger, I never would have been able to carry him when he transformed into stone form.

"I know it's important to you," I consented. "But you need to believe me that Max only cares about meeting you. He doesn't care about the cake."

Dorian grimaced. That was the wrong thing to say to a chef. "Max Liu will remember this night for years to come. Thus, he will also remember my culinary creations. He will truly understand how the act of baking is similar to alchemy—and how I have created the perfect complement to the tea he will no doubt serve after dinner. You understand that food served with tea must not be too overpowering?"

"Otherwise, the subtleties of the tea are drowned out."

"*Précisément.* Nuts and dried fruits are a perfect complement. Yet they alone do not make a dessert. The light, fluffy cake, with a creamy, subtle frosting will be perfection." Dorian gave a satisfied smile as he tasted a second spoonful of frosting. "*Bon.* A hint of sweetness, but it is not too strong. A perfect complement for the cake."

"Why aren't you slathering it on the cake then? We're late."

"Patience, Zoe. The cake needs a few more minutes to cool. One cannot simply 'slather,' as you crassly put it. As one cannot rush the process of alchemy, one cannot rush the steps of baking."

Which was why until I had a chef for a roommate, I focused my alchemical processes on plants themselves, not on complicated cooking. My idea of a good meal was tossing fresh or preserved ingredients I'd grown myself into a blender to make soup or a smoothie. My ingredients did all the work.

"Do you think Max will wish to become a true alchemist?" Dorian asked as he wiped down the kitchen counters, careful to avoid the gift he'd wrapped for Max.

"He already is, in a way."

Dorian clicked his gray tongue. "Yes, yes, I understand he is using his intent transforming the leaves of the tea plants into an elixir. Yet it is not the Elixir of Life."

Alchemy, at its core, is about elevating substances through transformation. Regardless of whether you're talking about elements found in rocks, plants, or oneself, the idea is to transform the impure into the pure. The quest to turn lead into gold is often the shorthand used to explain alchemy, but it's so much more than that. The three core elements of sulfur, mercury, and salt can be used in different ways to transform the impure into the pure. Sulfur represents the soul, mercury the spirit, and salt the body. Various elements and alchemical processes can be used as the ingredients to transform disposable metals into gold, a failing body into a healed one, or a disturbed mind into one of clarity and purpose.

"Max picked the name of the new shop because of the Chinese idea of alchemy," I said, "which is an Elixir of Life that gives an energetic essence and rids the body of toxins. In other words: tea."

"Does he truly have a whole section of tea blends sold as hangover cures?" Dorian inspected the clean countertop and tossed the kitchen towel aside.

"I don't know how you knew that, but yes."

Dorian chuckled. "I have very good eyesight in the dark. I saw the placard through the window late in the night. I was curious, since I knew I would not be able to visit like you and Tobias." He nodded as he checked the temperature of the cake. "*Bon.* I will frost the cake now. I will be ready to depart in ten minutes."

"A whole ten minutes to frost a cake?"

"Patience, Zoe. This will be one of the best cakes you have ever eaten." He turned and selected a proper utensil, muttering about how his culinary genius was not being properly recognized.

I stepped into my back garden, which would calm me. A tangle of vines from the summer squash mingled with tendrils from the Persian cucumbers. I picked a handful of Blue Jay Blueberries from a bush, leaving more than enough for local birds to feast on. I'd be eating dinner soon, but I've never been able to resist fresh-picked berries.

I settled into a chair on my back porch. I'd fixed up this once-falling-apart Craftsman house, and it was now the cozy home I'd always wanted. The garden might look overgrown, but my plants were thriving. I only trim back what's necessary for the health of the plants, not for curb appeal.

My phone rang as I was enjoying a burst of flavor from the ripe berries. It was Max's sister, Mina. I steeled myself for her admonishment. I knew how important this night was for Max, and Dorian and I were more than fashionably late.

But Mina's words weren't the ones I'd expected to hear when I answered.

"Dinner's off," she said. "Max's shop was fire-bombed. It's utterly destroyed."

The phone nearly slipped from my fingers as my mind conjured an image of the man I'd met earlier that day.

This was my fault. I should have taken that man more seriously. *The Alchemy of Tea will be open tomorrow morning*, I'd told Blue's admirer. His reply ran through my mind: *Not if I can help it….*

Not if I can help it.

How could I have thought him harmless?

I found my voice. "Max. What about Max?"

The connection went dead.

CHAPTER 3

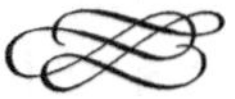

"Sorry," said Mina as soon as my phone rang once more a few seconds later. "I slipped on some of this fire extinguisher foam."

"So Max—?"

"Nobody's hurt," she assured me. "No one was here when it happened, but we're all over here now, going through the wreckage." She lowered her voice. "Max wanted me to call you and tell you the dinner party was off and you and Dorian shouldn't come over. But he's really depressed, Zoe. If you could come over here to the storefront—"

"I'll be right there." I squeezed my eyes shut and imagined the enchanting shop that Max had spent months preparing to open tomorrow morning. "And I'll tell Dorian the party's off."

"Dorian!" I called as I ran into the house through the back door. "There's an emergency at The Alchemy of Tea—a *real* one."

"Max?" Dorian scampered down the stairs. "He has suffered an early heart attack? I knew he was pushing himself too hard. And he has always been rather uptight. It is not good for one's physical health. He—"

"His shop," I explained as I donned my silver raincoat, having given up on waiting for Dorian to pause for breath before I corrected him. "Max is fine, at least physically, but someone has destroyed his shop."

"*Mon dieu!*"

"I'll let you know more as soon as I do."

I hurried out the door and jogged down the street to The Alchemy of Tea. Hawthorne Boulevard, the main street of shops in my neighborhood, was only a few minutes away from my house, so it was easier to go on foot.

As I grew closer, the acrid scent of smoke hit my nostrils. I rounded the corner and saw the once-beautiful front window of The Alchemy of Tea smashed to pieces. Max and his sister Mina stood on the sidewalk directly in front of the shop. Shards of glass covered the ground, and as I grew closer, I saw the glass wasn't only from the window, but also glass teapots and some of the jars storing loose-leaf tea. Shattered porcelain comingled with the fragments of glass. At least the iron teapots weren't broken, though they looked quite forlorn toppled and no longer artfully staged and instead lying askew in the rubble.

"It wasn't him," Max's sister Mina was saying to him as I reached them.

"It was," Max snapped. His normally well-tamed black hair was askew, as was the collar of his jacket.

"You know who did this?" I asked. Maybe it wasn't my fault after all.

"I do," Max said. He turned his furious gaze from his sister to me. "It was my father."

I blinked at him in stunned silence. Max's *father* had destroyed The Alchemy of Tea?

That's why the man who'd threatened the shop had looked so familiar. Not because I knew him, *but because he was Max's father.*

"I think you two had better tell me what's going on," I said. It was all I could do not to choke. The air was filled with dissipating smoke, and other scents mingled in the air with the smoke: burnt tea, charred cotton, and smoldering wood. I cast my gaze around the shop until I found the source of the burnt wood. One section of the shelving Max had hired local artisans to build was completely destroyed.

Max swallowed hard and swept me up into his arms.

"I'm so sorry," I whispered into his ear.

"I didn't think he'd go through with it," Max whispered back.

After Max and I realized our relationship was blossoming in spite of its challenges, I had grown close to Max's mom, Mary, and his sister, Mina. I'd also heard about his beloved grandparents, who had both passed away. But I had never met his dad. Max hadn't ever spoken of him. The only thing I knew about Andrew Liu was what I'd learned from Max's mom, and it wasn't much. She'd met Andrew in college, fallen in love, gotten married in her early twenties, and had two kids. Mary and Andrew divorced when Max and Mina were young.

I had my own complicated family issues, so I never pressured people to speak about their families. I knew Max would tell me when he was ready. But I never expected it to be because his father had physically destroyed his fledgling shop. The start of Max's second career that he'd put so much time and love into was being destroyed by his own father.

"Can you tell me what happened tonight?" I asked softly.

Max held onto me more tightly. "I should have anticipated something like this when he came to see me this week."

"Your father came to see you?" I tensed. *Why hadn't he told me?* "You knew he was here? Was I going to meet him at the dinner party tonight?" I unconsciously glanced down at my simple forest green dress. I wouldn't have dressed differently, but I still would have liked to have known if I was going to meet my boyfriend's father.

Max shook his head, still holding onto me and his breath warm on my shoulder. "I didn't invite him."

"He came to town to convince Max to not open The Alchemy of Tea," said Mina. "Since Max wouldn't listen over the phone."

Max let go of me and looked sharply at his sister. "You finally agree with me that it was him?"

"You're the one who used to be a detective." She swept her arm across the damage. "Shouldn't you be detecting?"

"Actually," I said, "shouldn't you call the police?"

"They've already been here and left," said Mina. "They bagged up the evidence: a brick used to smash the window and the flaming cloth it was wrapped in. And took a few fingerprints from the area where it looks like they ransacked the shelves."

"The person who smashed up the shop came inside?" I stepped around Mina and looked more closely at the shop beyond the smashed window. The Alchemy of Tea wasn't utterly destroyed, as Mina had initially told me, but it was bad. Very bad.

Along with scattered loose leaf tea, broken fragments of pottery and glass dotted the floor—at least what I could see of the floor. Foam from a fire extinguisher coated a swath of the interior, including the Valentine typewriter in the front window that Dorian had given to Max as a gift for the store. A soggy sheet of paper curled on top. Max had typed one of his grandmother's poems about tea on the typewriter, and the idea was to vary the poetry and quotes about tea on the type-writer, so that people who passed by the window could have their curiosity piqued.

"One of the workers at a nearby shop was the one who heard the sound of breaking glass and called the police," said Max. "He extin-guished the fire as soon as he saw smoke, but he didn't know who owned the shop, so the officers who responded had to track me down. That's why they're already gone. I was the last one to get here." He kicked one of the few shards of glass on the sidewalk. "I should have been here."

"What were you going to do?" asked Mina. "Sleep at your shop each night? I admit it's cozy—"

"*Was* cozy," Max said.

I squeezed his hand. "Where are Tobias and the Flamels? I'm so sorry Dorian and I were running late, but I assumed everyone else was already at your house."

Max and Mina exchanged a glance.

"*What?*" I asked.

"I can't say it," said Max, pinching the bridge of his nose.

"Perenelle managed to distract the officer gathering the evidence," said Mina, "while Nicolas snipped a fragment of the burnt cloth wrapped around the brick."

"Wait," I said. "You mean Nicolas *stole* a piece of evidence?"

Mina was once more the one who answered, while Max scrunched up his face as if he'd just tasted an especially distasteful medicine. "He wanted to test the accelerant himself. The two of them are back at their alchemy lab at their house. Nicolas needed Tobias to help with something, but I expect he'll be back shortly."

That sounded like Nicolas. As much as I appreciated the zest with which he approached all things in life, I didn't see what he could do better than a police lab—*unless this was related to alchemy.* And the only destructive force of alchemy I knew was backward alchemy. None of my encounters with backward alchemists had ended well. I considered the fact that my friends and I weren't dead after crossing their paths to be a success.

Mina knew that Nicolas and Perenelle Flamel were alchemists because she was the doctor I'd turned to after I rescued the Flamels from where they'd been imprisoned and discovered that they both suffered from serious injuries that needed special treatment. Mina practiced integrative medicine, so I had hoped she'd be open to the fact that their injuries weren't quite normal. She'd been as curious as I'd hoped, accepting that they were hundreds of years old, which enabled her to help them both through their recovery.

Max, on the other hand, was open to *some* aspects of alchemy. It wasn't just the name of his shop, but he was indeed practicing many alchemical processes with his handling of tea. But he hadn't fully embraced the whole package. Mina's presence was another reason we thought it was a good idea for Dorian to make an appearance at dinner. She understood there was far more to medical science than she'd been taught in med school. She was the one we were counting on to keep Max calm in case he didn't believe his eyes when he met Dorian. But, of course, that meeting wouldn't be happening tonight after all.

"Are you all right, Zoe?" Mina asked. "*Dammit.* It's the air quality, isn't it? The fire didn't really take hold, but people with sensitive lungs should all be wearing masks even with this amount of smoke." She rummaged through her bag.

"It's not the smoke." I put my hand on her arm. "It's what just occurred to me. Why did Nicolas think he needed to help?"

Max gave me his first smile of the night. In spite of the circumstances, my whole body lit up at the sight of that smile. "I assured him this had nothing to do with alchemy. My dad has serious issues, but he's the furthest thing from an alchemist. Nicolas is the most curious guy I've ever met, and he's a good scientist. I can look the other way here, because the evidence doesn't matter. I already know who did this." Max pointed to a camera on a shop across the street. "As soon as they look at the footage, I know I'll be proven right."

"It's not him—" Mina began.

"If you're not going to help me clean up," said Max, "you don't have to stay." He turned back to me. "Zoe, go home."

"I can help." I took his hand in mine and squeezed. "I've cleaned up the wreckage of setbacks like this before." I consciously avoided the word disaster, even though I knew that's what this was.

"It means a lot that you came." He squeezed back. "But I know nighttime is tough for you, especially with the stress of this mess instead of the camaraderie of the dinner party. Mina, you too. I don't expect you to help me clean up the ruins of my shop. I'm sorry I snapped at you. You're wrong, but—"

"He always has to be right," Mina said to me. "But you know that by now."

"He also knows we both want to stay and help."

Max swept both me and his sister into a hug. "Thank you," he whispered. "I love you both, you know that?"

"In spite of how wretched I was when I was a ten-year-old terror," said Mina, "I'm glad you're my big bro, Maximilian."

Max laughed and let us go. "You really *were* a terror. I have someone coming to board up the window who should be here any time now, so I don't need more help. Blue recommended the guy who fixed her café while she waited for a replacement window—he's one of her customers—and he agreed to come right away. I also need to call the insurance company. The rest of the cleanup…" His eyes fell as he surveyed the ruins of the space he'd poured so much of himself into. "I'll get started cleaning up this wreckage tomorrow."

I picked up an unscathed ceramic mug from the floor. "See, not all is lost. It'll look better in the light of day."

"I wish I could believe that."

Mina took the mug that Max hadn't accepted. "He's not telling us something. What are you going to do after we leave, if it's not cleaning up?"

"Can't you guess?" Max crouched and lifted a shard of porcelain. I cringed as I recognized one of the most expensive items he'd purchased. "Tonight, I need to find the man who did this."

CHAPTER 4

After a concerted effort, Mina and I convinced Max not to go in search of his father that night.

I wasn't at all convinced that our arguments persuaded him. It was the reality of the situation. Max's initial call to Andrew Liu's cell phone went unanswered. He didn't know where his dad was staying, and the police were in the process of pulling surveillance footage. Regardless of what made him decide not to go in search of his dad, I was glad he wasn't pursuing it that night. He promised he'd meet us back at his house a little later.

We left Max once the window repairman arrived. The cheerful young guy with a mop of black hair was dressed in head-to-toe corduroy and was bopping his head to whatever music was playing in the wireless headphones in his ears. He'd taken the call while at a friend's birthday party, but he was happy to help even though it was off hours. I wondered for a moment if it had been a costume party, but I'd seen more and more 1970s style clothing around the neighborhood lately, so it was more likely he was simply more fashionable than me. The 1950s had been my favorite fashion decade of late, but that was mainly because I could still easily find high-quality tailored clothing that was simple but lasting.

"Come on." I pulled Mina away from micromanaging the young

man's work. Though her specialty was medicine, not construction, I'd learned she was interested in minute details of all kinds. It's one of the things that made her such a good doctor.

When I first met Mina Liu, she'd immediately noticed that my white hair, which everyone else assumed I dyed to be fashionable, was real. She wasn't an expert on hair dye. She'd simply noticed that the fair hair on my arms was also white. So obvious, yet something nobody else noticed.

Mina and I walked in companionable silence to Max's house, both processing the strange events of the evening. We both had a set of keys, so we let ourselves in.

In contrast to the turbulent scene at The Alchemy of Tea, Max's house was an oasis of calm. A white couch and pewter coffee table rested on the hardwood floor. Two six-foot canvas paintings of forests covered the main wall, and a sliding glass door provided a view of Max's tranquil backyard garden.

"You really think Max is wrong that your dad is the one who destroyed the shop?" I asked as she shrugged out of her sleek black coat.

She stayed focused on the coat rack for longer than was necessary as she hung both her coat and purse on the smooth metal hook. Was she considering how much to tell me?

Mina stood a few inches shorter than my five foot six, so her hands were poised high above her head as she gripped the hook. Her silky, straight black hair flowed midway down her back, but that wasn't her most striking feature. That would be her empathetic eyes. Always taking in the details of the world surrounding her. Curious, like Nicolas, but looking for existing answers first, before she sought out new ones.

"I retract the question," I said. "You don't know the answer. How old were you when your dad left?"

She tensed.

"I'm sorry to ask, but—"

"It's all right." Mina faced me and smiled. It was a genuine emotion, albeit a sad smile. "You're right that we need to figure out what's going on. I was only ten. Max was thirteen. I'm three years younger." She turned toward the kitchen. "Let me put the kettle on. I'm sure the bruschetta and spiced nuts appetizers have gone cold, but I can fix something—"

I insisted she not worry about food, and over mugs of tea in the living room—Mina drinking caffeinated tea from the true *camellia sinensis* plant and me sticking to a lemon balm—Mina told me more about when their dad left.

"I still don't know what's real and what's the memory of a ten-year-old," said Mina as she tucked her feet underneath her on Max's white couch. "But I remember Dad being a completely different person before my grandmother died. Since my grandparents were living with us, we were all close to her, but Dad took it especially hard. It changed him."

"Grief affects people in different ways. You probably remember him grieving."

"It makes sense, because it was his mom. But Max and Mom remember him ignoring us in favor of his work even *before* my grandmother died, and he accepted that job on the East Coast without consulting Mom. But I don't."

"That all happened the same year?"

Mina nodded and closed her eyes. She breathed in the steam from her mug while I let my eyes wander from the paintings of forests to the sliding glass doors that led to Max's backyard garden. The edible portion of his garden wasn't as extensive as mine, but a few herbs and berries grew in one section, plus wild stinging nettle I'd convinced him not to remove because it's wonderful both as tea in the summer and in soup in the winter. We'd also planted a few tea plant cuttings together, but those wouldn't be ready to harvest for quite some time. The black tea in the cast iron teapot on Max's pewter-topped coffee table was store-bought, but high quality with a spicy, earthy scent that I could enjoy even though I couldn't drink black tea this late in the day.

When my gaze fell back to Mina, her eyes were open, and she was looking intently at me. "He wouldn't have done this, Zoe. Not to Max. As screwed up as my father is, I know he loves us."

Footsteps sounded outside the house. A key turned in the lock, and Max walked in.

"I'm sorry I don't get to meet Dorian tonight," he said as he hung up his jacket. "But it's for the best, because I just learned—"

Before either Mina or I could reply, a fist pounded on the door. I don't believe in summoning someone with the power of suggestion, so I knew it wouldn't be Dorian.

Max flung open the door. I recognized the man standing in the doorway. It was the same man who said The Alchemy of Tea wouldn't open if he could help it. Max's dad, Andrew Liu.

Max stood eye to eye with his father, glaring at the older man. "You have the nerve to come here, after what you—"

"Please," Andrew said. He didn't attempt to push his way past Max to step through into the house (if Dorian had been with us, he would most likely have wondered aloud if the man was a vampire unable to cross the threshold unless invited inside), but his voice was firm. "I need to explain."

Max glared at him, but stepped aside and held the door open wide for his father to enter.

"Tea?" His father said when he saw the tray of tea on the coffee table that Mina had made. "You're serving tea?"

"Here, Dad." Mina poured the rest of the pot of black tea into her empty mug and shoved it into his hand.

He nodded appreciatively and took a long sip, not waiting to test if it was too hot to drink, as if he'd been walking in the desert and needed hydration above all else. He wasn't curious about me at all. If I was being honest, that stung a little bit, but since he and Max weren't in touch, he didn't know who I was.

Banging sounded on the door once more.

"What now?" Max looked toward the ceiling as he pulled open the door.

Two police officers stood in the doorway. "Andrew Liu," said the older one, looking past Max toward his father, "would you accompany us to the station to answer a few questions?"

"What's this about?" Mina asked.

"Can you account for your whereabouts this evening?" the younger officer asked Andrew. The older one glared at his partner.

"My whereabouts?" Andrew answered. "This evening," he said slowly, then paused to finish the last sip of the cup of tea. "Yes, this evening… If you're referring to about two hours ago, I was destroying my son Max's tea shop, The Alchemy of Tea."

Mina gasped and gaped at her father. Max's jaw tightened, but he didn't otherwise react. I watched Andrew. I didn't know the man, but there was something stilted and unnatural about the way he spoke the last sentence.

Andrew held out his hands in front of him before the officer even spoke the words that followed: "Andrew Liu, you're under arrest."

CHAPTER 5

While Andrew Liu was led away in handcuffs and the police car eased away from the curb, yet another person arrived at Max's house.

"This isn't the scene I imagined returning to." Tobias Freeman looked from one shellshocked friend to the next.

"It's about time." Mina ran into Tobias's arms.

Tobias Freeman was one of my oldest friends. He and Mina had started dating after meeting this past year, but I wasn't sure how serious the relationship was. From the look of things, rather serious indeed.

They were both healers who believed in combining modern medicine with more traditional remedies. Mina was a doctor and Tobias worked in medicine in positions that didn't require as much formal training. Not because he didn't have it, but because he was an alchemist. It was easier to hide in plain sight when one moved from place to place every several years, as soon as people would catch on that we didn't age, so Tobias worked as an EMT. In his off hours, he delved deeper into various types of healing.

"Dammit." Max watched the police car drive away. "Dad didn't do it."

"Hang on," I said. "You thought your dad was guilty *until* he confessed?"

"Exactly." Max scowled in the direction the car had driven off, before turning back to me. "I know him. He was lying. I just don't know *why*."

"I was about to say I'd fix a pot of tea," Mina said. "But forget tea. I'm opening the champagne in your fridge. I'll buy you another one when we're ready to celebrate your grand opening."

Max stopped her. "Come with me to the police station to see if we can talk to Dad."

"That was your dad being taken away in the cop car?" Tobias let out a low whistle.

"You think they'll let us see him?" Mina's expression was hopeful.

"I'll call in however many favors I have to." Max stepped back inside and grabbed the jacket that he'd just taken off.

"Hang on," I said. "What were you going to tell me and Mina as soon as you got back. Something you'd learned—"

"It can wait." He leaned in to give me a kiss. "You and Tobias can stay here if you'd like. But I'm not sure how long Mina and I will be."

"We'll clean up everything that was set up for the dinner party before we get out of here," I said, "and we'll lock up."

Max gave me another quick kiss, then he and Mina were off.

"I've had many miserable days in my life," said Tobias as he closed the front door, "when people I thought I could trust let me down. But I don't quite know what to make of this one. Max and Mina's own *father*?" He peeked out the window through the white curtains, as if expecting him to appear once more.

"Max has never mentioned him to me," I said.

"Mina never talks about him either." Tobias tapped on his phone screen a few times, then music began to play.

"Accidental Life." I gave him a hug. It was Tobias's own song. And one that meant so much to me, even before I knew he was the songwriter and performer behind it.

First recorded in the 1950s, the song was written and sung by a musician called the Philosopher. Who was really Tobias Freeman. The song told the story of a man who wandered the earth for a thousand years. Tobias had written it on his hundredth birthday, five decades after discovering the Elixir of Life, when it was finally hitting him that he'd outlived everyone he loved. I hadn't known he'd become an alchemist, and he hadn't known if I was still alive either. We hadn't found each other until a little over a year ago, and it really did feel like coming home to have a good friend back in my life.

I first knew Tobias Freeman only as Toby. It was 1855, and slavery hadn't yet been abolished in the United States. I had volunteered my herbalism skills to help care for formerly enslaved people who'd escaped but were too weak to travel, until they were well enough to carry on. Toby was six feet tall and barely 100 pounds when I met him. I had thought, at the time, that he was too ill to watch my herbal preparations carefully. But I was wrong. I used alchemical techniques of both the processes to extract an herb's healing properties and my own intent. He watched and learned, unbeknownst to me. We parted ways as friends who never expected to see each other again.

But last year, when Dorian was dying and I'd reached the extent of my own alchemical knowledge, I sought out other alchemists. Not an easy task, since alchemists are secretive by nature, plus I had never been a part of any brotherhood of alchemists. For obvious reasons. I'd lost touch with my mentor Nicolas Flamel long ago as well (the only alchemist of the seventeenth century to be interested in having a female apprentice), and I hadn't known what had become of him until I was able to rescue him and his wife Perenelle earlier this year. It was a strange and comforting feeling to have so many old friends back in my life. People I thought of as family.

By the time the song ended, we'd danced our way to the kitchen, where cold appetizers and evidence of Max's dinner preparations were on display on the counter.

The playlist shifted to other songs from the 1950s, many of which I had on my 8-track tapes. My old Chevy truck still had the 8-track I'd installed. I'm good at catching up with the times in terms of my vocabulary, since I don't want to draw attention to myself, but aside from my basic laptop computer and cell phone, I'm not eager to keep up with modern technology. Definitely not what you'd call an early adopter.

"Dorian was really going to introduce himself to Max and Mina tonight?" Tobias tasted the homemade spiced nuts and offered me some before packing them into a glass container.

"We weren't late because he got cold feet. His first dried berry nut cake with coconut frosting wasn't perfect by his standards, so he baked another one, which is why we were late."

"Mina would deal just fine, but you didn't prepare Max for Dorian being a gargoyle."

"I've tried to tell him before." I pointed a wooden spoon at him. "He didn't believe me, so Dorian and I thought the best thing to do was be surrounded by alchemist friends when he introduced himself."

"A gargoyle with *fruit cake* as a peace offering?" Tobias chuckled.

I winced. "Don't let him hear you say that. It's not a fruit cake like the heavy ones made during the winter with brandy or rum. But nuts and dried fruit are a good accompaniment to tea. Dorian really wanted to make a good impression. Let's finish cleaning up. I should get back to him."

"To me?" Dorian climbed in through Max's kitchen window and slid back the hood covering his face. "Do not look so scandalized, Zoe. I am wearing my cape, so I was not detectable. You did not return home, Zoe, so I wished to see what mischief was afoot."

"How long have you been outside?" I asked.

"I saw a man who looked like an older version of Max being taken away by one grumpy police officer and one gleeful one. I waited several minutes until I was certain they were not coming back, and in case you were leaving yourself. Neither transpired, so here I am." He bowed, stretching his wings as he did so. "I am glad I heard you say you wished to return home to update me. Otherwise, I would have been quite hurt that you did not think of me." Dorian folded his cape and crossed his arms indignantly. "Have you two begun discussing the mystery without me? That is not very sporting of you."

I sighed. I had created a monster. Before Dorian met me, he thought himself above what he considered pulp fiction. But when he discovered my small collection of paperback classic detective novels and was bored enough to give them a try, he fell in love with Agatha

Christie's Hercule Poirot mysteries. The fictional Belgian detective brilliantly solved countless mysteries and spoke of the "little gray cells" of his mind assisting him. As a gargoyle, Dorian *literally* had little gray cells throughout his body, as well as an interest in solving baffling mysteries, so he had come to think of himself as a modern-day Poirot.

"No mystery," said Tobias. "Only complicated family dynamics. Max's dad destroyed his shop—he admitted it. No mystery."

Dorian frowned. *"C'est vrai?"*

"It might be true," I answered. "But Max doesn't seem to think his father is guilty." And though I didn't voice my observation aloud, there had been something odd about Andrew's confession.

"Andrew Liu confessed, Zoe," said Tobias.

"He admitted his deed?" Dorian's black eyes grew wide.

"Not only to Max," said Tobias, "but he admitted it to the police. He said, in his own words, that he was the one who destroyed the shop."

"After drinking Mina's tea," I murmured. There had been a sense of relief on his face after sipping the tea.

"Aha!" Dorian cried. "You are thinking the same thing as me."

"What are you thinking?" I like to think that Dorian and I have a special connection, since we've saved each other's lives, but it doesn't include mind reading.

"*Monsieur* Liu Sr., was worried about his son's shop opening." Dorian steepled his clawed fingertips together. "But *why?* Surely, he would not wish to destroy his son's life right before The Alchemy of Tea was set to open."

"Families are complicated," Tobias pointed out. "You both know that well. Max's dad might have … issues."

"*C'est vrai,*" Dorian agreed. "This is true, yet what if two things are true at once? *Monsieur* Liu admitted he destroyed his son's new shop. Yet Max said his father was lying. Therefore, there was something *inside this shop* that the man wished to suppress."

"Making his words both true and untrue," I said. "Whatever is going on, that tea he drank tonight triggered it. Which doesn't make sense, since tonight's tea wasn't even made from one of the teas Max was selling in the shop. It was high quality store-bought tea Mina found in Max's kitchen."

"Hang on," said Tobias. "What makes you think it's this tea at all?"

"Andrew insisted on having a cup of tea as soon as he arrived," I said. "Mina had brewed store-bought tea for us tonight—*but Andrew didn't know that.*"

"Poison!" cried Dorian.

"Not poison." I thought back to the look of relief on Andrew's face as he drank Mina's tea. "I've already sampled Max's tea. It's not poison." I'm sensitive to natural substances, including detecting poisons in smaller doses than other people would recognize.

I turned from Tobias and Dorian and rummaged through the kitchen cabinet where Max kept tea, in search of the tea he'd prepared himself and would be selling.

"You are searching for poison?" Dorian asked.

"Here," I said, yanking open a tiny tin. I recognized the scent and felt its energy. "It's the *opposite* of poison. This is the tea Max had cultivated, picked, and dried by hand."

I brewed a small pot of tea. Normally, Tobias and I wouldn't have caffeinated tea this late, but there was something strange going on here. Information was more important than sleep.

I steeped it long enough for a full brew, poured it into three porcelain teacups that I distributed, then took a sip. Then another.

I frowned. "It's just tea."

"Excellent tea," said Tobias.

"Tea for a special occasion." I breathed in the subtle, calming aroma.

"I prefer coffee." Dorian wriggled his horns. "My constitution is stronger than that of your average alchemist. Still, I am able to discern that this is high quality tea. It would have gone perfectly with my cake. *Bof.* Now I am reminded of the tragedy that Max will not get to sample my cake!"

"Another time," Tobias said.

"It is always 'another time,'" muttered Dorian. "Yet now that a mystery is afoot, it is imperative that I be introduced to Max as soon as possible. He is investigating, and I am a master investigator."

"Is he always like this?" Tobias asked me.

"You don't know the half of it."

~

Max called while I was getting ready for bed a short time later.

"What's going on with your dad?" I asked.

"They wouldn't let us see him. It's probably for the best, because I would have yelled at him and made things worse."

"I'm sorry, Max."

"What are you up to tomorrow morning?" he asked.

"I finished mailing Elixir orders yesterday, so I could be free to spend the day with you at the new shop. I'm free all day."

"What do you think about visiting the Posh and Punk Rock Tea Club with me tomorrow morning?"

"Cute name for a club. But you want to take a break to visit a group of tea enthusiasts?"

"Zoe, the section of tea leaves wasn't just damaged like I thought. One of the tins of tea is gone—it was *stolen*."

I stifled my gasp so Max wouldn't hear how concerned I was. "So it wasn't just vandalized. What else—"

"Only one container of tea was missing. I know I said I wasn't going to clean up after you and Mina left, but I couldn't help it. But it's not just the fact that it was an expensive batch of tea—it was my alchemically produced homemade tea."

"From your own tea plants." My heart ached for Max. He'd put so much of himself into that shop, but especially into the tea leaves that he was turning into specialty tea. He'd been learning plant alchemy through the tea plants he planted with his grandmother when he was a child.

"The only other people to have sampled my tea besides you and my mom were the members of that tea club. Now that I know that jar of tea was stolen, they're the most likely suspects."

"How much were you going to charge for it?" Max's tea had an elevated quality that made all handmade products special, but our whole neighborhood was lined with small shops selling homemade goods. That's one of the things I loved about it. "I didn't think you were pricing it high enough that people would resort to theft."

"I didn't. And it's not that valuable. Not in a monetary sense. But it's my hope that my alchemical processes create more elevated tea. And this group… well, they take their tea seriously."

"Enough to wreck your shop to get their hands on it instead of waiting until tomorrow to buy it? I don't know…"

"I wouldn't have thought so, but… Just come with me tomorrow. I need your help."

"With what, exactly?"

"You'll see what I mean when we get there."

I frowned, even though Max couldn't see me on the phone. It wasn't like him to be so cryptic. "Why are you being so vague?"

"I don't want you going in with any preconceived notions."

"You realize that now you *have to* tell me."

"Tomorrow."

CHAPTER 6

"The Carpathians?" I read aloud from a hand-painted sign at the base of the turnoff from the main road onto a narrow, private drive. "We're crossing over from Multnomah County, Oregon, to a mountain range in Central Europe?"

"That's only the beginning," Max answered as he eased onto the steep road.

The light held a special quality today. It was the summer solstice—the longest day of the year. We should have been celebrating the season at The Alchemy of Tea instead of entering this overgrown road that might give us answers about the destruction of the shop.

The strong sunlight of the summer morning faded away as we were enveloped by a canopy of moss-covered trees along the side of the road. We drove in silence for a few minutes, the earthy scents of the forest seeping into the car as we drove higher into the hills.

I let out a gasp as we rounded a corner and entered a clearing. A grinning Loch Ness Monster loomed over the jeep.

"Monster topiary?" I laughed and shook my head as we drove past the boxwood topiary plant, an evergreen shrub that could be shaped into detailed figures. "The plant monster is charming. I can handle eccentric people, you know."

"I met their groundskeeper, Gary, when I was here." Max

continued past the plant monster. "He's a skilled gardener and sculpts the topiary, but the owners are the ones who request the subjects."

Beyond the bush shaped to look like a sea serpent emerging from the earth as if it was water, a kraken and a dragon followed. Finally, beyond the rest of the topiary bushes was a lone bush, shaped into the figure of a man but one who was eight feet tall.

This last figure was different. It was shaped not from the more common boxwood bush used for the other topiary, but from a tree-size tea plant. It had squared shoulders, a lopsided head, and two symmetrical branches jutting out from its neck.

"Frankenstein," I whispered, the smile vanishing from my face. While the other monster likenesses had a whimsical feel, this one possessed an added eerie element. I couldn't place what it was, but he felt like he was about to walk away from where he stood.

"Don't forget to look that way." Max startled me from my thoughts as he pointed to the other side of the road, toward what looked like ruins of a stone castle. "That's Dante's Inferno."

"That's being a little overdramatic, don't you think? It's rather bewitching. I bet it's a great spot for a picnic."

"That's not my commentary. It's the name of those ruins. And possibly the whole mansion, according to some people on the internet. But I'm pretty sure Dante West only uses the name for the ruins."

"Ah." I still thought Max was being a bit unfair about not wanting to influence my impression ahead of time, until we rounded the drive and were met with a conservatory straight out of Victorian England. Now I saw why he wanted me to see this for myself. It wasn't one eccentricity. It was the whole package.

Glass windows stretched three stories high. These weren't the flat sheets of glass you'd see on a modern skyscraper, but an intricate pattern of smaller windows held together with metal bars. 'Conservatory' was such an old-fashioned word, but I didn't know of a more modern one to describe it. It was essentially a massive greenhouse, but on a grand scale and attached to the house. Tendrils of ivy and moss climbed one section of the glass walls, and even with the windows of Max's jeep rolled up, I could have sworn I detected the scent of a peaty bog like one would find in the highlands of Scotland.

"All right," I consented. "*Very* eccentric people. You didn't want me to look up whatever it is we're walking into."

"I want you to meet them first, without a biased opinion based on anything I told you. And…"

"And *what*?"

"I want you to help me sniff out the stolen tea."

"You think it could be here if one of them stole it."

"You might even be able to tell if one of them handled it in the last day, right?"

"Maybe." I'm much more sensitive to detecting nuances in plant substances than most people—like the fact that one of the branches of the elm tree we passed a moment ago was secretly rotting and needed to be cut or a larger section of the tree would likely break off during the next big storm that came through Portland—but I didn't know if I could be the miracle worker Max needed right now.

"I don't think my dad did this, Zoe. Since my homemade tea was the only thing stolen when my shop was ransacked, if we grant that my dad didn't do it, these are my main suspects."

"How did you get them together?" I asked. "Surely you didn't simply tell them you think one of the members of the Posh and Punk Rock Tea Club destroyed your shop last night, and oh-by-the-way would you all mind gathering together to have me question you, and bring the evidence with you in your handbag or pockets?"

That got half a smile. "It's their weekly tea club gathering this morning." Max pulled to a stop behind an old car covered with bumper stickers, even though it didn't technically have a bumper any longer. It wasn't as old as my 1942 Chevy truck, but it was at least thirty years old. A much fancier car was parked under an awning that sheltered it from the sun and rain.

"Which is why you wanted to come here right away, instead of assessing your shop in the daylight."

"I know I should be sorting through the wreckage." Max gripped the steering wheel more tightly. "I stopped by there briefly this morning, and I'll get back there afterwards."

"They know you're coming?"

"I thought the element of surprise was best. Follow my lead."

Follow his lead? Normally, I can trust Max more than anyone in my life. But now? Because of the emotional baggage of whatever was going on with his dad, he wasn't thinking straight. Still, this was Max. He took a step forward, and I followed.

We walked up to the side of the conservatory. It was even grander than it had looked from the bottom of the hill. Max knocked on a glass door.

"Detective Liu, how lovely to see you!" A smiling woman who looked to be in her late sixties held a skein of midnight blue yarn and knitting needles in her hands, but this was no delicate knitting project. The stitches hadn't formed a scarf or baby booties—but a creature that looked a cross between a gargoyle and a sea serpent. Her long and frizzy hair was dyed with black and white stripes, and she wore plaid pants covered in silver studs and a black lace blouse. I understood where the "punk" in the Posh and Punk Rock Tea Club came from.

"Just Max now, remember?" He gave her a charming smile.

"Of course, of course. You remembered it was our tea club meeting today. Did you bring us a special treat again?"

"Shouldn't you be at your new tea shop at this hour?" asked the man who came up behind her. Tall and broad-shouldered, his salt-and-pepper hair flowed past his shoulders. His features suggested he might have been of South Asian ancestry. He was around the same age as the woman, and he put a hand on her shoulder, barely missing one of the sharp knitting needles. He was dressed in a slightly more subdued manner than his wife. Or at least that's what I thought until I noticed his black trousers were adorned with a dozen zippers adorned with mini silver skulls. He walked with a swagger that gave me the impression he'd strode onto a concert stage many times before.

"Don't be forgetful, Dante," said the woman. "His shop hasn't opened yet. I'm Carla West," she added for my benefit. "This is my husband, Dante."

Ah. That explained "Dante's Inferno."

If I hadn't known Max as well as I did, I would have been convinced that the easygoing smile that lit up his face was genuine. Even now, I could tell Max really did like Dante and Carla. But there was a nervous edge to his expression. He didn't want to believe one of them had destroyed his fledgling shop.

"This is my girlfriend, Zoe," said Max.

I shook hands with both Carla and Dante. I didn't detect any of Max's tea, so if they were the thieves, they hadn't handled the tea this morning. They each gave me a broad smile as they shook my hand. Both of their faces were a curious juxtaposition of health and hard living. Sunspots covered Carla's thin face and neck, and neither had tried to disguise or combat their wrinkles, but they both wore the contented inner smiles of people who'd lived life on their own terms and were happy with their choices, sunspots and all.

"Do join us," said Carla. "There's plenty of tea. It's a pu-erh today."

I couldn't be certain if it was my imagination or whether Dante's calm fell away for a moment, but it looked as if he frowned as his wife invited us inside. Even if I'd imagined it, the look was gone a second later, and they led us inside the conservatory.

Stepping into the glass room was like stepping into a tropical jungle. Or a tea plantation of Munnar, India. Combined with the scent of the air, that was the climate I felt like I'd stepped into. It had been a long time since I'd visited India, but the scenery details of the fragrance of the air created a strong sense of déjà vu. I spotted an Ashoka tree next to a coconut tree. Both were trees I'd expect to find in a rainforest in India or Sri Lanka, not a hillside in Portland, Oregon.

Beyond the towering trees was a row of smaller tea bushes and a few taller tea trees. Both *camellia sinensis*, sometimes known as "China Bush," and *camellia assamica*, known as "India Bush," were here. The *sinensis* plants were smaller shrubs with smaller leaves, whereas the *assamica* variety was both a bigger tree and had larger leaves. Two of the *assamica* trees had been shaped into topiary. The dense tea trees no longer looked like trees in large planter boxes next to each other, but rather the figures of two people dancing in each other's arms.

As I leaned closer, I realized they weren't *exactly* people. One figure had the curled horns of a ram, and the other a narrow tail. Dancing demons.

"Gary is really talented," said Dante. "I'd never seen tea plants used like this, but after he did so much with more standard plants, he tried his hand with our tea plants. It's like magic how he coaxes leaves into these shapes that look so alive."

"We've never gotten good at harvesting and drying our own tea," Carla added, "so this pair of lovers is a better use of them."

"We're serving tea just through there." Dante pointed the way through a small break in the plants just past the dancing demons. He and Carla lagged a few steps behind us.

"Did I see Joyce's boots by the *asssam*?" Dante asked Carla. It wasn't exactly a whisper, but there was a quiet urgency in his voice.

"Just your imagination," Carla replied.

I hadn't noticed any boots, but I doubt I would have seen them in the thick greenery. And after a few dozen paces, we were now in a subtly different microclimate. Still moist, but now more like a chilly bog—this was the section that smelled like a peaty bog from Scotland. I know plants better than most people, but I didn't recognize many of the ones surrounding me, until I came to one that looked like a snake —or rather, *dozens* of snakes.

"A cobra lily," I said, leaning over the cobra-like hoods of the leaves of the plant I'd last seen deep in the forest growing amongst redwood trees.

"Yes!" Carla's eyes lit up as she reached my side, narrowly avoiding stabbing my arm with one of her sharp knitting needles. "You know about carnivorous plants? Besides the Venus flytrap, I mean."

That's what these plants all had in common. Now I recognized a couple more of them—the aquatic Waterwheel and of course the famous Venus flytrap—but most I still didn't recognize. Unlike Charles Darwin, I'd never been fascinated by what he'd called "insectivorous" plants. Darwin thought insectivorous was a much better descriptive term for the strange plants that trap insects than what we now call carnivorous plants. When I first read that he'd published a book on the subject, I was surprised, but I shouldn't have been. He was interested from the angle of plant evolution.

"I'm an herbalist by training," I said, "so I know a lot of plants in general, and I recognize a few of these, but most of them are new to me outside of books."

"The trick is creating the conditions they need to thrive." Carla touched a clump of loamy dirt. "They only survive in the most inhospitable conditions. If you care for them too well, they die. I thought we might lose our cobras until I got their desolate bog just right."

"And they need rainwater to survive, right?" I looked up at the glass ceiling, which allowed sunlight in but not rain. "Not water from the tap."

"Bottled water will kill them as well," Carla said. "We have barrels to catch rain outside."

We emerged from the tangle of plants into a clearing, where a formal tea service was set at a table. It was such a jarring shift that it took a moment for me to be certain I hadn't conjured it from my imagination.

We were being served a formal tea while deep in a jungle of carnivorous plants and devilish tea topiary. What exactly had I gotten myself into?

CHAPTER 7

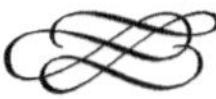

The steam from the tea reached my nose. The fermented pu-erh tea smelled earthy, rather like harvesting mushrooms in a fairy tale forest.

"Lena and Elias are already here," said Carla, "but Frederick is late. Typical. This is Lena Tamraz and her brother Elias. Lena and Elias, you remember Max? And this is Zoe."

"A pleasure." Lena stood and shook my hand with a firm handshake. She looked to be in her early twenties, but rather than being dressed informally, she wore her dark brown hair rolled into a precise chignon at the base of her neck, and her polished white flats matched her pristine white pantsuit. She wore a delicate gold band on her right ring finger, and small pearl earrings adorned her ears. Definitely the "posh" of the Posh and Punk Rock Tea Club.

"Hey." Elias gave me a friendly nod from where he was sitting on the other side of the table. His features betrayed that he and Lena were related, but aside from the genetic forces he couldn't control, he was the mirror opposite of his sister. His hair was short and wild, and he wore artfully askew black clothing down to his heavy, scuffed steel-tipped black boots. "Welcome, Zoe. Good to see you again, Max."

I stepped around the table and offered my hand to Elias. Normally, I wouldn't have insisted on the formality, but I wanted to shake hands with all of them. I didn't detect the presence of Max's tea on any of the four of them.

"Unfortunately," said Max, "the reason I'm here is because someone vandalized my shop. My grand opening was supposed to be today, but it's been postponed, so I felt like being around fellow tea people."

"That's awful!" Carla gripped her knitting needles tightly and smothered the sea serpent she was knitting. It struck me that she was overacting, as if she already knew the news about Max's shop. Then again, she might simply be a dramatic person. Which wasn't a farfetched assumption about a woman knitting a sea serpent who grew carnivorous plants and asked her gardener to create dancing demons.

"Sorry to hear it," added Dante.

"Zoe and I were going to fix tea to drink in my backyard," said Max, "but then I remembered you were all meeting today, so I took a chance that you wouldn't mind if we crashed the tea club meeting."

"So glad you did," said Elias. "We were having an argument about whether this brick of pu-erh is fermented to perfection or went too far. Now that we have guests, we'll have to be civil." He grinned.

"I'll grab two more teacups for Max and Zoe." His sister Lena stood and disappeared into the foliage as a new figure appeared.

"Sorry I'm late." A white-haired man in fashionable oversize glasses stepped into the clearing in the conservatory.

"Fred," said Dante, "Max and his girlfriend Zoe are joining us for tea this morning. "Max needs cheering up after his new shop was damaged."

Fred frowned. "Frederick," he said curtly, offering me his hand. "Frederick Rasmussen." He turned to Max. "Your shop was damaged? You mean your new Alchemy Tea for You and Me whatnot?"

"Afraid so," said Max, ignoring Frederick's jab. "The Alchemy of Tea won't be opening today as planned."

"Didn't put enough money into proper security, eh?" Frederick sneered.

"Was that really necessary?" Elias snapped.

"It was a simple question." Frederick spread his arm out with his palms up in a placating gesture that rang false. "Why are you all looking at me? Shouldn't someone be serving tea?"

Lena returned carrying three small teacups and glaring at Frederick.

"Forgot how to count on your trip to the kitchen?" Frederick chuckled and waved a beautiful porcelain cup more haphazardly than the centuries-old porcelain deserved. "You only needed two more cups. My cup is already here on the table."

Lena's face remained impassive except for faint spots of red that appeared on her cheeks, all the brighter since her attire was entirely white. "Gary was pruning some plants at the side of the house when we arrived, so I thought he might want to join us for tea as well." She set down the three cups, then lifted and swirled one of the two tea pots before pouring two cups for me and Max. She ignored Frederick's empty cup.

"That barbarian isn't interested in tea." Frederick poured a small amount of the fermented tea into his own cup, then sniffed the tea like it was a glass of wine.

"Of course he is." Carla pointed one of her sharp needles at Frederick. "You can't have forgotten that Gary always used to join us."

"That was before," Lena said softly. "He was only here for—"

"How bad was the damage to your shop?" Dante asked Max.

Dante's body language had once again shifted, his relaxed manner tensing. Had he cut Lena off on purpose, to prevent her from whatever she was about to reveal? In spite of his outward presentation of a rebel, I didn't get the sense that Dante was a rude person. He must have had a reason for interrupting. What didn't he want Lena to say?

Max sensed it too. He looked as if he might ask Lena what had happened "before," but he changed his mind and turned to Dante. "It's bad. And *not* because I forgot to lock up." He glanced sharply at Frederick. "But I can tell you all what happened."

That was my cue. "May I use your bathroom?" I asked.

"Of course," said Carla. "It's the seventeenth door to the left."

I blinked at her. I've visited some grand estates in my time, but I didn't think this one was quite that big.

Dante chuckled as my eyes grew wide. "In the hallway past the lounge, it's the *first* door on the left. Carla still makes fun of the fact that we bought and live in this huge mansion."

On my way to the house, I walked through a section of *camellia sinensis* tea plants growing in pots. Small white blossoms were blooming on one of the smaller plants, even though it was too early in the season for the plant to flower. The sweet perfume from the flowers overpowered the scent of the sandy soil. I nearly stopped to examine the little plant, to see how I could help it thrive, but I reminded myself I wasn't here to be a plant whisperer. I was here to help Max find out who'd sabotaged his grand opening and stolen his tea. Only two of our suspects lived in this house, but it was the gathering spot for the tea club, so it was worth searching.

The lounge was connected to the conservatory, with a full wall made of glass, making it feel as if this massive greenhouse was part of the house itself. Of the two walls of the lounge that flanked the glass one, one was lined with photographs from their punk rock days in the 1970s, including a poster-size black-and-white photo of Carla on stage, her lips curled into the scream of a song and her hair mid-flip.

I glanced behind me. Nobody had followed. Instead of turning left when I reached the hallway, I turned right, toward the kitchen.

Stainless steel appliances filled the open plan kitchen. Half a dozen tins of loose-leaf tea and two fermented bricks of tea were gathered on a marble countertop. Before my hand reached the closest tin of tea, I was startled by the countertop itself. The lines running through the marble weren't arbitrary—they were in the shape of a skull.

I pulled my eyes from the curious countertop, wondering how they'd etched the lines of a skull into the marble while keeping it a smooth countertop, and opened each tin of tea. Like Max, this group appeared to consider "tea" the drink made from the leaves or stems of the *camellia sinensis* plant or its *assamica* variation, not simply a warm beverage created by steeping a medicinal plant in hot water.

To get by over the centuries, I'm much less precious about the original meaning of words. Whatever terms people use to best communicate are the words I use. I consider peppermint and lemon balm infusions to be "tea" just as surely as black, green, or white tea from the true tea plant.

None of the tins on the counter contained Max's homemade tea, so I did a quick search through cabinets. In the darkest corner of the kitchen, I found a whole cabinet devoted to tea. I took a deep breath and wondered how long it would be before they missed me.

Ten minutes later, I made my way back outside, having sniffed each tin of tea I'd found in the kitchen or any of the downstairs rooms, but not having had time to search the whole house. It was too big to conduct a full search without raising suspicion. I'd been gone too long as it was.

"Those photographs from the '70s are amazing," I said as I rejoined the group. "I got waylaid by looking carefully at them. I especially love the one that captures a moment when you flipped your head and your hair was flying through the air."

Carla smiled and hugged her knitted creation to her chest. "Thank you. That was a great Carla and the Carpathians show." She looked fondly at her husband. "We've had some good times."

"That we have," Dante echoed, raising his porcelain teacup.

Everyone raised their cup to their lips and enjoyed a sip, even Max. I was the only one paying attention to our surroundings—and the sound of a twig snapping behind us.

I glanced around but didn't see anyone else. But I could have sworn something had moved behind me. Someone—or something—was watching me through the leaves of this tropical forest.

CHAPTER 8

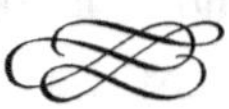

Max and I said our goodbyes half an hour later, no wiser for our visit to the Carpathian Conservatory and Dante's Inferno.

Dante and Carla asked if we needed help finding our way out, and Max replied that he remembered how to get out, so there was no need for them to get up. They thanked us for stopping by and wished Max good luck with his shop, but they didn't rise from their seats. Surely, if they were worried about us sneaking around the house, they would have shown us out.

"Nothing?" Max asked quietly as we stepped around the corner of the sprawling conservatory.

"Nothing related to tea." I glanced up at the windowpanes above, thinking of the eyes I'd felt watching me. From what I could see through the greenery, the windows weren't spotted with rain or debris. They had been recently cleaned. Someone must spend a lot of time keeping up the house and grounds.

"What does that mean?"

"Let's just get out of these claustrophobic plants."

"I never thought I'd hear those words come out of your mouth in relation to each other. Claustrophobic plants?"

"There's something unnatural about this place," I whispered, pushing through the red stems of a dogwood. I came to a halt. I hadn't known the half of it. "These two sundews have been stitched together."

I leaned closer to the rotting leaves of two sundews in a boggy patch of dirt that was equal parts peat and sand. The shapes of a sun and a moon were carved on the front of the planter box. Someone had used lightweight green yarn, made of flax, to sew together the leaves of two different varieties of sundews. The two plants looked nothing alike, but that wasn't unexpected. There are over one hundred fifty varieties of the *drosera* flypaper plant. I've never planted them, but I've encountered them before. They've been used as medicinal plants to treat respiratory infections. But neither of these plants would survive long themselves. Both plants drooped from the damage.

"We should go." Max tucked his hand through my elbow.

"Why would someone do this? Both are dying."

"Let's get out to the car. Then I'll tell you everything else I know."

We found the glass door leading outside, and walked in silence through the monster-shaped topiary toward the driveway.

I was still shaken by feeling like we were being watched by someone hiding behind the plants, but with how strange the whole setup was, I could easily have let my imagination run away from me.

"Oh!" I tripped on a boot. There was a foot inside it. I guess it wasn't my imagination that we weren't alone.

"Sorry," I said to the wearer of the boot as I steadied myself on Max's arm.

A man with massively large shoulders was kneeling next to a bed of wild cosmos flowers, thick, dirt-covered gloves covering his hands. His face was obscured by a well-worn baseball cap.

"Hi, Gary," Max said as the man stood. "Sorry we didn't see you there."

Ah, the groundskeeper.

"Nice to meet you." I introduced myself and extended my hand, forcing him to stand up and take off his gloves to shake my hand. "Your topiary creatures are beautiful."

His handshake was firm, earthy despite having been inside gloves, and, disappointingly, without a hint of Max's tea. Gary wasn't our thief either. He gave a silent nod, acknowledging the compliment. The gesture was friendly enough, but he didn't otherwise reply.

"I'm sorry we missed you for the tea tasting this morning," Max added. "I wouldn't have been here this morning if I'd been able to open my shop as planned, but unfortunately it was vandalized, so the opening is delayed."

"Sorry to hear it." Gary put his gloves back on.

"Didn't you used to come to the tea club gatherings more regularly?" Max asked.

"That was before." Gary looked up at the sun and adjusted his baseball cap. "Looking to be a hot day. I should finish up before the sun gets too high. Nice meeting you, Zoe." Without a backward glance, he walked away from the conservatory and disappeared around the side of the house.

"Was it just me," I asked once we were safely inside Max's car, "or was he acting suspiciously?"

"The strong and silent type," said Max. "He's exactly what I remember. They're *all* quirky Portlanders, but I didn't have a gut reaction about any of them being guilty of wrecking my shop. Did you sense my tea anywhere?"

"No. Nowhere. Right now, I'm much more interested in Carla's plants."

Max started the engine. "Like I said, a quirky Portlander. She, ah, doesn't just knit clothing and stuffed animals. You saw that she also stitches plants together."

"But *why*? Why would she intentionally kill such rare plants?"

Max didn't put the car in gear, but instead turned to me. "I still can't tell if she's joking about this … but she says she Frankensteins plants together. And … that they grow together within a few days."

"She must have been joking. There's no way those sundews will survive."

"I couldn't quite tell if Carla and Dante were pulling my leg, or if they really believe she splices together plants with her knitting needle and green yarn."

"It's creepy." Through the car window, I eyed a smaller topiary monster I hadn't spotted before. One that was only a couple of feet high and resembled a goblin. Had he been there before? I shook my head. Of course that plant had been there before. I simply hadn't spotted him, with so much else to take in at this sprawling estate. "Let's get out of here."

"I thought you would have said that it was natural to combine plants in unexpected ways. Isn't that what both herbalists and alchemists do?"

"Transformation is more than taking some string and sewing together two things you wish would fit together."

"Doctor Frankenstein did it." He took his eyes off the drive for a second to grin at me, but I didn't smile back. His smile faded. "It was a devil's advocate question, I admit. I don't think she's really creating new plants by stitching them together with yarn."

"Sorry." I reached for the locket I wear on a chain around my neck and looked out the window. "You inadvertently touched on a subject that frightens me."

"Frankenstein?"

"It's called a horror novel for a reason. I already feel like I messed with more than I should have when I went far beyond healing remedies and found the Elixir of Life."

"Which you only did for your brother." Max swore. "I'm sorry. I shouldn't have brought it up. I didn't think—"

"It's all right." I was already thinking about it, which is why I'd reached for my locket that had a miniature portrait of Thomas. Max knew the story. My beloved younger brother was the person who'd saved me when the people of Salem wanted to put me on trial for being a witch, because I saved their dying crops. He came with me to Europe when we fled, and he succumbed to the plague. I had tried to save him, but only ended up cursing myself with eternal life. Eternal life is something I think of as a curse on some days, and a blessing on others. But it's not something that should be forced upon anyone. Dorian and I were both accidental alchemists.

"Many alchemists went mad," I said, "because of their quest for gold or for the Elixir of Life. They wanted so badly to become true alchemists that they grew further and further away from getting there, because in their desperation, they did things exactly like those leaves sewn together with yarn. They lost sight of what they were truly after and tried to shove pieces together that just didn't fit."

Change, growth, and transformation are all worthy pursuits, but not if the cost is making things worse and driving yourself mad in the process. Purity of intent is the core element of alchemical transformation. But sometimes the harder we strive for perfection, the more that drive turns into frustration, corrupting the very purity of intent we were seeking.

"I can understand the temptation," said Max. "That's why I needed to spend time on my own when I was learning alchemical processes for working with tea. I didn't want to be distracted by you—which was inevitable if I'd seen you—and I didn't want to take shortcuts."

Max wasn't learning alchemy in the same way as alchemical disciples sought to turn base metals into gold or discover eternal life. Max was a wise man. He had no interest in living forever.

Instead, he was practicing the underlying principles of alchemy in turning tea plants into drinkable tea: listening to the plants rather than taking exact measurements; taking the time to learn about the chemicals in plants; and adding one's intent as one worked with the plants. That's how he'd created tea he'd be selling at his shop—at least the tea he was *supposed to* sell at the shop, before it was destroyed. His personal tea blends would only be a small portion of the tea he sold, but it was something that made the store special and that made him excited about the shop. He hoped having his own homegrown tea would inspire others to learn more about tea than simply drinking it, maybe even entice them to grow it themselves, even if they had no desire to do more with it than enjoy it as a plant in their yard. Being surrounded by the energy of plants is therapeutic on so many levels.

"We didn't really learn much from them," I said. Except for the creepy setting, of course.

"I was hoping you'd sense the tea on *one* of them. Or that one of them would have been nervous about my being here and telling my story of what happened last night. But they all seemed genuinely surprised. Well, except for Gary, who had no reaction whatsoever. I wish one of them had a terrible poker face, so I'd know it wasn't my…" he trailed off.

"So you'd know it wasn't your dad who damaged your shop. What do you say we get back over there and start fixing it up?"

"But my tea is gone."

"Max. Your homemade tea was a lovely addition to the shop, but only a small fraction of why it's so enticing. That's not why people will be excited to shop there."

"If they ever get to."

"Max—"

"I should check on my dad again, and then on to the shop. I'm supposed to meet the handyman there in a little while. He boarded up the window last night and is going to help with the shelving today. I'll drop you—" His words were interrupted by the sound of his cell phone.

Max picked up, and his eyes grew wide as he listened to whatever was being said to him. He swerved sharply and pulled over on the side of the narrow drive down the hillside, jostling us as a tire clunked over the rocky soil at the edge of the road.

"I appreciate you letting me know," he said before he hung up. His eyes blazed with confusion as he stared out the window.

"What's wrong?" A sense of unease came over me. We'd gotten far enough that we could no longer see the house, nor could we see the end of the long private drive. The canopy of greenery enveloped us, and I felt as if we were isolated in a strange forest.

"Nothing." Max answered, though his tone said the opposite. "Or everything. I don't know."

"Who was it that called?"

"My dad has an alibi for the whole evening. A good one. The police have verified it. He's being let go."

I stared at Max, who looked every bit as confused as I felt. "Why did he confess if he was innocent."

"I have no idea. The most common reason people falsify a confession is because they're protecting someone they love. A close family member. But that can't be the case here."

"Because there's only you, your mom, and your sister."

"Something very strange is going on here, Zoe."

Why would Max's dad have hurt his son by confessing to have ruined his shop, but then been proven not to have done it? If he wasn't protecting someone, and he wasn't guilty himself, why lie?

Who was Andrew Liu protecting?

CHAPTER 9

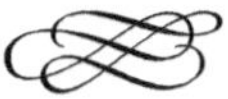

"Dorian?" I called out when I came through the front door.

No answer. I expected he'd be cooking lunch in the kitchen, so I pushed open the swinging door. The kitchen was empty of all signs of life. He must have been in the attic.

But he wasn't.

I frowned. Dorian didn't leave the house during daylight hours. That's why we'd fixed up the attic so it would be his cozy space, and I was also sure to leave all the curtains closed for rooms he used.

I trudged down the creaking stairs to the basement alchemy lab. It, too, was empty. That's when I started to get truly worried. I needed to figure out what my next step would be, when I heard a car pulling up.

I opened the front door as Tobias stepped out of his car.

"Statue delivery," he said.

"Stat—" I groaned. "Dorian?"

Tobias nodded, then hefted Dorian—frozen in statue form—out of the trunk. "We'll explain inside."

Inside the house, the three-and-a-half-foot stone gargoyle statue began to shake slowly in a hum of movement, as if an earthquake was shaking underfoot. From there, Dorian's wings began to flap, his horns twitched, and his clawed toes tapped on the floor. Within thirty seconds, the rest of the still figure was moving. The stone statue was once again Dorian.

"*Merci, monsieur* Freeman," Dorian said to Tobias. "I appreciate the favor."

"Why," I asked, "did you need a favor?"

"I believe this is an instance where I should 'Plead the Fifth' as the Americans say, *n'est-ce pas?*"

I looked to Tobias. He shrugged his shoulders and looked at Dorian. "I need to tell her."

Dorian sighed and retracted his wings. "I snuck into the back of Max's car when he came to pick you up this morning."

"You—"

"Zoe, you wished me to accompany you!" Dorian cried. "You served Max a cup of tea on the back porch before you departed. In those ten minutes in which you dawdled, his vehicle was unattended in your driveway."

"Max always locks up," I pointed out. "It doesn't matter if it's a house, car, or shop."

"What is a lock between friends?" Dorian chuckled as he tapped his clawed fingertips together. His stone claws were as good as lock picks. I didn't know he'd become adept at breaking into cars as well as houses.

"You crept into the conservatory after we arrived at the West's mansion?"

"You were investigating without me," Dorian huffed. "True friends do not abandon one another." He held up his clawed hand. "Yet I understand why you proceeded without me in this instance. You could not very well introduce me to the tea club members, especially since my introduction to Max in person had been delayed as well. I took the only measure at my disposal. I followed."

"You were who I saw watching us!" Now my sensation of being watched made sense. "That was reckless. Someone else could have seen you as well."

Dorian's expression turned serious. "*Non.* I was careful. You know this of me, Zoe. It is how I have survived since my father brought me to life more than one hundred fifty years ago. How could I do this if I was careless?"

It was a fair point. Dorian had lived in the shadows since being brought to life in 1860, and he'd been on his own since 1871. Famous French state magician Jean Eugene Robert-Houdin read the Latin from an antique book without knowing real alchemy was contained within its pages, so he was ill-prepared for the life he had accidentally brought forth. The combination of Robert-Houdin's fantastical stage show props and the backward alchemy within the book's pages had created a transformation unlike any other, bringing Dorian to life. The pair had to figure out how to keep Dorian's existence secret from the world, and Dorian was left on his own only a decade later when the retired stage magician died of old age.

But the old magician had cared very much for the gargoyle. He ensured that Dorian could work for a chef friend of his who had lost his sight in a kitchen fire. The chef understood Dorian to be a disfig-ured man—a condition he empathized with after the fire—so he taught Dorian to cook gourmet food for them both. Dorian was a natural, and from then on, he was able to secure employment as a chef, always in the shadows and usually working for blind people who needed live-in assistance.

My own curse was that I could never stay in one place for too long. After I'd been in a certain place for a few years, people I'd come to care for would begin to notice I wasn't aging, which meant it was time for me to move on. I wasn't sure which of us was better off—me for having the opportunity to live in the open but being ripped away from people I loved, or Dorian for having the freedom of the shadows but never able to reveal his true identity. But now? Here in Portland, we'd both found a place where we could reveal our true selves. I hadn't been so happy in nearly a century, but part of me was still holding my breath and wondering if this blissful existence with Dorian, Max, and all of my dear friends here in Oregon was real.

"I know you're careful," I said.

"Truly, *mon amie*. I was nowhere near you. Yet..."

"Yet *what*?"

"There was *another creature* inside the conservatory. An unnatural creature hiding in the shadows." Dorian gestured theatrically.

"I know you don't like to feel attacked, and I really didn't mean to yell, but you're only making it worse by making up—"

"You accuse me of falsifying what I saw with my own eyes?" Dorian thrust up his gray chin with indignation. "There was a monster lurking amidst those leaves."

Tobias chuckled. "You continue to amaze me with that wild imagination of yours, Dorian."

"I don't think he's joking." I stared at Dorian. He wouldn't lie about something like this. And that feeling I'd had… "If you were as close to me as the sound I heard behind me, I would have seen you. It wasn't you I felt watching me."

Dorian pursed his gray lips together before speaking. "I wish it was only my imagination, *mes amis*. But no. It was not only those carnivorous plants and leaves knitted together in the conservatory. Zoe, it was not I you were afraid of when you grew nervous while the others were distracted by their beloved tea. There is an unnatural creature lurking in the shadows of the conservatory."

"Frankenstein's monster," I murmured.

CHAPTER 10

I shivered as I thought back on that sensation I'd had in the conservatory of being watched.

"You two are serious?" Tobias's lips moved in what I assumed was a silent prayer.

"Carla, one of the people who owns the mansion, stitches plants together with yarn," I explained. "Max thinks it's a joke, since she and her husband Dante are rather eccentric, but I don't know.... She's taken pains to use yarn made of flax, a natural fiber that I've often used to tie up herbal preparations. If someone was serious about performing this type of plant transformation, that's the type of material they'd select."

"She has to have a proper workspace if she's truly transforming plants that way," said Tobias.

"Did you get a good look at the creature?" I asked Dorian.

The gargoyle shook his head, giving his wings a solitary flap of frustration as he did so. "Only his eyes. He was looking out at me from between the leaves—or perhaps he and the leaves were one in the same!"

"A plant monster?" The topiary had indeed been monsters made of plants, but surely, they couldn't come to life.

"*C'est possible.* The vegetation was too thick to see if the creature was made of plants, or simply hiding within them. I thought it prudent to retreat. Alas, you and Max were leaving sooner than I could safely return to Max's car. You returned, yet you were accompanied by an angry man."

"How did you get hold of Tobias?"

"The West household has many telephones in various rooms. I was fortunate that this couple still maintains a landline telephone number, as we do. I crept into the house and used one of their home phones to call Tobias's mobile phone."

"I'm sorry you had to drive all this way to get him," I said to Tobias.

"It wasn't far. Mina and I both stayed over at Max's house in the spare room, so we could help with the shop today, so it wasn't far. We're both off work until this afternoon. But I should get going soon. I wish there was more I could do to help Max."

"There is already an internet funding campaign to save Max's shop," said Dorian. "Veronica set it up. Do young people not know of insurance? Surely Max would have been sensible enough to have purchased insurance."

"He did," I said.

"But it's rarely enough," said Tobias. He'd taken care of his wife in the last years of her life.

"And it's a nice gesture," I added. "I'm less worried about the money needed to fix up the shop, but the fact that something strange is going on with Max's dad."

"Because the rogue was the one responsible for the destruction of Max's shop?" Dorian asked. "I am glad you are still not cynical after centuries, *mon amie*, but we must accept that family members can be as vile as anyone—"

"That's not what's strange. I haven't had a chance to tell you both what I just learned: Andrew Liu has an alibi for the time Max's shop was broken into."

"*C'est vrai?*" Dorian scowled. "*Non.* How can this be true?"

"Didn't he confess?" asked Tobias.

"He did," I said. "That's what's so strange. The police released

Andrew Liu after they confirmed he has an alibi for the whole evening.”

Dorian wriggled his horns. “The man’s confession was a lie? How baffling.”

Tobias twirled his car keys in his hand. “I need to get going, but call me if there’s anything I can do.”

“*Merci, monsieur* Freeman.” Dorian hid behind the couch while I opened the front door for Tobias.

Dorian poked his head out from his hiding spot once I closed the door once more. “We face a strange quandary indeed.” Dorian clasped his hands behind his back and paced across the floor.

A knock on the door sounded. Had Tobias forgotten something? Since Dorian was downstairs with me, I didn’t open the door. Instead, I looked through a sliver in the curtains. It was *Andrew Liu.*

“It’s Max’s dad,” I whispered to Dorian. The walls and windows of the old house were thick, but I was still overly cautious when it came to Dorian. The curtains were drawn, as they always were.

Dorian’s liquidy black eyes grew wide. “*Mon dieu*! He has snuck out of his hotel. He has—” Dorian broke off as another knock sounded.

“I’m answering the door,” I whispered. “You can turn yourself into a statue or go upstairs.”

Dorian frowned. “Turning into a statue is difficult to do when I have done so recently. I will retreat to my sanctuary, if you promise to leave no detail untold when next we meet.”

Once Dorian was out of sight, I opened my front door.

Andrew Liu was already walking down the driveway. I jogged to catch up with him. His salt-and-pepper hair was damp, and the faint scent of hotel soap lingered, as did the fragrance that dryer sheets had left on the clothing he’d changed into. But there was no trace of the tea that he’d confessed to stealing.

He turned and smiled, and I was again struck by how handsome he was. His face was rounder than Max’s, and his nose wider, but how could I have missed their resemblance?

“I gave up and thought you weren’t home.”

"Want to come around to the back garden for a cup of tea, Mr. Liu?"

"Andrew, please." He extended his hand.

"Zoe." I shook his hand, which wasn't as soft as I'd have expected for a university professor. He had the callouses of someone who spent a lot of time with their hands in the earth. I led him to the side gate that led to the back garden.

"You're a gardener like Max," he said as the garden game into view. "It's beautiful back here. I… I'm so sorry for the circumstances under which we met."

"You mean you lying about attacking Max's shop?" I surprised myself by how blunt I'd been, but I was truly angry at him for hurting Max. "It really hurt him, you know."

He winced and shrank back as if I'd physically attacked him. "I'm so sorry I wasn't myself last night. I only came by to apologize. That's not the impression I wanted to make when I first met you."

I offered him a seat on the back porch, and went into the kitchen through the back door to make tea. I brought out two mugs of hot water with tea infusers filled with mint tea.

He accepted the smaller of the two mismatched mugs. "Thank you."

"How did you find me?"

"I'm in touch with Mary, and she told me about the wonderful woman Max was involved with…. Don't take it for granted."

"The garden?"

"Max. I regret many things in life, including losing Mary."

"You're a professor on the East Coast now?"

He gave me a sad smile. "A professor of history. I teach at a small liberal arts college in New England that I doubt you would've heard of. I teach world history and Chinese history."

"That's pretty broad."

He smiled. "My own research is in how tea spread across overland trade routes and played a part in shaping cultural and spiritual traditions across Asia. I'm working on a new paper with my assistant, Jon. I shouldn't even be here…" He looked out over my garden.

"I'm glad to have a chance to get to know you," I said, "but we're avoiding what brought you here. Why did you come? Not just here to my house today—but to Portland."

"I didn't want Max to open his shop." Andrew looked from my blackberry brambles to the steaming mug as he spoke. "He gave up his old life too quickly. Being a small business owner is difficult. He knows I only want the best for him."

"Which includes lying to him and telling him you're the one who vandalized his shop?"

Andrew kept his gaze focused on his mug. "I wish I could explain, but please know I truly am sorry for any pain I caused him. And you."

"He thinks you're taking a nap in your hotel."

"I was. I couldn't sleep. Is that bitter melon you're growing?" He walked over to the vine. "I hear that you're interested in herbal remedies. This one has great medicinal purposes, though I know it's an acquired taste." He took a gulp of the hot tea. He grimaced, since the water was still far too hot to gulp, but he took another large sip.

"I like to experiment with different varieties of plants."

"You might have the greenest thumb I've ever seen." He walked back to me and set his empty mug on the small table on the porch.

"I'll refresh your tea and be right back." I scooped up the empty mug and pushed open the kitchen door—but when I came back outside only a minute later, he was nowhere to be seen.

On the table underneath my own half-empty mug, a note had been scribbled on the back of a green sheet of stationery. The note read, *I'm sorry.*

A set of fresh footprints was visible in each row of the soft dirt of my garden, and Andrew Liu was gone.

CHAPTER 11

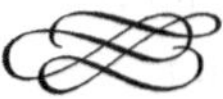

Using an arm of greenery, the verdant creature swatted aside the curious Venus flytrap blocking its path.

It appeared, at first, as if the entangled leaves of the towering plant had only swayed in a sharp gust of wind. Yet there was no wind here.

It also appeared that the leaves shaped to look like Frankenstein's monster was only a bush shaped around metal wires. Two of the wires were cleverly placed to end as bolts on the creature's neck.

Had they but known that this was only an amusing illusion.

For as soon as the sun set and the moon rose, the plant creature stepped off his platform.

He did not need the electricity of the metal coursing through his branches. All he needed was the moonlight. The moonlight which would cause him to rise and wreak havoc on the village—

Dorian wrinkled his gray nose as he reviewed the lines he had typed. The great Dorian Robert-Houdin was capable of far more Gothic prose than these simple lines. Zoe was becoming too great an influence on him. Was he becoming too skilled in the art of recognizing different types of plants? Was this detail what slowed down his prose?

Non. Knowledge was to be treasured. It was his sentence structure and vocabulary that were becoming far too Americanized. He was losing the complex phrasing of his mother tongue, Latin, and his first learned language, French. Zoe believed in high quality simplicity in all aspects of life—food, shelter, clothing, language. This was perfectly acceptable for Zoe, who he admitted grew the most flavorful fruits and vegetables, and nurtured the most potent herbs, in the humblest of gardens. But for Dorian? *Mon dieu!* Such humble simplicity would never do.

He yanked the paper from the typewriter, the claw of his index finger ripping the paper as he did so. He crumpled the paper into a ball and tossed it into the trash bin, where it came to rest on top of a dozen other crushed sheets of paper. He stamped on the papers for good measure, nearly getting his clawed foot stuck in the bin.

He sighed. Perhaps he should stick with cooking.

Non! Again, it was the American mentality to specialize in one field, not to enjoy the various realms of life as a Frenchman. He was certainly as talented at detection as the fictional Agatha Christie creation of Poirot, so why could he not learn to craft fiction as well? As a gargoyle sleuth, he had a unique perspective. A Gothic sensibility, innate to his stone bones, that went beyond the skill of merely crafting a devious puzzle.

The teeth-lined leaves of the Venus flytrap curled into a smile as the living plant watched his hedge compatriot free himself from the confines of the shrubbery.

Bof! Bushes? Shrubbery? These were not the words of Gothic fiction, Dorian scolded himself. *Hedge* was slightly better, for its connection to Gothic hedge mazes, but only slightly.

Moonlight filtered through the hand-forged glass into the conservatory, casting a ghostly glow over the flora. Saplings slept while the larger vines craned towards the light.

A tendril of ivy snaked its way across the cold cobblestones, peeking into crevices—spaces where it might need to hide.

As the moon rose higher, the ivy's fears were realized. It tried

*to press its heart-shaped leaves into the space between stones,
but there was not room. It should have climbed the glass, though
even that would not keep it safe. Not if the creature roamed free.*

Crunch.

The monster lifted itself from its verdant pedestal.

Crack.

The monster broke a branch as it stepped onto the ground.

Snap.

*The monster crushed a twig in its hands as it peered out of the
frosted glass.*

Smash.

It was free.

Dorian pulled the sheet of paper from the Remington, more gingerly
this time. This was not bad. Not bad at all.

He frowned. His displeased expression was not directed at his prose.
He was quite satisfied that even in English, he had found a way to convey
the oppressive feeling of that conservatory. It was because his words
were *too* good. They transported him back to the Carpathian Conservatory. He had not meant for his novel to mimic real life so closely. Yet how
could it not? Not after what he had seen.

Yes, it was true he had not exactly laid eyes on the full body of the
plant monster he had seen in the conservatory. But he had not imagined
those monster-like eyes peering out at him. *Those eyes.* He shivered
despite the warmth of the day.

Could Zoe be right that the plants simply appeared animated, even if
they were not?

This Carla woman was a strange creature herself, stitching together
plants as if she were Dr. Frankenstein. Dorian knew all too well how
dangerous it was to imbue alchemical life forces onto others, rather than
looking inwardly.

Could Carla have glued eyes onto plants? He did not think such false
eyes would look so real, yet perhaps the modernization of automata had
led to them looking truly alive. It was *possible*, he admitted, yet some-

thing in his soul told him this was not the case. The eyes that he had seen were alive.

A man?

This was a possibility he had, of course, considered. Yet could a man climb so high? There might have been a ladder, had it not been for the placement of those eyes. If he were not mistaken—which he was assuredly not—there was no room for a man, or even a small woman or child, to climb into that spot.

What else remained?

Carnivorous plants. Such curiosities were a provocative choice of houseplant, yet they were not nearly as large as portrayed in fiction, nor as dramatic. A Venus flytrap would not actually consume a man.

Perhaps Dorian would return to investigate further… His novel would, of course, be a masterpiece, if he were to pursue it, but he could not ignore the fact that it was far more than words on a page. Yes, Dorian Robert-Houdin would return to Dante's Inferno and the Carpathian Conservatory to catch the monster.

CHAPTER 12

"You'll never guess who showed up at my house," I said as I sat down at a two-person tree ring table at Blue Sky Teas, next to Max.

I was meeting Max for lunch at Blue Sky Teas. Blue's cozy café didn't have a cook working during the day. She served pastries along with tea, plus sandwiches made using Dorian's freshly baked bread and fresh fillings sourced from local farmers.

Dorian was the secret chef and baker for Blue Sky Teas. Under cover of darkness, he arrived at the tea shop kitchen around three o'clock in the morning and was finished before six o'clock, when he'd sneak back to the house shortly before sunrise. In the summer, he'd begin even earlier to make sure he was done before the five o'clock sunrise. He would also prepare heaps of sourdough bread a day ahead of time, so that there were always several loaves ready to bake each morning.

"Dorian?" asked Max. "Geez, I'm so sorry I didn't get to meet him because of—"

"Not Dorian," I said.

Max didn't know that Dorian lived at my house. The gargoyle didn't need to sleep, so there was no extra bed in the attic. Instead, it was set up as a cozy office and storeroom, which it was. An unsuspecting person would assume it was my desk and collection of typewriters next to my shelving of antiques for my home business, Elixir.

"It was Andrew," I said.

"My *father* Andrew went to your house?" Max frowned at me. "Just now, he wasn't napping at his hotel?"

"He said he couldn't sleep, so he wanted to apologize for his behavior last night."

"Which he chose to tell *you*, rather than his own son." Max's cheeks flushed. "The line has died down. I'll place our order. What would you like?"

"I like everything here. Surprise me." I found myself holding my gold locket for comfort.

"That's a beautiful piece." A young woman at the table next to mine smiled and indicated the locket I wore as a necklace. "Those old boots are amazing as well. Did you find them at one of the second-hand shops on Hawthorne?"

I smiled back. "The shops in this neighborhood are a treasure, but I got this locket while traveling abroad, and I can't remember where I found the shoes." I remembered well, but I couldn't tell her I'd bought them new in a post-war Sears catalogue and had them repaired by cobblers many times. "If you like shopping for antiques online, here's a card for my shop." I handed her my letterpress business card for Elixir.

"Elixir." She ran her fingertip over the handwoven paper and indentations of the letters created by the printing press that had created the short run of cards. "You *are* old school."

I've collected "antiques" long before they were old, because over time, I'd acquired a sense of which types of items would be of interest once time had gone by. I wasn't always right, but my educated guesses often paid off many-fold. I've never been great with money—either making it the traditional way or transmuting lead into gold as an alchemist—but I appreciate the joy that old objects can bring to people who care for history, so it was a perfect fit for me to keep history alive while bringing some happiness to others.

In the past, I was an apothecary and herbalist as well, but now that so many talented modern herbalists were filling a void, I gave up the herbal side of my business and gave up selling products in person. I now run Elixir as an online antique shop, making enough money to live comfortably.

To others, my modest income might not seem like much, but I've learned that once basic needs are met, money isn't what leads to a rewarding life. It's the people in our lives, followed by the simple pleasures, which can mean different things to different people. I've always been drawn to plants, so one of the things I love about having bought my modest fixer-upper is its backyard garden. In my small plot of land, I don't have room for crops such as rice or oats, but I can grow many of my own vegetables and herbs, as well as summer fruit.

Until I bought my crumbling Craftsman house in Portland, which I've been slowly fixing up for the last year and a half, I lived out of my Airstream trailer for more than half a century. I'd closed up my shop in Paris in 1942 and put my larger wares into storage. I hadn't had a stable home since then, until now. I only sold small items at flea markets out of my Airstream, such as vintage postcards from Paris and other small items that had increased in value.

I rarely need to buy clothing, because most of the time I mend high quality items that last for decades. After water leaked through the roof and damaged my limited wardrobe, my friend Heather had taken me shopping to buy new clothes. Heather was one of my good friends here in Portland, but it was her teenage son, Brixton, who I'd met first. Heather didn't know about Dorian's true existence as a gargoyle, but Brixton did, and was one of Dorian's closest friends and defenders of the gargoyle's secret.

The breezy summer blouse I was wearing today was something Heather had helped me pick out when she'd taken me shopping. I still found it odd to wear off-the-rack clothes. That type of clothing used to be thought of as a luxury, as opposed to the other way around. I much preferred hand tailored clothing like these lace-up ankle boots and the charcoal gray slacks that were a perfect fit. But I admitted how much easier so many things in life were in the twenty-first century.

Max sat down with a pot of gunpowder green tea. "Blue is

toasting our sandwiches. How did Dad even know where to find you?"

"Your mom told him who I am, so he wanted to make a good impression—or at least do damage control after last night." Max's mom, Mary, hadn't been at the ruined dinner party last night, even though Max had invited her, because she said she wanted the "young people" to have fun without her. I wondered if she thought she'd be a third wheel, with three couples in attendance: Me and Max, Tobias and Mina, and Nicolas and Perenelle Flamel. Once Mary said she wasn't planning on coming, that's when Dorian felt he could introduce himself to Max. But now, that would have to wait.

"The disturbing thing," I continued, "is that he rushed off quickly without saying goodbye. As if he had somewhere urgent to be."

"Well, he didn't come back here. Are you sure you just didn't hear him say goodbye? He was always distracted when I was young. Maybe he mumbled a farewell?"

"I don't think that could be it. Andrew and I were having tea on my back porch, and he finished his cup of tea, so I went to get us another cup. When I got back outside, he was gone."

"Unbelievable." Max shook his head and tensed his jaw.

"Are you planning on meeting up with him later?" I asked.

"Not that he's committed to. We have a strained relationship."

"I'm sorry. I don't mean to pry."

"I have a complicated relationship with my dad, Zoe. He left when I was a teenager, and we haven't been close since. In truth, we weren't close for quite some time before that as well."

"So you don't know who he's protecting by lying about destroying your shop and stealing the tea."

"I tried talking to him when I picked him up at the station, but he wouldn't talk to me beyond apologizing for the anguish he caused me. He said he wanted to get some sleep, so I dropped him off at his hotel."

"You saw him go inside?"

"I did better than that. I watched him head toward the elevator, then I told the front desk I was there to meet him and asked if they could call up to his room. He didn't have time to reach the room, so I knew he wouldn't answer."

"But the front desk put through the call, so you know he's really staying at the hotel."

"He's not under an assumed name, and he doesn't care that I know where he's staying. But he won't tell me anything besides that he's sorry."

He reached across the small table and took my hand. "I love you, Zoe. I want you to know things about me, even when they're difficult. He left when I was thirteen. I was angry about it, but honestly, I was more angry that his mom had passed away and his dad went back to China. It all happened the same year. My grandmother dying, my grandfather going back to China, and my parents' relationship falling apart. I think in some ways, it was my grandparents living with us that kept them together for so long. Not in a bad way. They had some issues, and my dad was always way too obsessed with his work at the expense of his family, but I could tell they loved each other. But then it all fell apart. I thought it was because he loved his work more than us, but as an adult, I know it's not that simple."

"Andrew told me about his job as a professor. I know he—oh!"

"What is it?"

"When Andrew left, he did leave a note saying he was sorry." I pulled the green notecard from my bag. "Still an odd departure, but not completely running away. I wasn't being fair to him."

Max's expression wasn't what I expected. Color drained from his face. "Zoe, do you know what this is?"

I raised my eyebrows and looked again at the paper. "A piece of green stationary?"

"It's the paper Carla West uses for the Posh and Punk Rock Tea Club correspondence."

I gaped at Max as he left a tip under the tea pot on our table and stood.

"We need to get back there," said Max.

"How is your dad involved with a neighborhood tea club on the other side of the country from where he lives?"

"I have no idea, but I don't like it." He took a step back and nearly bumped into Blue, who was heading our way with two plates.

"Two hummus, wild arugula, and cherry tomato baguettes." Blue's smile disappeared when she looked at our distressed faces.

"Sorry, Blue," said Max. "We need to take these to go."

～

Max was driving too fast as we approached the turnoff to the private drive. He slammed on the brakes as a tiny car pulled off the one-lane road onto the larger thoroughfare.

He swore, but we hadn't hit the car or driven into a ditch, so as soon as he'd asked me if I was all right after the abrupt stop, he continued up the steep road to Dante's Inferno.

His tires screeched as we rounded the Loch Ness monster and pulled in front of the mansion.

Their car wasn't in the driveway like it was last time.

Max banged on the door. No answer.

We circled the large house.

"Max." I pointed to the conservatory's glass open door. "The door's open. They must be inside."

"Hello?" Max called out as we knocked on the door.

Stepping into the conservatory, I was transported into a tropical climate far away from Portland, Oregon. It was a sunny summer day, and the warmth was stifling.

My curiosity got the better of me, and I headed straight for the spot where I'd seen the Frankensteined carnivorous plants yesterday. I reached the two ailing flypaper trap plants in the stone planter with the image of a moon and sun—but *the sundew plants were no longer sick.*

Instead, I stood in front of a healthy sundew with healthy, vibrant leaves in a rosette pattern, its flypaper-like hairs ready to catch unsuspecting bugs. This wasn't possible. I must have gotten turned around.

No. I remembered the spot. And the sun and moon were unique. This wasn't a mass-produced box. I leaned closer. This was the planter box I'd seen before. I was sure of it. I was also certain I'd never seen a sundew quite like this one, which appeared to be a mix of the two varieties that had been stitched together. It appeared as if Carla's transformation had worked—this was the alchemical child created by the merging of the original two plants, rising from the once-putrid dirt. But that wasn't possible…. Was it?

"There you are," said Max.

"This sundew plant—" I began.

"We should stick together. Nobody's here in this section. Let's check the clearing where they serve tea."

Nobody was there either. At least that's what we thought at first. But we were wrong.

Frederick Rasmussen, the unpleasant member of the Posh and Punk Rock tea club, was next to the table where we'd been served tea—not in a chair, but on the floor.

I didn't need to call his name to know there would be no answer. Frederick's unmoving body lay face up on the floor, the translucent, snake-shaped leaves of a carnivorous cobra lily clawing at his neck, and the teeth-like leaves of the Venus flytrap covering his face.

He'd been killed by two of Carla's carnivorous plants.

CHAPTER 13

"Frederick can't have been killed by a carnivorous plant," I said as Max and I waited for the authorities. "Plants don't strangle and eat people. Even carnivorous plants." I paced anxiously back and forth on the concrete floor of the conservatory. "Darwin was right that they should be called 'insectivorous' plants, since they trap insects. And not even actively. The insects come to them."

Max had immediately called the authorities after checking Frederick's body to make sure the man was beyond saving.

Frederick was indeed dead, though I didn't understand what could have happened. It couldn't have really been the carnivorous plant that had killed him. I didn't know much about carnivorous plants, but what I did know was that they weren't lethal to people. The Venus flytrap isn't like it was in the play made into a famous movie, and the cobra lily doesn't actually behave like a snake. The cobra couldn't have wound its way around his neck and on its own, nor could the flytrap have jumped up to snap onto his nose.

"Could he have been allergic to the Venus flytrap or the cobra lily?" I mused aloud. If he was handling it and fell, perhaps it could have landed like that.

"What?" Max's attention was elsewhere, looking around at the plants that surrounded us—the scene of the crime.

"Frederick," I said. "I don't know of any carnivorous plants that contain toxins dangerous to people, so that cobra lily can't have killed him unless he was allergic to it."

"It wasn't the plant that did this to him. Blunt force trauma to his head—looks like the mark of a hammer."

"Oh!" I jumped back involuntarily. "This couldn't have been an accident?"

"Get back to my car." He tossed me his keys. "Lock yourself inside."

"Leaving you here? You think the killer is still here?"

"I don't know what to think. Hang on—" He held up his hand and hit a button on his phone. "Yes, I'm still here with you," he said into the phone. "Dad!" he yelled as soon as he'd muted the phone once more. "If you're here in this damn conservatory, it's better for you to come out now."

"You think your dad—?" I whisper-screamed, but Max cut me off.

"Zoe, please. My dad isn't going to hurt you. If he's the one who's here, you're in no danger. But we don't know that he's the person who did this."

"Then you shouldn't be here either."

Max scowled at me, but he knew I was right. After one final sweep of the scene, he left with me. As we retraced our steps to find our way out of the conservatory, I had the strongest sense that someone—or some*thing*—was watching us.

Could it have been the "monster" Dorian had mentioned? Carla's strange Frankenstein plants were also here in this bizarre conservatory. And, of course, there were the names Carla and Dante West had come up with: the Carpathian Conservatory and Dante's Inferno. Cheeky names for people who liked the punk aesthetic that was designed to shock. But the names felt quite eerie as we stood in this inferno-like greenhouse with the dead man.

An odd smell hit my nostrils. Not poison. Besides, Max said he'd died by being struck, not from poison. I knew what the smell was. Several plants I wasn't too familiar with had recently been damaged. My first thought was "damaged" rather than cut, because the harm was caused by being ripped or trampled, not from being cut cleanly, or even from having been stitched together like I'd seen yesterday. Had someone trampled through the conservatory? But I didn't see any footprints—only plants. No matter where the evidence led, my thoughts kept circling back to the "monster" Dorian had mentioned.

Max ushered us out of the conservatory and back to his jeep, where he locked the doors and crossed his arms over his chest. We were close enough to keep an eye on the crime scene, at least from one angle. From the driveway, the towering glass windows of the conservatory loomed above us.

"You really think this could have been your dad?" I asked.

"Anyone can kill someone, given the right circumstances."

"You don't seem to think highly of him. Just because he had a scrap of paper from Carla—"

"There's a lot you don't know about him."

"Then why don't you tell me?"

A voice from his phone squawked. He unmuted himself. "Thank you. Yes, we're outside now. We're safe." He turned to me. "Help will be here soon."

"So you can tell me about—"

"Frederick," he finished. "Frederick Rasmussen was their next-door neighbor."

All right, so he didn't want to talk about his dad anymore. Fair enough. "That's it?" I asked after Max fell into silence.

"I barely know most of these people, Zoe. That's why it's so strange that my dad—" He stopped himself. "I did talk to Frederick a little bit when I was visiting the tea club. I know he hadn't lived there for very long. At least that's what he told me. But he wouldn't necessarily have told me the truth."

"Why would you say that?"

Max considered the question. "There was something guarded about him. Like I was getting a censored version of him."

"Which makes sense, since something got him killed."

"From what Frederick said about himself," Max said, "he's Dante and Carla's only nearby neighbor. That much is easy to check.

There's only one other driveway that leads from the private road leading up here." Max tapped his fingers nervously against the steering wheel. Was he worried that we were trapped with only one road out?

"It looks like we're the only ones here." I pointed at the drive that was empty aside from our car.

Max shook his head. "There's a garage and more parking along the side. We have no way of knowing who else is here." He forced a smile. "I'm sure it's fine. I don't think there's a homicidal maniac on these grounds. Frederick wasn't a nice guy. The Wests told me that after a failed business venture a couple of years ago, Frederick moved in with his elderly mom, since it was something that helped them both. It allowed her to stay in her home and helped him to get back on his feet. They were close and had many things in common, such as enjoying tea. They were both members of the Posh and Punk Rock Tea Club, until she had a heart attack. She died not too long ago, at 90. At least he seemed shaken up about that, since he was with her when her heart attack struck. He's probably still grieving. I shouldn't be so judgmental."

"He was horrible to everyone this morning, not just you. I know that doesn't mean he deserved to die—" I broke off as a robin flew past and landed on the nearby Loch Ness Monster topiary. "It's odd that Frederick would be here alone. Did he know Carla and Dante well enough to be over at their house without them at home?"

"I don't think Dante liked him much. Frederick wasn't as open to the parties Dante threw in those ruins he calls Dante's Inferno—he complained about the noise."

"So he was Carla's friend?"

"I'm not sure about Carla either. I got to know Dante more than Carla years ago when I was a beat cop and Dante was involved in an altercation downtown."

"An altercation?"

"A fan of Carla's accosted her, and there was a fight. I hadn't heard of her band, Carla and the Carpathians then, but I found it interesting that even though this was at a bar, Dante was drinking tea. I learned he'd been sober for more than a decade already—it's been multiple decades now—and tea is his drink of choice."

"I haven't heard of Carla's band either."

The hint of a smile appeared on Max's lips. "And you didn't look them up online after we met them." He spoke the words as a fact, not a question, but as if he were still incredulous that someone who looked twenty-eight wouldn't immediately pull out their phone to look something up.

"They both were in punk bands back in the day," Max continued. "Dante's band Mayhem wasn't semi-famous like Carla's. His parents were well-off, so he inherited their wealth, which is how they have this big mansion they've been able to expand with topiary gardens and a huge conservatory. He gave up alcohol after struggling with addiction. Tea is the thing he's found that helps him still feel satiated. Plus, nobody thinks poorly of you if you begin drinking tea five minutes after waking up in the morning. Not that he cared what people thought of his alcohol problem when he was young. But by his late thirties, he was both feeling bad and not liking the constant confrontation with others."

"He didn't strike me as the idle rich." I surveyed the grounds, with the monster topiary, sprawling conservatory, and those preserved stone ruins of an older section of the house.

"Because he's not. He was into punk rock and rebellion, but he did something with that energy. His father was a big-name music producer, so he was indoctrinated into the music scene. His mom was from Sri Lanka, so unfortunately in the 1950s, when Dante was born, that was an issue and made them even more of an outcast family. Not everywhere, of course, but even then—"

"I know, Max. I lived through that decade."

Max's breath caught. "I know. I mean, even though *I know,* it's still…"

"A lot."

Max tucked my white hair behind my ear and caressed my cheek. "This life I've fallen into… Sometimes I have to remind myself it's real."

"Even I'm having trouble with today. Those carnivorous plants that were stitched together, and the ones left on Frederick Rasmussen's body…"

"Right. Back to reality." Max sat back in his seat and ran both hands through his hair as he looked up at the massive glass conservatory. "And back to what I know about the people who fixed up this strange menagerie that's now a crime scene. This was originally their vacation home, which they moved into full-time when they retired. Carla convinced Dante to retire early from his work managing bands, so they've been here a while."

"Does it strike you as eerily quiet?" The chirping of two robins and cawing of a solitary crow were the only sounds besides our voices.

"I'm far more worried about the fact that my dad might have been here." He paused. "I didn't get a good look at the driver of that small car that was peeling out of here, but it had a rental car company sticker. My dad rented a car."

"I got half the license plate," I said softly.

"You did?"

"As I was tossed forward into my seatbelt when you braked, I was also hit with the scent of sunflower seeds, and I saw some bits of the plant stuck to the back bumper of that car."

"Sunflowers?"

"I'm not going to go all Sherlock Holmes on you and tell you I know where that particular variety of sunflower came from. But because I smelled that scent, I looked for where it came from. The bumper covered with plant matter wasn't far from the license plate, and I remember four letters."

Max grabbed a pen and pad of paper from the glove compartment and wrote them down.

I didn't have time to say more, as the promised help arrived, and Max hopped out of the car.

The following hours were a blur of plants and people, though I was mostly relegated to the car. I wished I had a travel mug of tea with me, as adrenaline only got me so far, and I was beginning to feel the weight of what I'd seen in the conservatory.

I feared I'd be caught up answering questions for the rest of the day, but it appeared they'd already found the killer. Fortunately, it wasn't a sentient plant. Unfortunately, it was the last person I wished it to be. Unlike last night at Max's tea shop, Andrew Liu *didn't* have an alibi for this crime.

Worse than that, Andrew had been at this mansion. He was captured on security camera footage. Video footage showed Andrew Liu peeking into the conservatory windows.

Max's dad was taken in for questioning on suspicion of murder.

CHAPTER 14

Max and his sister were at the police station dealing with their father. Max's mom, Mary, drove down to provide support for her children. Andrew Liu wasn't talking, at least not at first, and Max was helpless. I was back at my house with Dorian, feeling helpless myself.

"*Mon dieu!*" cried Dorian. "A humble gargoyle cannot leave his closest confidante alone for even the lunch hour before a murder transpires!"

We were in the roomy attic, with me sitting at the small writing table that held the typewriter Dorian was using to write his novel, and Dorian pacing the length of the space, his wings flapping at his side. He nearly clipped a vintage turntable with the edge of his wing, but I thought it best not to mention it. He rarely broke things, even at his most excited, and I didn't blame him for feeling like he missed out on so much of life because he couldn't venture outside during the day.

"Dorian, they got video footage of Andrew Liu. When you crept into the conservatory this morning—"

Dorian batted away the question with his clawed hand. "You take me for a sloppy chimera? *Non.* I have survived in the shadows for more than a century. I have adapted with the times. I know what a surveillance video camera looks like. Even ones that are petite and hidden behind ivy encircling a structure. Though I must say, it is unwise to place a camera next to such a plant. Ivy grows quite quickly. It might have obscured the lens."

"Well, it didn't. And it captured Andrew Liu arriving and leaving."

"He should have used the unlatched back window."

"Not everyone can climb high like you can."

Dorian shook his head and wriggled his horns. "The window of the conservatory was low enough for anyone taller than a small child to easily climb through."

The conservatory was constructed entirely of glass window panels. I had assumed they'd been solid panes of glass that didn't open because of the temperature-controlled environment, but that was a foolish assumption. "Someone else could have gotten inside without being seen as well."

"If they knew that window opened. Most of them do not. I had to test many of them before I found it. But this discussion is pointless. I already know who killed this man."

"It wasn't one of the carnivorous plants. The killer must have put those plants over his face after they killed him."

Dorian clicked his tongue. "You think me a fool? I am well aware that a fly-eating plant, no matter how deadly in musical theater fiction, cannot eat a person. It was not a plant. It was the monster."

"*That's* your rational explanation?"

Dorian blinked at me. "You are speaking to a gargoyle, *mon amie.* You think it is not possible that Carla Carpathian has gone beyond her stitched-together plans? She could very well be a modern-day Dr. Frankenstein! The authorities should raid her home. They will discover the laboratory of a mad scientist."

I stared at the gargoyle. What else was he keeping from me? "You found a creepy lab when you were at the house?"

Dorian shook his head and flapped his wings. *"Non!* If I had known the West property would become a crime scene, I would have looked more carefully when I visited previously. I speak of the creature, Zoe. I am certain I saw it roaming through the plants."

"What exactly did it look like?"

"I do not know… I saw it hiding behind plants. But its eyes! I have never before seen such vicious eyes. They were the eyes of a killer. Someone with those eyes could easily have killed this man."

"Frederick."

"Dead Fred," said Dorian, drumming his fingers together.

I thought about pointing out that it wasn't a very respectful nickname for a dead man, but from what I'd seen of Frederick, he wasn't a very respectful person in life. "I don't think he was a very nice man, but now that he's dead—"

"Yes, the hypocrisy of not disrespecting someone once they are no longer amongst us."

"What's gotten into you, Dorian?"

He gave a single flap of his wings. "I apologize for my rude behavior. Yet you know what has shaken me. The monster."

"If you didn't get a good look at the 'monster,'" I said, "how do you know it wasn't a normal person? Someone could have been hiding in the thick greenery that day, and this morning."

"The monster moved too quickly. And there was no space for a normal person to have squeezed behind the plants and the glass. Yet a creature with narrow plant limbs—"

"In that environment, are you certain it wasn't the motion of one of the carnivorous plants? They can have tendrils that look like monstrous eyes, and they can snap shut quickly, making it look like a fast person's mouth."

"It was as alive as you or I, Zoe. I wonder if this is why they keep these types of plants. Perhaps the creature both hides among them and eats them. A Frankenstein's monster who feeds on carnivorous plants?"

I groaned. "You saw the topiary Frankenstein's monster out front, too, didn't you?"

Dorian blinked his liquidy black eyes at me. "Of course. I am a most observant gargoyle, Zoe."

"That's why you think it was a monster. The power of suggestion." I sighed. "You could write that into the novel you're working on, but in real life we need more to go on than the fact that you saw something moving in the distance."

"Perhaps," Dorian mumbled. "I must first return to the scene of the crime to gather more evidence of my theories before I can—"

"Absolutely not."

Dorian narrowed his eyes at me. "We have discussed your superiority complex before, *mon amie*. I am an equal partner in our investigations business."

I pinched the bridge of my nose. "You know I don't think I'm better than you. Only older. But more importantly, we don't have an investigations business."

"Brixton and our other young friends call it a 'side hustle.'"

"I know the term. I don't care what it's called these days. I object to the meaning behind it as it applies to us. We don't accept money for looking into crimes. We've accidentally become involved in sleuthing when we had to." I was glad that Brixton was keeping his friend Veronica company as she did volunteer work at the behest of her parents, after her recent reckless actions. Otherwise, I was certain Dorian would have roped them into his investigation. "We're *not* actively investigating Frederick's murder at Dante's Inferno."

"But we must. Max's estranged father is accused of a crime he did not commit! This is the perfect case for Dorian Robert-Houdin to investigate!"

CHAPTER 15

Dorian could see that I was less than enthusiastic about his plan. "You get cranky when you have not eaten, Zoe Faust. I will return with snacks momentarily."

He returned five minutes later carrying a silver platter. On it was a plate of toasted sourdough bread, a jar of homemade summer berry jam, and a pitcher filled with a fizzy beverage. He poured the shrub—a tart drink flavored with vinegar and herbs—into the fanciest cut glass tumblers from the kitchen, which I'd had for seventy-five years. I'd known the person who made them. Dorian knew these items would relax me, and they did. A calming energy tickled my tongue as I took a sip of the shrub.

Dorian always cooked with seasonal ingredients. That was one of the first things we'd agreed on when we first met. I've always felt a connection to plants and had an interest in both helping plants heal and drawing out their healing properties to people, and I follow a plant-based diet that prioritizes fresh, seasonal foods. Dorian had trained as a chef in France, studying under the tutelage of a chef who'd lost his eyesight in a kitchen fire.

As a French chef, Dorian was at first horrified to discover that I didn't stock bacon or butter in my household. I had pointed out both that he had broken into my shipping crates as a stowaway to end up in my home and that it was possible to cook delicious meals without relying on ingredients he thought of as staples. He didn't believe me when he saw my own simple creations like soups and smoothies, but as soon as I let him loose in the kitchen, both our fates were sealed. Dorian now thought of himself as an unrecognized genius of plant-based cooking and baking, who deserved a Michelin star for his creations. He was now the sole chef at our home and the pre-dawn baker at Blue Sky Teas. I rarely cooked these days, and instead spent my culinary energy growing herbs, fruits, and vegetables, as well as foraging and turning plants into dried herbs, infused oils, and healing tinctures.

"*Bon.* Life is returning to your pallid features. Sometimes I worry about you, *mon amie.* You spend so much time in your garden, yet you remain pale."

"Hats and sunscreen do wonders."

Dorian chuckled. "There. Affable Zoe has returned. Eat the bread while it is still warm. I toasted this morning's fresh bread. The far corner of Blue's top oven rack is lopsided, so the far left loaf always comes out crooked."

"I'm sure that's easy to fix."

Dorian shrugged. "Perhaps I wish for an excuse to bring some imperfect bread home."

I leaned over and gave Dorian a hug, nearly toppling the platter. "Thanks for cheering me up."

Dorian straightened his wings when I let go, similar to how a man might straighten his lapels. "This is what any good friend should do. You realize what else a good friend should do?"

"I do want to help Max, but…"

"You must avenge this injustice to your beloved! Save his good family name. Sacrifice your own desires for that of the man you love." Dorian paused his dramatic speech and watched my expression. "*Non. Non,* it cannot be true. You believe *monsieur* Liu senior to be guilty?"

I hesitated before speaking. "I'm worried that Max thinks he could be involved," I admitted. "I don't have enough facts to know what really happened. But from Max's reaction, I think he believes his father might have killed Frederick by accident."

"Then it is even more imperative that we investigate."

"Why would you say that?"

"Without even his own son believing in him, you and I must be the impartial hand of liberty. The bringers of truth and justice—"

"That's what the justice system is there for. They're not going to toss him in prison without proving their case."

"Zoe, Zoe, Zoe," Dorian *tsked*. "You are not this naive. You are simply reeling from having seen a dead body. Let us turn to less gruesome aspects of the crime."

"Such as?"

Dorian grinned and wriggled his horns. "The plants in the conservatory. How there are Frankenstein plants that have been stitched together and miraculously coming back to life?"

"That's what I was thinking of as well. I know those plants can't really be reanimated after stitching them together, but there's something odd going on in that conservatory."

"Are you certain the yarn is not alchemically infused natural fibers? What if Carla and Dante have discovered not only how to reanimate their Frankenstein's monster plant into a real man but also bring their plants back to life with yarn."

"Because that's not how plant alchemy works. Transforming the healing properties of plants on a higher level than herbalism is fundamentally different than stitching plants together."

"Is it?"

"Have you been reading Socrates again?"

"If someone would bring me my latest list of requested library books, I could enjoy less philosophical texts than the vintage books here in the attic."

"I know. Brixton and Veronica aren't available for the rest of the summer, and my library card is still suspended thanks to your vandalism—"

"It was not vandalism to correct the bad advice in the cookbooks! I have been unfairly condemned."

"*I* have been unfairly condemned, but what I was going to say is that I'll ask Nicolas if he can pick up the books for you. He's been buying all of his books at Powell's Books in Portland these days, so he should be able to use his card to get your books. But no more writing in them."

"But—"

"I know, I know. It's painful to see unclear recipes in cookbooks. How about you leave a sticky note with the corrections, rather than defacing the books?"

Dorian considered the question and consented. "This is a fair compromise. You are correct, *mon amie*, that sometimes there is a balance."

Dorian couldn't read e-books, only print books or audiobooks, because the screens of modern electronics didn't respond well to his clawed fingertips. I'd tried to get him to use a stylus pen that he could hold and would work on the screens of various devices, but his refusal made me think his lack of adoption of modern technology was more of an aesthetic choice. He could type on my laptop computer, yet he preferred to work on his novel on an old typewriter.

"Do not distract us with a discussion of library books," Dorian continued.

I could have pointed out that he was the one who brought up library books, but I've learned that it's best not to argue with a gargoyle.

"How about we wait to see what Max has to say about what's happening to his dad," I said instead. "There's nothing to suggest that rare plants and a possible monster brought to life from plants had anything to do with Frederick's murder."

"You were the one who told me a cobra lily and a Venus fly trap were placed over his face. This sounds as if unique plants had very much to do with his murder."

"Those carnivorous plants didn't have anything to do with his death. Murderers who have remorse often want to cover the face of their victim, so they don't have to look at it."

"Or to send a message."

"Oh no…" An idea was forming in my mind.

Dorian perked up, flapping his wings as he watched me think through the horrible revelation that had entered my mind. "What have you realized? Have you recalled some key element of your visit to the conservatory?"

"Max's new shop is named The Alchemy of Tea," I said, thinking through how it might be connected. "It's a good name for what his shop is, and it fits in perfectly with the Portland vibe. It doesn't lead anyone, alchemist or not, to believe that Max is claiming that his tea shop will offer the Elixir of Life and the secrets of eternal life. Good health and a bit of what people call plant magic these days, but not eternal life."

"*Oui.*"

"Carla's Frankensteined plants are more than that. There were no dead plants in that conservatory. Carla's stitched-together plants we saw aren't alchemy. Plants sewn together won't miraculously grow together, even if stitched with intent—unless she's discovered something new."

"An alchemy lab to create Frankenstein plants?"

My voice was desperate as I spoke. "Who does unnatural alchemy make you think of?"

Dorian gasped. "The backward alchemists."

Backward alchemy was the antithesis of true alchemy. Rather than looking inward and working with respect for the natural world, backward alchemists used death and destruction as their fuel. They achieved their selfish goals by taking from others and twisting the rules of reality.

A backward alchemist had taken my first love from me. I had a second chance here in Portland, and I wasn't going to let anyone steal my life from me once again.

CHAPTER 16

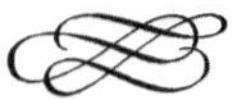

I stepped to a far shelf of the attic's Elixir inventory and picked up the top postcard from a stack of vintage postcards of Notre Dame Cathedral in Paris—a place of power filled with many alchemical secrets.

I'd purchased these cards nearly a century ago, when they were brand new, knowing they would be of interest in the future. Many faux-aged cards are created now, but very few of these originals exist.

I ran my finger over the textured card, marveling once again at the detailed line work the artist had incorporated into the line drawing of the majestic cathedral. You could even see outlines of the gargoyles and the reliefs that contained alchemical secrets hiding in plain sight. Very few people knew what had once been hidden underneath the cathedral, near the catacombs.

Dorian and I had faced our most formidable foes in the backward alchemists. After many attempts, we had defeated them—*mostly*. Their source of power was gone, but there was still at least one of them left: the person who'd killed my beloved Ambrose nearly a century ago. A former friend of mine, and the one other living gargoyle I knew of, might also be out there somewhere, and I hoped they hadn't been tempted once again by backward alchemy.

Without being able to steal the life force of others, they would all be aging rapidly, so I wasn't sure what had become of them. Nor had I heard of any living gargoyle sightings in Prague, Paris, or elsewhere in the world. I hoped they had all found peace. But even if they hadn't, I couldn't feel too bad for them, after what they'd done.

I put the postcard down. When I turned around, Dorian was watching me with a concerned expression. He hated it when I grew maudlin. He wasn't one to dwell on the tragedies of the past. I'd heard more about the grand meals he'd cooked when learning to become a chef than I had of the loneliness he must have felt when his only companions were blind people who didn't know he was a gargoyle.

"Stitching plants together," I said, "or turning plants into living monsters, is something far different than stealing the energy of other people to speed up alchemy."

Dorian smiled. "*Bon*. We are back to the matter at hand. What if there is a new band of backward alchemists? Crafter alchemists!"

"Knitting alchemists as backward alchemists?"

"*Oui*. It makes perfect sense, *non*? Knitters transform yarn into wearable clothing. They are comfortable using dangerously sharp needles and use their intent to create beauty and comfort from base materials." Dorian flapped his wings, clearly excited about his theory. "Knitters also employ alchemical principles of transforming the impure into the pure. Just as your mother figure, Perenelle, does with her paints. She takes raw elements, transforms them into pigments, then mixes these pigments with other ingredients to paint truth and beauty. Once people understand alchemical principles, they can learn how true alchemy works and apply the steps to different mediums."

"Creating a truly new transformation."

"Carla must have a laboratory in her mansion," said Dorian. "What if she is holding innocent people captive to draw their energy to fuse her plants and bring her monster to life? We must stop her, Zoe!"

"You're a dozen steps beyond the facts we know."

"Do not exaggerate. It does not become you," Dorian huffed. "I will grant that perhaps I am *five* steps ahead. I cannot help it that my little gray cells help me connect the dots of a mystery unfolding before us so quickly."

I needed to get used to the fact that this wasn't a shiny new phase that would wear off soon. He was never going to stop thinking of himself as a modern-day Poirot. After realizing that my paperback mysteries were more engaging and intelligent than he had been led to believe, he had devoured the entire Christie collection, available at our local library.

Unlike Poirot, Dorian often acted before he finished thinking through the direction his little gray cells led him. He'd gotten us into a fair amount of trouble in the short time I'd known him. He'd also saved me and our friends. I couldn't fault his motives. Though sometimes I wished he'd slow down a bit. Still, I wouldn't have traded my best friend for anything in the world.

"I think you're falling into Portland stereotypes to think that knitting is the path to alchemy," I said, though even as I spoke the words, I realized they weren't as far-fetched as I'd initially imagined.

"Or at least," I added hastily, "let's not go down that path before we have more evidence. For now, the thought that worried me wasn't about anything we might imagine as brewing in Portland, but rather that the opening of The Alchemy of Tea was widely publicized, so what if our old friends were monitoring what we're up to? Did the backward alchemists learn of the tea shop? I know now *I'm* the one who's jumping to conclusions. I just think we should be on the lookout for anyone from our past."

Dorian scampered away from me, running around the bookcase to the most shadowy corner of the attic. I followed, and I reached him as he was carefully lifting a painting from the wall. This was no ordinary work of art. It was one of Perenelle Flamel's portraits. We kept it safely in the attic, where it was turned to face the wall, rather than outward.

"*Bon*," said Dorian, looking at the charismatic face of alchemist Edward Kelley.

Edward was another of our former adversaries. I wasn't thrilled with how many of them I was accumulating. Still, Edward wouldn't be doing us any harm. Not anymore. He was imprisoned—inside this painting I kept in my attic.

Perenelle Flamel was brilliant at both art and alchemy, and she'd invented an alchemical paint that allowed her to transform people and paintings, using her skills creating natural alchemical pigments to paint life-like scenes to draw people into the world of a painting. Like this one that was keeping the world safe from Edward Kelley.

There was still so much I didn't know about alchemy. Not only because I had only been formally taught for a few years, or because alchemy is usually passed on secretly by men who choose who they impart their wisdom to, or even because I had run away from alchemy for so many years after losing my brother. Even for those of us who've discovered the Elixir of Life, there are countless unanswered questions. No alchemist before Perenelle Flamel had discovered that alchemical paint was possible. What else was waiting to be discovered? It's why even after hundreds of years, Nicolas Flamel had boundless curiosity.

"I know who can help," I said.

CHAPTER 17

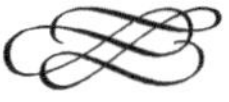

I was introduced to Nicolas Flamel in the year 1700, when I was twenty-four years old, eight years after my brother and I fled from the witch trials. Nicolas was one of the few—possibly the *only*—alchemist of that era who'd take on an apprentice who was a woman. The healing tinctures I sold to survive in London were special enough that they attracted the attention of the underground world of alchemists. However, they all thought my brother Thomas was the one with spagyric skills and alchemical potential. When they found out I was the one with the elevated herbalism aptitude, they lost interest—except for Nicolas. He'd seen my aptitude for plant alchemy in my herbal preparations and believed I was worth tutoring.

I lived under their roof in their French countryside home, not the one they'd abandoned in Paris after faking their deaths, and I studied as Nicolas's apprentice. I learned a lot in those four years of study, though I should have needed many more to find the Elixir of Life, if that's what I sought. All I sought was a life free from persecution. And if I was lucky, a life surrounded by people I loved and doing something that might make the complicated world a little bit better.

I only began seeking the Elixir when my younger brother Thomas fell ill with the Plague. I could tell his life force was ebbing away more and more each day. If I could find it, I could save him. Or so I thought. Once Nicolas realized what I was doing, he cautioned me that the Elixir wasn't something that could be transferred from one person to another. It had to come from within. Perenelle suggested I should spend my time not in the laboratory, but spending time with Thomas. If the worst happened and he didn't survive, that time together would be especially meaningful. But as an exemplar of the folly of youth, I didn't listen to them. I knew I was special. I believed my alchemical aptitude could find the Elixir of Life and save Thomas.

I was only half right. I found the Elixir, but Thomas passed away while I was working. In my grief and bleary-eyed state, I didn't realize it had taken effect.

I was too heartbroken to continue my studies, so I left the Flamels. I didn't realize my quest to find the Elixir had succeeded and I had stopped aging until my hair began turning white yet the rest of my body didn't age. When I attempted to find them once more, enough time had passed that they were gone. It was only this past year that I found out what had become of the Flamels and I was able to rescue them from the painting where they'd been trapped for more than two centuries.

They were adjusting well to life in the twenty-first century. They'd learned a bit about the outside world during their captivity, when the painting was hung in homes in which they could see the world going on around them, including exposure to the modern world through television when the portrait was hung in rooms with a TV, so they were able to acclimate relatively quickly when I found and extracted them earlier this year. I was also glad that being trapped in a painting had changed their perception of time, so they had no idea so much time had passed and hadn't been mentally scarred by the experience. Only physically. Perenelle had recovered from being poisoned by a murderer, but Nicolas still grew tired quickly and had trouble with his vision.

Nicolas had always been great at making gold, so even though they emerged from the painting with few possessions, shortly after I rescued them, he and Perenelle Flamel were able to buy a house down the street.

They were eager to come over to talk through ideas with me and Dorian, so they walked over to my house as soon as I called.

"You look tired," Perenelle declared as she swept through the front door with her massive skirt rustling. "You aren't getting enough sun."

Perenelle Flamel was an imposing figure, with fiery red hair and full skirts made partly of woven gold. Much like me with my hair that people assumed I dyed white because I wanted to be trendy, Perenelle's old-fashioned skirts and dresses were perceived by others as a bold fashion statement. In truth, as well as she was adjusting to many aspects of modern life, she couldn't fathom wearing trousers. She found skirts far more freeing. She had always sewn hidden pockets into her skirts, so I suspected this was the primary reason for their appeal.

"Don't fuss, dear." Nicolas swung my front door shut behind them. "Zoe is naturally pale. But she's clearly dehydrated."

Did I mention they're the closest thing I've got to parents? That was both a good and bad thing.

Nicolas scratched the scruffy beard forming on his chin as he studied my face more carefully. "I should have brought some of my home brewed beer with me. It's quite invigorating. Shall I go back for it?"

Like his wife, Nicolas looked like a modern bohemian. For him, that meant wild hair and wilder eyebrows, elbow-patch jackets with hidden pockets inside, and the thick tortoise shell patterned glasses he'd picked out completed the look. Not that he bothered looking in a mirror more than once a week. He'd never been concerned with appearances, only science. It's why he hadn't given a second thought to taking me on as an apprentice, when all the other alchemists of the late 1600s had believed him mad. I doubted he'd even noticed that his stubble had grown into a beard. Even with the beard, he looked nothing like the most famous image of him recorded by history and widely shared online. Which is for the best. It wouldn't do to have anyone recognize him for who he really was.

The Flamels had been misfits in their day, and they were misfits today. They fit in perfectly in Portland.

"I have a pitcher of water with mint and cucumber from the garden, so there's no need for beer." I grabbed the glass pitcher from the dining room table and poured the refreshing flavored water into four tumblers. "But thanks for the offer."

Nicolas was great at many things. Making beer was not one of them.

Dorian cleared his throat. "Zoe always forgets food."

"Good man," said Nicolas. "Shall we hear from you two about this plant monster before we turn to food?"

Dorian, clearly torn between his culinary and detective inclinations, hovered between the kitchen and living room, before his little gray cells won out. He accepted a glass of water and took it to the green velvet couch as I explained what we'd seen.

"It's not impossible to imagine that using natural fabrics a person has created themselves could add a transformative boost to knitting," said Perenelle. "It might make the fabric feel as if it was the softest on earth, or have some purifying effect when used. That is one level of transformation. I cannot imagine a plant being brought to life as you posited."

"But we have Dorian Robert-Houdin here with us, dear," Nicolas pointed out. "He was originally carved in stone, and yet through alchemical intent, he is every bit as alive as each of us. Could not the same thing be true of a plant shaped as a sculpture?"

"Dorian is different," said his wife. "The alchemical link that brought him to life was broken. There is no longer a powerful connection to the ancient alchemical teachings at Notre Dame Cathedral."

"*Madam* Flamel," said Dorian, "are you not yourself powerful enough to imbue life onto others through your alchemical artwork?"

She smiled. "I can *transform* life, moving where it resides. I cannot *create* it."

"Ha," said Nicolas. "This is a fair point. My wife is the most powerful alchemist I have ever known. Yet even my darling Perenelle cannot do such a thing. No, I agree it is impossible. And yet…"

"Yet *what*?" I prompted.

"In my recent reading of books considered classics that were written during our imprisonment, I have read this novel, *Frankenstein, or The Modern Prometheus*, by Mary Wollstonecraft Shelley."

"A most impressive novel," said Dorian. "Especially for someone so young. A true genius."

"She may have been inspired by alchemist Johann Konrad Dippel," I said, "who conducted his experiments at Castle Franken-stein and was interested in *soul transference*. Which sounds quite like Frankenstein's monster."

Nicolas's face soured. "Ah, Dippel. Quite the fraud."

"You knew him?" I shouldn't have been surprised. Nicolas had known everyone, and Dippel was a contemporary of mine, though I'd never known him.

"In name only," said Nicolas. "He claimed to have found the Elixir of Life, named it Dippel's Oil, *and* claimed he could sell it. The audacity!"

"Then you don't believe he succeeded in soul transference?" I asked Nicolas.

"Not as realized by Dippel or in Shelley's novel, no," said Nicolas. "But it is presumptuous of us to think we understand everything in this world. Did you know that in the novel, the young Victor Franken-stein was inspired by alchemists?"

"Everyone should be inspired by alchemists." Dorian chuckled. "We are most enlightened souls. But we must nourish our bellies in addition to our minds. Shall I prepare dinner?"

Since Dorian didn't want to miss anything I discussed with the Flamels, we huddled together in the kitchen. This wasn't a kitchen made for four people, even if one of them was a three-and-a-half-foot gargoyle.

Still, it was a cozy kitchen, and I felt more at home than ever with three people I loved here with me. I hadn't replaced the appliances that were left in the house when I'd moved in. The porcelain stove and pink fridge reminded me of another era in time, but much like my own collection at Elixir, these models from the 1950s were back in style as retro. Popular because it was a time that people remembered or imag-ined was simpler, even though it really wasn't.

It was the height of summer, so Dorian sent me to the backyard to harvest leafy greens and berries for a salad, as well as herbs to make a dressing for the salad and to sprinkle over the summer squash and chickpea main course. The bounty from the backyard garden made up the bulk of the meal. It was a quick meal for Dorian to put together, and I was setting the dining room table in no time.

"I'm sorry for the occasion that brings us together," said Nicolas as he raised a glass of mineral water, "but I'm delighted to be dining in all of your company."

"And to be enjoying this food." Perenelle moaned in happiness as she bit into a scoop of salad that included mizuna, baby collards, blackberries, and a sprig of dill. "We could never have a live-in chef because our work needed secrecy, but even if we had, I doubt he could have rivaled Dorian's flavor combinations. And the vibrant color combinations in this salad!"

"*Merci, madame* Flamel." Dorian gave a satisfied bow.

"Now," she said, "back to what you both saw in the conservatory. Did it look as it did here in these magazine photos?" She held up her cell phone, showing a local magazine's professional photographs of the interior of the conservatory. "Do the colors truly have this much vitality?"

I shouldn't have been surprised that when it came to thinking about the murder and a possible Frankenstein's monster made of plants, Perenelle was more interested in the vibrant colors of the greenery than the fact that one of the topiary shrubs might have been transformed into a monster. She had once been a world-famous artist —but only under an assumed name. That of a man. It was the only way for her to be taken seriously at the time. Her artwork still hung in prestigious museums of the world, unattributed to her. I hoped to help her remedy the injustice one day. In the meantime, I was pleased that we'd been able to get back a painting she'd made of me and my brother Thomas. It now hung in my house.

"That's really what it looks like," I said. "Their gardener has both a green thumb and artistic tendencies." I swiped across her screen until I came to a photo of the dancing demon topiary. Only here in the photo, there was only one horned tea plant figure, not its partner with a tail.

Dorian scowled at us both. "There is no need to bring a telephone to the dining table."

Perenelle gave a last fond glance at the rich tapestry of colors on the screen before slipping her phone into one of the many hidden pockets of her full skirt.

"You think one of these plants resembles a monster?" she asked. "This horned figure, perhaps? It looks more like a satyr to me than a monster—"

"*Non!*" Dorian cried so forcefully that a chickpea dropped from his fork and rolled across the table. "One of these plants *is* a living monster. You do not believe me either, *madame* Flamel?"

"The vibrant contrasting colors might resemble the eyes you saw. There is certainly enough contrast and other sensory details to fool the senses—"

"I have no need to put up with this humiliation," Dorian huffed.

"Forget about the monster for a minute," I said. "Let's grant that there might be a plant that was brought to life through alchemy or something inspired by alchemy, like Victor Frankenstein's monster. Does that mean the creature is violent and killed Frederick Rasmussen?"

"A valid point," said Nicolas. "We have no reason to think a plant would be more violent than a person. Quite the contrary, I would expect. Even if we find a plant that has been transformed in an unexpected way, there is no reason to think the plant itself is dangerous. It is humans I fear."

CHAPTER 18

After dinner, during which we didn't come to any insightful conclusions, Dorian insisted on cleaning the dishes himself. He packed extra slices of cake for our guests, and I left my house with the Flamels to walk them home before heading over to Max's house. The most important parts of my life were within walking distance of my house—my *home*. That wasn't a coincidence. I'd found the house because I'd fallen in love with the neighborhood, and I'd met Max because he lived in the neighborhood as well.

Max put a finger to his lips when he opened the front door. He led me through the house to the kitchen.

"I know it's early, but mom is already asleep in my guest room." Max leaned against his kitchen counter and lifted a mug of tea, gripping it as if for dear life. "She was really upset, so Mina gave her something to help her sleep. We should talk in here rather than the living room, but we don't need to be too quiet."

"How many cups of tea have you had?" I pointed at his shaking hands.

"That's rage jitters, not caffeine shakes. I have some herbal tea as well. I can fix it—"

"I'm fine." I took the teacup from Max's hands and wrapped his shaking hands in mine.

"I don't want to believe he did this, Zoe," Max whispered.

"I know. But he was there—"

"He admits that, which he has to, since he's on camera, not to mention that was his car we saw peeling out of there. He insists he ran away because he panicked when he came across a dead body."

"Why was he there in the first place?"

Max shook his head in frustration. "*He won't say why.* I got him a good attorney. She's talking to him now. And I hope he's at least telling her what's going on."

"Your mom didn't get anything out of Andrew either?"

Max shook his head. "Since she's staying here at least for tonight, maybe she'll have some luck tomorrow. It was too far for her to drive home to Astoria, and like I said, she was really shaken."

"Do you want me to stay here with Mary while you go back to the station?" I stepped away from Max and moved his teacup away from the edge of the counter. I didn't trust him not to accidentally break one of his favorite mugs.

"No. It's best that my dad talks with the attorney alone. For anything … confidential he needs to tell her."

I spun around and nearly dropped the mug myself. "You think he *could have* done it?"

Max ran his hands through his dark hair and looked away from me. "I do believe anyone is capable of taking another life—under the right circumstances. I don't believe my father is a bad man, or one who'd kill in cold blood. Given the right circumstances? Anyone can be put in a position where they see no other way out. But this? I don't believe my dad killed Frederick Rasmussen."

I took a deep breath to steady my voice. I didn't want to guide Max's memories by mentioning a monster. "Did you notice anyone else hiding in the conservatory when we were there in the morning?"

"You saw someone besides the members of the tea club I introduced you to? Zoe, why didn't you say—"

"It was more of an impression."

In the midst of those eerie plants, I knew I could have imagined the sensation that someone else had been in that conservatory. Dorian had actually seen someone—or something, but of course I couldn't tell him Dorian had been there. Besides, eyes watching from among the odd plants was hardly the same thing as truly having seen a monster. Or even a person. Many of those carnivorous plants looked like they had eyes, and Dorian had a very active imagination. That had to be it.

"What do you mean, *an impression*?" asked Max.

"You know how sometimes you get the feeling of being watched?"

Max's shoulder slumped. "It's those plants of Carla's. I had the same feeling when I had tea with them last week. It's not only the topiary shaped into life-like monsters. That hothouse environment feels like you're in a claustrophobic jungle, so it's easy to imagine people hiding behind the shrubbery. It's certainly thick enough for someone to hide there, but the cameras would have picked up on anyone leaving."

"There's another way into the conservatory. One that the cameras don't face."

Max groaned. "Really? Why didn't you say so earlier?"

"I did. I already told the detective. I saw it when I went through to the house. It's a window in the side of the conservatory, large enough and low enough that I'm pretty sure a person could slip through it." As a gargoyle had done. "I'm not totally certain the cameras don't capture it, but I did mention that I'd seen it when we were there."

Max squeezed his eyes shut. "Why was my dad there? It doesn't make any sense."

"Are the authorities looking into Dante and Carla, since it's their property? They're the ones who could have gotten into the conservatory without being on camera."

"It's true," Max agreed, "but that's not the *entire* truth. Their security system cameras only show the easiest access to the house and the conservatory. As you pointed out, there are blind spots to access the conservatory. Anyone with knowledge of camera placements and that window could have done it—and if you saw that window so easily, I'm sure others knew as well."

Dorian was always looking for ways to remain hidden in the shadows, so he was extraordinarily careful about staying unnoticed. He was adept at climbing drainpipes, like a good gargoyle, which gave him an advantage for how to get inside buildings without being seen. Did the camera's blind spots apply to people walking on the grounds as well?

"If the blind spots were large," I said, "it could have been anyone."

"Definitely any of the people in the tea club. I'm sure Lena and Elias know the grounds well, as does the groundskeeper."

Or Max or myself. We showed up on video when we came in through the open conservatory door, but someone could think we were covering our tracks. What if they thought we'd killed him earlier and left trace evidence behind. It would make sense for us to then show up later on camera and pretend to "find" the person we'd killed. I shivered at the thought. I remembered so well what it was like to be unjustly accused of a crime. The helplessness was terrifying.

"Zoe?" Max squeezed my hand. "Are you okay?"

I squeezed back and shook off the memory. "I'm fine. This is just a lot to process. I'm used to death, but the way we found Frederick?"

"I'm so sorry I brought you with me. I had no idea—"

"I know."

"Why would Dad have been there? I just don't get it. He was never into plants like my grandmother."

"He was, though," I said.

Max gave me a sharp look.

"Tea," I said. "Your dad cares very much about tea, both in his academic research and in drinking it. And a big section of the plants your grandmother cared about when you were a kid were those tea bushes you planted with her."

"But tea is only a small fraction of the plants they've got in that sprawling glass conservatory. It's not like they were growing anything of interest to Dad. You didn't see or sense anything—"

"No. Their own tea plants were hardly the focus of their energy. It was clear the carnivorous plants were the ones they put their energy into, creating those boggy, desolate microclimates where the plants thrive."

"Maybe that lawyer will talk some sense into him, and he'll tell us why—" Max broke off and reached for his ringing phone.

I watched as his face transformed from hopeful to fearful. "Wait, *what*?" His forehead creased with worry as he listened. "You mean —?" He broke off once more as he listened to the caller. I couldn't hear what was being said, and he didn't offer to put the phone on speaker for me to hear.

Finally, after what felt like minutes but was most likely only thirty seconds, he spoke again to the caller. "I understand. I appreciate you keeping me in the loop."

He hung up and looked at me with frustration and confusion in his eyes.

"What is it?" Whatever it was, it wasn't good.

"They're holding him," Max said. "They haven't formally charged him yet, but it doesn't look good. There were only six people they think could have been at the house during the time window when Frederick was killed. My dad is one of them—and the only one who left like he was fleeing after committing a murder. He's the main suspect."

"But those cameras at the house have blind spots—" I began.

"There's a camera on that road leading to those two houses. It captures cars, not the people inside. But it's got the Wests' car, Elias and Lena's car, Gary's truck, and a rental car."

"Your dad's."

"Bingo. Meaning we have seventy-two hours to prove he's innocent."

"That's how long they're allowed to hold him until deciding to charge him or let him go?"

Max nodded. "My father is keeping something from me, and from all of us, which isn't helping his case. He has three days, maximum, for them to find enough evidence to charge him—or for me to find enough evidence to clear him. I'm going to find out what my father is hiding and who really killed Frederick."

Less than three days to solve a murder.

"*We*," I corrected. "We're doing this together. One of the five remaining members of the Posh and Punk Rock Tea Club killed Frederick—and *we're* going to find out who."

CHAPTER 19

This called for more tea. I put on the kettle to make another pot.

"They all have secrets." Max kicked the floor of his kitchen like a frustrated fourteen-year-old, not the mature man in his forties that he was. "Everyone we met at the tea club. That's who the police should be looking into."

"We all have secrets." I certainly had plenty. And I understood Max's frustration that his father was implicated in a murder. "But would their secrets lead to murder?"

Max glared at me. "Well, no. Not the ones I'm aware of, at least. I did some digging this afternoon and found that two of them have police records, but neither remotely like murder."

"Who?"

"Elias was charged with assault a couple of years ago, but the charges were later dropped. The charges were brought by a patron of his hair salon, but it turned out it was simply someone unhappy with their hair who'd thrown a hand-held mirror at him. He took hold of her arm to lead her out of the salon before she did more damage—thus the claim of assault. After the case was investigated and the charges dropped, she sued him in small claims court."

"Did she win?"

"No. He didn't take any money from her before he asked her to leave. And apparently, all her friends thought it was the best haircut she'd ever gotten. One of them even testified in favor of Elias." Max's lips ticked up into a small grin for a second before the smile vanished. "And Dante has been in several bar fights, both before and after he got sober. Only one ended up with charges filed, and that was because of the damage he did to another band's equipment. Each time was supposedly defending Carla."

"She looks like she can take care of herself."

"My thoughts exactly, but from my own experience when I first met Dante, I'd say it was more about not letting guys get away with harassing her more than her physical safety."

"Frederick could have been harassing her." I turned away from Max to pour the near-boiling water into a teapot with a sachet of lemon balm tea.

Max stepped up behind me and wrapped his arms around my waist, resting his chin on my shoulder. He smelled like lavender. "I wish I could rewind two days and be here with you, like this, cleaning up in the kitchen after my dinner party that wasn't meant to be."

"Me too." At Max's touch and the calming scent of the flower's essence, the tension of the situation dissipated from my shoulders and was leaving my whole body as Max rocked back and forth—until his next words brought me back to the present.

"I was honestly surprised to find something on Elias but not their gardener. Gary is hiding something. I know, I know, we're *all* hiding something. I didn't find out much of anything, did I?"

He was right. We couldn't hit rewind. We needed to figure out how best to move forward. "You're sure the detective on the case isn't looking into other suspects?"

Max let go of me. "I don't know what exactly is being investigated. I can't be sure of anything. This detective isn't someone I know, so he's not keeping me in the loop. But yeah, it's standard procedure that if you're sure you have the right person, that's where you focus your energy. That's when the evidence is freshest, so you can best make your case, rather than chasing figments."

I watched the steam from the teapot disappear into the air like figments of my imagination. Like the eyes I'd felt watching me through the plants—or from one of the plants itself?

We poured our steeped tea and took our teacups to his back porch. It was a warm night, with a light glow of sunlight all we needed. The summer solstice sun was low in the sky, with orange and purple swaths of sky visible.

"You left out the women when you went over the suspects," I pointed out.

"Carla and Lena. Both smart enough not to have police records."

"Something strange is going on with those plants Carla is stitching together." Darkness was falling, but the greenery in Max's backyard was soothing compared to the strange plants resembling creatures in Carla's conservatory. Here, the shadows felt like a cozy blanket wrapping around us as we settled in for the evening.

"Those plants didn't kill Frederick." Max ran a finger around the rim of his teacup. "Carla is more of an open book than any of them. Not like Elias's sister, Lena. Flawless in her appearance and outward actions. Which, in my experience, means she's probably hiding the most secrets of any of them."

"That logic makes no sense."

"Of course it makes sense," Max snapped. "Sorry. I'm on edge. I didn't mean to snap at you. I just wish I knew more. It's customary to keep a fellow officer up to date. You'd think after all my years of service, they'd have some courtesy—"

"You're no longer a detective," I pointed out. "And it *is* a conflict of interest."

"But that's also why I can help them." He stopped spinning his finger around the rim of the teacup and grabbed the clay cup so tightly that I was scared he'd break it.

"You're not going to listen to the facts," I said softly.

"Zoe, you don't really think my dad—"

"I only met the man yesterday," I said. "But if you say he's innocent, that's what I'll believe until it's proven otherwise."

"Thanks for the vote of confidence," he said sarcastically.

"Max." I took his hand and moved the teacup from his reach. "I'm with you. I'm simply saying we need to have an open mind for whatever we find."

"So you *are* expecting him to be guilty?"

"Actually," I said, "I'm not. I'm expecting that he's innocent, but that in the process of figuring out why he's been lying and acting strangely, you're going to learn something about him that you wish you hadn't."

Max opened his mouth but had second thoughts about whatever he was going to say. Instead, he stood and set down both of our teacups before lifting me from my seat and pulling me into a hug. He held onto me as if for dear life. We stood there in silence, rocking back and forth, for several minutes.

"I know you're right," said Max after he finally pulled away. "But I know him better than anyone."

"You don't, though. You admitted you're not close." I would have gone so far as to say "estranged," but I knew it would upset Max, which wouldn't help anything right now.

"I mean I know my dad better than anyone working on the case."

"Let them do their job from that angle," I said, "and we can think through what we know on our end. Starting with the murder scene."

"Where my dad was fleeing? Why won't he say why he was even there—"

"Maybe we should start even earlier."

"Two nights ago, when he *didn't* destroy my shop, but claimed to." Max clenched his jaw.

"I was thinking even earlier," I said softly. "As soon as your dad came back into your life."

"When I decided to open The Alchemy of Tea? Dad was upset as soon as he learned about it from my mom."

"Which is strange, since he learned about tea and herbalism from his parents. I know he told you he worried about how many small businesses fail, something he repeated to me when he came to see me as well, but—"

"It doesn't sound like him. I think that's why I was so angry when he got in touch."

"Exactly. He's not a very good liar."

"Which I suppose is a good thing. But also explains why he won't say *anything* right now."

"Your dad was so close to his parents that they lived with you for many years. And they were apothecaries in China before they emigrated to the United States."

"You know all this, Zoe. Why are you—"

"Bear with me. Everything points to your new shop being a catalyst, but we don't yet know why. We need to find the connection."

Max took two deep breaths before speaking. "My grandmother, Ling, was the skilled herbalist. Granddad, Jim, helped with the business side—"

"Jim?"

"It's pronounced sort-of similarly to his real name, Zhen, and it was easier for Americans to say, so he used Jim. He came over with my grandmother in the late 1940s."

"After the Chinese Exclusion Act was repealed in 1943... It couldn't have been easy for them. Public opinion didn't change as quickly as the law."

Max stared at me with a flash of irritation or frustration, but it was gone a moment later. "I'm sorry. It's still a lot, getting used to knowing that you lived through all this history. I'm not exactly envious—"

"You shouldn't be. It's not something I'd wish on others. I love my life *now*, but I haven't always. And it's still hard sometimes."

Max took my hand. "It was hard losing Granddad shortly after he celebrated his hundredth birthday, so I know. It's never easy outliving our loved ones, even when they've had a full life, like he did."

"Back to your apothecary grandmother. She's the one who taught you about tea. You two planted those tea plants together."

"We did. I was a toddler when she and Granddad came to live with us. Granddad constructed treasure hunts for me, and Grandma taught me about tea's magical properties. That's what she called it. When I got older, I thought she was embellishing facts for a small child. I was frustrated, and that's what sent me totally in the direction of rationalism. I rejected everything she'd taught me when I was little, thinking it was all a game."

"Until you learned about alchemy."

Max nodded. "She wasn't practicing alchemy on the same scale as you, but she extracted the healing properties of plants, especially tea. Her use of tea wasn't anything like the formal Chinese tea ceremonies you might have experienced. She didn't have patience for formality." He smiled at the memory of his grandmother. "Mom was busy teaching elementary school, and Dad was busy as a professor, so they loved having Dad's parents live with us to help with me and Mina."

"And your sister was the one who embraced the teachings of your grandmother."

"Sort of. Mina sees everything in the world as science, even things that scientists don't think of as science. Like those tea plants I planted with my grandmother."

"But you were the one that planted them with her."

"Only because of my age. Mina's three years younger than me. She was a baby when I helped plant those tea bushes. Now that I think of it, I bet it was just a way to keep me occupied while my parents were busy with a newborn."

"Regardless of why it happened, you were the one whose energy went into the tea plants."

"I didn't know anything about alchemical energy or intent at the time."

"But as a kid, everything you did would have been pure. Your heart was fully in it. And that's the key to alchemical preparations working—putting your own energy fully into a preparation."

Max looked out over his kitchen garden into the semi-darkness. "I hadn't considered that something I did more than forty years ago might be relevant."

"Your grandmother died when you were how old?"

"Thirteen. Around the time my parents' marriage was breaking up. Without her, and with me and Mina no longer little kids, Granddad went back to China to be with his extended family. It's funny. I always thought he'd been the one to assimilate to life in the United States better—that's why he went by the name Jim, after all, and he was the one who got a traditional nine-to-five business job to care for his wife and child—but he didn't feel like it was home without his wife."

"Because it's people who make a place feel like home." I took Max's hand and traced it with my fingertips. I'd gotten to know his strong hands so well. His well-tended fingernails, the faint scents of lavender from his own backyard flowers and the coconut oil in his hand lotion, the little mole on the side of his thumb, the small scar on his palm.

Max looked at me with a vulnerability that nearly cracked open my heart. "Stay here tonight."

I let go of his hand. "As much as I'd love to, you've got your mom here to look after. I'll come over in the morning."

"I'll drive you home."

"It's not far to walk."

"There's a murderer out there, Zoe." Max grabbed his keys. "At least humor me. Let me drop you off at home, so *I'll* sleep better."

"It's a deal." I hadn't warned Dorian we'd have company, so I hoped he wouldn't ask to come inside when he dropped me off. I hated that I had to hide the fact that Dorian was a gargoyle from the man I loved. We'd been so close to having Max finally meet Dorian. How much longer could I keep the gargoyle's secret?

CHAPTER 20

"You and Max are getting nowhere," Dorian said half an hour later. "I am disappointed in you both. You must think in a more logical manner!" He slapped his pointing stick at the oversize cork board resting against a shelf in the attic, dislodging a strip of red yarn.

The words MURDER BOARD were written in neat, calligraphic handwriting on a thin sheet of typewriter paper, which was affixed to the top of the board with thumb tacks. Dorian didn't watch much television, but as a voracious reader he had read about the concept of a cross-referenced suspect chart in a 1970s spy novel. Then he'd stumbled across the term "murder board" when reading a more recent novel about a true crime podcaster.

I scanned the headers on the murder board, which was so covered with yarn that I could barely make out details beneath the headings of each section. But the headlines spoke for themselves:

- Max's father, professor Andrew Liu.
- Topiary sculptor and groundskeeper Gary (surname unknown).
- Retired music producer Dante West (former guitarist of punk band Mayhem).

- Carnivorous plant enthusiast Carla West (former lead singer of Carla and the Carpathians).
- Young hospitality services worker Lena Tamraz.
- Hair stylist punk rocker Elias Tamraz.
- Victim: Failed businessman Frederick Rasmussen.

Beneath these headlines were photographs and a combination of handwritten notes and computer printouts.

"You found all of this information online?" I wrapped a thread of yarn that had come loose around the nearby thumbtack. I was fairly certain it was the right location, though I couldn't be certain. The web of thick red yarn looked more like a sinister spiderweb than a collection of logical thoughts.

"Your printer needs more ink," said Dorian. "I have added that to the list on the refrigerator."

Despite the importance of each of the people on Dorian's murder board, I felt my body succumbing to the absence of sunlight. I stifled a yawn.

Dorian scowled at me and drew his horns together. "Am I boring you with my meticulous research, Alchemist?"

I pointed at the attic's skylight. It was well past 9 o'clock at night, and Max had dropped me off at home half an hour ago. The summer sun had nearly set, and the light from the skylight above had long since disappeared. It was now truly late enough that I could no longer draw any energy from the sun. The room with its high, sloped ceiling was illuminated only by the soft light of two vintage lamps. "You know it's difficult for me to stay alert after dark."

One of the downsides of being so attuned to nature is that I wilt like a flower after dark. It's not like a fairy tale in which I turn into a pumpkin at midnight, but it feels as if my energy is being siphoned out of me. The opposite is true as well. No matter how early the sun rises or how much sleep I've gotten, the sunrise fills me with energy.

"Hot cocoa," Dorian declared, raising his pointing stick above his head triumphantly. "This is what you need. The heartiness of chocolate with a smidge of caffeine will be enough for you to stay alert until midnight, so we may discuss the facts and have solved the case in time for your *petit déjeuner* with Max and Mary."

"I'm fine," I insisted. The hot chocolate would keep me up past midnight. There was enough stimulation on Dorian's cork board to keep me awake, and I needed to think through what I knew with an unbiased friend. Max had too many preconceived notions about his father to see the case clearly. I didn't know if Andrew Liu was a murderer, but he was definitely involved.

"I don't see more about Andrew Liu than his profession on that murder board." I cringed. I shouldn't have given in to calling it that. Or maybe it was a lost cause and I needed to adapt to the times.

"He is here, in the corner. He is not as prominently featured as the members of the Posh and Punk Rock Tea Club, as I have not yet had time to read his scholarly books and articles, only a recent paper co-authored with Jonathan Jin that made me wish I was capable of sleep. Yet my main motivation for focusing on the others is our working assumption that he is innocent."

"I didn't think you'd be sentimental enough to consider him a lesser suspect because he's Max's dad."

Dorian shrugged. "We are only investigating to assist your beau, *n'est-ce pas?* Therefore, our starting assumption must be that Professor Liu is most likely innocent."

"Which is why we need to learn more—" I broke off as I opened the screen of my laptop and eyed the gargoyle. "Why is my browser open to a social media platform I don't use?"

Dorian cleared his throat and had the decency to look chagrined. "I neglected to return your computer to the state in which I picked it up? I do apologize, *mon amie.*"

"Why are you on social media? I don't begrudge you if you'd like to make online friends, but you claimed you hated it."

Dorian sniffed. "I do. This was simply reconnaissance."

"Reconnaissance?"

"Yes. Gathering intelligence—"

"I know what the word means. Reconnaissance on social media?"

"I am an old friend and business associate of Frederick Rasmussen, who was greatly saddened to learn of his passing…"

I groaned. "You made up on online identity to get information about the funeral, where you're guessing the killer will appear?" I wondered how Dorian proposed to disguise himself to sneak into a funeral service. Perhaps as an elderly woman with a black veil?

Dorian grinned. "It is so much better than a silent funeral gathering. The Wests are throwing a memorial concert in his honor!" He tapped a key on the laptop and a flyer appeared.

"They're honoring the memory of both Frederick and Joyce Rasmussen with a memorial concert at Dante's Inferno," I read. "Joyce?"

"*Oui*. The mother of Frederick. She passed away of old age earlier this year. She was a member of the tea club as well. She was quite elderly, but it was still unfortunate to read that she died alone."

"That's why I've heard her name. They mentioned her when I visited with Max. And she was close enough to them to leave her shoes in their conservatory."

"Theirs was not a shoe-free home. Perhaps she practiced rewilding."

I had no idea how Dorian knew about the modern practice of rewilding, the act of transforming land ecologically back to its state before people meddled with it, and also the individual practice of going without shoes so that our feet could experience the world in their natural state. Then again, the gargoyle didn't need to sleep, so he both had time to see the world at night and to read all about it.

"Maybe," I said, "but my guess is that she was a fellow plant enthusiast who left her gardening boots at their house. Dante mentioned her boots were in the conservatory. I didn't understand why he was upset, but it makes more sense if they were close and she passed away."

I read the details on the flyer, which included an image of the stone ruins of Dante's Inferno and an invitation for friends and family to bring instruments to sing songs to remember their neighbors, or simply attend in the audience. A large note at the bottom stated, *Due to a severe allergy, no pets of any kind! Thank you for understanding.* "This concert is two days from now," I added, reading the date.

"One wonders what they are covering up by having people trample the crime scene," Dorian murmured.

"Max thought the crime scene crew would be there all night, so I'm guessing it'll be released in time. Still, it's awfully soon...." A flurry of thoughts ran through my mind, but it was only snatches of ideas, nothing clear enough for me to fully grasp.

Monster topiary with eyes watching us in the conservatory, carnivorous plants, leaves stitched together with yarn, an outdoor concert venue among stone ruins, all connected to an unpleasant man who was somehow connected to Max's estranged father…

"Zoe, you look as if you will fall asleep in this armchair!"

I jerked awake. I hadn't been asleep, had I? What was the thought that Dorian had interrupted?

"I will return in five minutes," said Dorian, "with stimulating cocoa."

I didn't object this time. And I only rested my eyes for a few seconds, but the next thing I knew, Dorian was lifting my laptop out of my lap and handing me a steaming mug of hot cocoa. I was more tired than I thought.

I breathed in the scents of cardamom, ginger, coconut, and cocoa, already feeling more energized. After three energizing sips, I was back at the murder board with one hand on my hip and the other wrapped around the mug.

"Can we please remove this yarn?" I asked. "Every single person on your board is connected, so we don't need the yarn. We know they're all connected. It's impossible to see what lies beneath the yarn."

"If you wish to destroy my painstakingly created masterpiece, I beg of you, at least take a photograph with your mobile phone before doing so."

I did so, then wound the yarn into a messy ball as I removed the tangle of connections, revealing a photograph of Frederick Rasmussen and several article snippets. "There's a lot here on the victim."

"But of course." Dorian tapped a claw on a flattering photograph of the dead man. "Frederick Rasmussen's headshot from one of his failed business ventures."

"If he was a bad businessman," I said, "he might have made enemies out of his investors."

"Unfortunately," said Dorian, "by all accounts, he was a man bad at securing capital in the first place, and equally bad at turning a profit. Therefore, he primarily used his own money, not that of others. Which is why he ended up with nothing and moved home to live with his mother, at age sixty, when she herself was in her late eighties. As we know, Joyce Rasmussen died at ninety, earlier this year, leaving Frederick the sole occupant of the mansion next door to the West estate."

"The only other house on the private drive on that hillside."

"*Oui*. Their homes were not visible to each other, through the thick blanket of trees, yet Frederick complained online about the noise from their concerts, so the Wests agreed to throw fewer outdoor parties using their Dante's Inferno stage. Have you read Dante Alighieri's epic poem, Zoe?"

"*The Divine Comedy*," I said. "Once, in the original Italian, and that was enough." I enjoy reading literature and poetry in its original language, when I can. Ambrose and I had been learning Italian together, and we read the epic poem together. I'm glad I did it, but I hadn't kept up on my Italian after Ambrose died. I still remembered the rhyme scheme of the epic poem, but the words were lost to memory—only the images they generated in my mind remained. I'm still not certain which images are ones I've seen in artwork and which ones my own mind generated when reading Dante's words.

"I wonder if Dante West has read it," mused Dorian, "or whether he only knows the cultural tradition of the famous work."

"We're getting off track."

"It is never 'getting off track,' as you crassly stated, to exercise one's little gray cells." Dorian tapped his gray forehead.

"What else did you learn about Frederick? Is there anyone you think we can remove?"

"Not one of the suspects had a good thing to say about Frederick. They are all suspects. Every one of them remains on my murder board."

CHAPTER 21

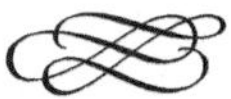

We had one murder victim, one destroyed shop, and six suspects.

Where did that leave us? I was sure the police were investigating. But so far, their investigations had led them to Max's dad, who was behaving suspiciously for unknown reasons. I desperately wanted to help Max get at the truth.

I looked again at Dorian's list of suspects in the murder of Frederick Rasmussen: Dante West, Carla West, Lena Tamraz, Elias Tamraz, Gary the groundskeeper, and Max's father. And Dorian had assembled numerous facts about each one, including everything from their friends and favorite restaurants to their addresses and where they'd gone to college.

I frowned at the board. "All of this information so readily available online." It had been hard enough to live in the shadows in the past. It was becoming more and more difficult to do so in the twenty-first century.

"*Oui*. These people share far too much of themselves online. Except for Gary. I found a website for his gardening business, but he does not list his surname. Gary the Gardener, a licensed landscaper providing service to the greater Portland area. He values privacy. An admirable trait."

"Or a suspicious one." Gary was smiling in the photo on his

website, surrounded by blooming rose bushes, looking far different than the silent man I'd met at the West estate.

"I could not learn much more, as he is not currently accepting new clients, so he has disabled his 'contact me' button. It appears that his duties as groundskeeper of Dante and Carla's estate take up much of his time. This makes sense if he is helping Carla with her alchemical experiments on plants—"

"Which we have no evidence for. So let's move on." I leaned more closely to the board. "Are Lena and Elias twins?"

"No. Elias is three years older than his sister. Yet they do look much alike, with those large, haunting eyes. When I began my research, I half-expected to discover they had been child actors in horror movies. But no, the closest they came to this was when they dressed as twins in a haunted house one Halloween. Another Halloween, they dressed as each other." Dorian pointed at a photo he had printed.

"Posh Lena abandoned her pristine white clothing and dressed as a punk, and punk rock Elias dressed in preppy clothing." I smiled at the thought of them. "They must be close."

"Close enough to cover up for each other! We must not believe anything they say. Do not fall for their youthful, innocent faces."

"What's this?" I asked, reaching for a blank sheet of paper tacked to the cork board.

Dorian scampered in front of me and blocked me from turning it over. "This is not for you."

"You're keeping secrets from me?"

"You did not take me seriously that I saw a monster in that conservatory, in spite of sensing it yourself. I am keeping my own notes as I consolidate my theories of a plant monster. I am a rational gargoyle." He flapped his wings once and then folded them to their resting place on his back. "I accept that we must first look at these suspects. But if the facts lead us to something else? I will be ready."

"Maybe I could help if I saw what you're thinking about—"

"*Non.* I am well aware that you may read my private notes after I have departed for the Blue Sky Teas kitchen in a few hours' time. Yet I must ask that you respect my wishes, and do not do so."

"I won't look at your notes about a monster," I promised, "but we agree to share what we know about everyone else, right?"

Dorian held his head high for a moment, then gave a curt nod. "Agreed. Dante West. Son of Clark and Lakmini West. Clark West was a successful Hollywood music producer, and Lakmini left Sri Lanka for Hollywood as a young woman, where she met Clark."

"I take it he was successful enough that you were able to get lots of information about them?"

"*Oui*. Dante is sixty-six years old. His parents were rich, so he inherited their wealth when they passed away a decade ago, not far apart. Even though he grew up with wealth, he wasn't a layabout. Yes, he was into punk rock and rebellion, but perhaps that's because his father was a famous music producer, so he was indoctrinated into the music scene and became a music producer himself. Dante both managed successful bands and was in his own unsuccessful one, Mayhem, and did things he loved with that wealth, like buying this mansion when it was an old, dilapidated building. Now, on to Dante's wife. Carla Carpathian—her legal name!"

"Really?"

"*Oui*. The pair met in the mid-1970s punk scene in Berkeley. Dante had departed Los Angeles for the university in Berkeley. Carla was at the time calling herself Carla Carpathian, because of her band Carla and the Carpathians. This was her high school punk band. Now some of her mail I saw in their house makes more sense—"

"You were snooping in their mail?"

"Not *in* their mail. That is a federal offense, Zoe. I am a good gargoyle immigrant. I know the laws of this nation, and our state of Oregon. Also the fundamental protections spelled out in the Constitution—"

"I believe you," I broke in. Though sometimes I couldn't quite believe my own life, having this type of conversation with a gargoyle in my attic. Not only the fact that Dorian was a gargoyle who considered himself a modern-day Poirot, but that I had *my own home*. After being on the road and living out of my Airstream trailer for so long, this was a life I hadn't imagined was possible for me.

"As I was saying." Dorian held his gray chin high. "I am aware that I must not *open* the mail of other people. Yet looking at the outside of mail? This is of no consequence to the law—yet possibly of much consequence to our investigation."

"You found something helpful?"

"Not as of yet," Dorian admitted. "Only the amusing fact that mail still comes to the house addressed to Carla Carpathian."

"Fan mail?" I asked.

"As I said, I did not open their mail."

"I don't suppose you found anything that suggests she was buying products for making a Frankenstein's plant monster."

"Veronica declined my request to look into their bank accounts—"

"You didn't really ask a fifteen-year-old girl to hack into a bank account?" But as I spoke the words, I knew he wasn't joking. He absolutely had asked her.

"You are the one who did not wish me to call her skills 'hacking'!"

"I'm glad that one of you had the sense to decline."

Dorian narrowed his black eyes at me. "Without access to their financial records, I was only able to read social media postings. Which are filled with much tedium—I am all for enjoying food, but why would I wish to see the meals of each person I am acquainted with? I was hoping I would find more hidden revelations, but alas, as of yet, I have not. Only the revelation that none of them were fond of Frederick."

"What about Carla's interest in making her own clothes?" I asked. "She's done punk-style knitting since her days in her band, which must have influenced how she began stitching together plants in that conservatory."

"How would this inform our murder investigation?" Dorian blinked at me.

"Because," I said, "it's a question of whether she's truly using some form of alchemy we don't understand to unite those plants she's stitched together. I didn't see—or smell—any rotting plants in the conservatory. That means either what she's doing *works* and leads to plants she then moves elsewhere—"

"Or monsters who walk away on their own! *Oui.* Good thinking, *mon amie.*"

"I wasn't *exactly* suggesting that she's created a monster. I'm only exploring the more reasonable ideas that she's performing alchemy to transform plants. *Something* is happening to those plants she's stitching together. If those plants aren't actually transforming, then she or someone else is replacing them."

"Why would someone else replace them?" Dorian asked. "Ah! I have answered my own question. If Carla is suffering from delusions, then someone close to her might wish to make her feel that her creations work! This also means she could suffer from *dangerous* delusions. If she thought Frederick was attacking her beloved plants, she might use her plants to attack him."

"Now we've entered the realm of wild conjecture." I was disappointed to find I'd finished the last of my cocoa. Dorian had a magical touch with all food and drink.

Dorian raised a clawed fingertip. "I am using my little gray cells to consider all possibilities. The easiest answer is not always the correct one. Life would be far easier if it lacked nuance."

"Let's get back to people. Dante would want to help Carla."

"Not their son."

"They have a son?"

"He is a great disappointment to them. A stockbroker. One who hoards his wealth instead of doing meaningful things with it. But he lives in London." Dorian tapped on his murder board. "Moving on to Lena and Elias Tamraz. Elias is twenty-five and Lena is twenty-two. Lena is a recent college graduate in the field of hospitality—such a strange profession! Studying to serve people at hotels and resorts? She is quite mature for her age, by every appearance, having graduated in the top group of students in her class, and already secured employment.

"Elias is their connection to Dante and Carla. He met them at a punk rock show, and they were the ones who ordered tea at the bar, and were served stale tea bags of Earl Gray tea, so they made plans to get together for good tea. They frequent Blue Sky Teas, but it is not their favorite, because Blue includes herbal teas in her mix of teas, whereas they believe that true tea is the *camellia sinensis* tea plant."

"Tea," I murmured. "We're back to strong feelings about tea once more. And the theft that started this whole string of events was the tea stolen from Max's shop."

CHAPTER 22

Frankenstein's plant monster wandered the grounds of the Gothic estate, frightening the black cat—

Dorian ripped the page from the typewriter. In his online research, he had discovered that Dante was deathly allergic to cats, so there would be no cat on the estate. Yet a black cat would have been perfect for his novel! With their connection to witchcraft and the occult, such creatures suggested mystery.

Bof! Dorian scowled at the wrinkled sheet of paper. Of course, he could include a black cat if he wished to do so. He was only writing fiction. Yes, it was fiction to assist his little gray cells puzzling out the truth, but still fiction. If he wished to place a cat in his fictional version of monsters and mayhem, he would do so.

Dorian had resumed work at his typewriter once Zoe departed to her bedchamber to sleep. With a few hours before he was due at Blue Sky Teas to bake, he could spend some time indulging in his novel.

He rolled the slightly wrinkled sheet of paper back into the typewriter and lined up the page.

The black cat arched her back and bared her teeth. Though she did not consciously understand the monstrosity of the plant crea-

ture before her, she instinctively knew this was a creature like no other.

The beast took a lumbering step forward, leaving three leaves and a trail of dirt in its wake.

This was an interesting question. Would a plant monster possess tree roots for its feet, or simply more curled tendrils of leaves with bendable branches? Would it need shoes to keep its form as it walked? Was it the wire he was shaped around that gave him a spine to stand upright? Strong gardening wire would serve this purpose.

Dorian scratched his chin as he read over his typewritten words. He had fixed the "B" key, yet it was still slightly off-kilter. No matter. The errant letter simply gave the manuscript more character. Now, if he were writing blackmail letters with this typewriter, that would be another story. Having such a distinguishable keystroke would be detrimental to such a plan. But Dorian had no current plans to blackmail anyone.

The black cat's fur stood on end in fear, her claws extended. She was now double in size than moments before, and her teeth bared like that of her fierce feline ancestor Bastet.

A cloud above shifted, enabling moonlight to light up the face of the monster, looming underneath a weathered gargoyle waterspout.

The cat retracted its claws. Slowly, the appearance of her thick obsidian fur returned to normal size. She began to purr.

This was an unexpected development. Yes, Dorian knew that he alone had tapped out the words on the old Remington. Yet it was as if he was not in control of his own story. *Mon dieu!* Like the Brontës, Christie, du Maurier, Poe, Tey, and so many other greats before him, he was a true writer. The characters had lives of their own. He wondered what would happen next.

The plant monster smiled. The shape of the leaves where his lips should be did not exactly resemble what we think of as a smile, yet the cat sensed this was his intention.

He reached out his green hand and stroked the cat between her ears. Her purrs grew louder.

This was an unexpected development indeed. Dorian had read Freud, yet he had never taken the man seriously. Perhaps there was something to this business of the unconscious mind. Perhaps the plant monster Dorian had seen was a victim himself. Or at the very least a harmless observer.

Dorian needed to find the plant monster *as a witness to the crime* of who killed Frederick Rasmussen.

He glanced at the grandfather clock in the attic. It was nearly eleven o'clock. In spite of the length of these long summer days, darkness had completely fallen. Zoe was fast asleep. He could wake her—she did not suffer from some fairy tale affliction, only the effects of being a plant alchemist. Yet once awakened, she would not be amenable to late-night breaking and entering at a crime scene. Of this, he was certain.

The mansion was too far for Dorian to travel on foot underneath his cape and the cover of darkness, and he had promised her he would not fly. He had also promised he would not drive her 1942 pickup truck, yet that had been an easy promise—he was too small to reach the pedals or see over the massive steering wheel and dashboard. There was simply no way for him to safely drive the vehicle. If he'd had need of one, he would have convinced her to invest in one of those miniature cars he sometimes saw parked in the more densely packed neighborhoods of Portland.

Dorian's young friends Brixton and Veronica were normally his co-conspirators, but Veronica was currently imprisoned by her tyrannical parents as punishment for her valiant actions on their recent escapade, and Brixton insisted on being a good friend and accompanying her on her involuntary volunteer work. No matter. At fifteen, they did not yet have licenses to drive. Only their friend Ethan had a fake driver's license, and he was spending the summer with his *grandmere* and *grandpere* while his parents completed their divorce.

Tobias? No, the man was too big a risk, his allegiances were solely to

Zoe. After all, she had once saved his life, so he could not begrudge the man. The Flamels were utterly devoted to Zoe as well. Although… Nicolas possessed a wonderful juxtaposition of character. One that allowed him to be both brilliant in intelligence and childlike when it came to people. Dorian could simply tell the man they were helping Zoe. Nicolas would have no qualms about borrowing Zoe's truck, driving without a license, or breaking into what was now considered a crime scene.

Dorian donned his cape and slipped out through the attic skylight, on his way to Nicolas Flamel's house.

CHAPTER 23

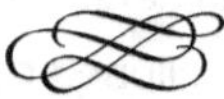

Le Chat Noir et le Monstre

Dorian's idea for a title to his novel sounded much more dramatic in French than its English translation, *The Black Cat and the Monster*. In English, it sounded more like a children's book, which was far from what Dorian was writing.

His mind was filled with titles and next steps in his novel as he crept through the neighborhood on the way to the Flamels' home.

Dorian was in luck. Perenelle Flamel had retired to their shared bedchamber already, but Nicolas was still wide awake, poring over a hefty book on engravings produced by the Metropolitan Museum of Art.

"Come in, come in!" cried Nicolas, ushering Dorian inside before spending nearly a minute looking for his glasses, which Dorian, once realizing what the man was looking for, pointed out were on top of his head.

"May I offer you a glass of my latest batch of home-brewed beer?" Nicolas offered.

Dorian frowned. "You have not been imbibing this evening, have you?" It was one thing to ask a man born in the thirteenth century to drive a car, and yet another to let him do so while intoxicated.

"Not this evening, no. Perenelle does not appreciate the flavor of my latest brew, so she has not wished to partake of it with me. It's quite grand, I assure you. Simply not to her taste. Are you certain I might not tempt you?"

"*Non, monsieur.* I have come to request a favor. One that only you can provide. This favor is for Zoe."

Nicolas's eyes lit up behind his thick glasses. "Of course. Anything for my dear Zoe."

~

When the engine of the green truck failed for the third time, the pair lurched to a stop in the middle of a deserted road.

"I believe you must also use that second foot lever," said Dorian, pointing at the clutch.

"Why did people give up the use of horses?" Nicolas lamented. "This does not seem to be a step forward in progress for humanity."

"*Oui.* As it appears in your hands, it is *très difficile.* Yet Zoe makes it look easy. Perhaps you could look up a video tutorial?"

"Ah!" Nicolas extracted a humungous cell phone from an inner pocket of his jacket, where the thick fabric also hid three glass test tubes. He tossed his glasses onto his thick head of hair and unlocked the phone screen. "How to drive an automobile." He enunciated each word as he spoke to the phone.

Nicolas was eagerly testing all forms of modern technology. He did not always like them, yet he gave them an energetic try before dismissing them.

"Two million videos?" Nicolas frowned at Dorian.

"Ask it how to drive a manual transmission," said Dorian. "And if this does not work, narrow it down to this particular make and model of car."

"Make *and* model," Nicolas murmured. "Such a complex metal beast this is."

~

Twenty minutes later, the pair of old alchemists was bouncing along the highway, nearly to the mansion. Dorian pointed out the private drive, and Nicolas downshifted to turn onto the narrow road.

"The Carpathians," Nicolas read from the sign. "Zoe gave me the novel *Dracula* to complete the gaps in my education after she rescued us, so I presume the person who named this hillside is a fan of Bram Stoker?"

"With all due respect, *monsieur* Flamel, perhaps you should stay focused on the road?" The bumper brushed into the bushes at the side of the road. Dorian would no doubt need to pluck leaves from the grate once they arrived home.

Nicolas righted the car. "This steering disc is lopsided."

"*Arrêtez!*" Dorian cried. "Stop! Pull to the side of the road."

Nicolas swerved and hit a topiary cut to resemble a gnome. No matter. Gnomes had always seemed to Dorian that they would be unpleasant creatures, so if this one were actually alive, he could use some humility.

"The cameras start there." Dorian pointed to a spot up ahead. "We are safe. But we go on foot from here."

He donned the hood of his cape and winced as Nicolas slammed the heavy door, oblivious to the fact that they were stealth operatives this eve.

"Stay close," said Dorian. "We do not wish to be captured on camera, or to wake the sleeping inhabitants of this mansion."

"Most magnificent," murmured Nicolas, coming to a stop as they snuck past one of the larger monster topiaries. "She resembles a serpent I once knew."

Dorian studied the old alchemist. "This is a likeness of the Loch Ness monster."

"Yes. I have to say, as I caught up on recent history, I was quite surprised to see she let herself be seen and photographed. She hated it when people she did not purposefully reveal herself to learned of her existence." He sighed. "I understand that times change, but I never imagined Nessie would become such a social creature."

"Are you pulling my leg, as the expression goes, *monsieur*?"

"Am I?" Nicolas gave him a mischievous smile.

They made their way to the conservatory in silence, Dorian careful that they remained in shadows and out of range of the cameras he'd seen when he last visited.

A solitary light illuminated a solitary window on the topmost floor of the house. It was far from the conservatory. Still, they would need to be careful not to make undue noise.

Dorian used a claw to pull open the windowpane of the conservatory that had swung open the previous day and allowed him to enter unseen. "Careful," he said to Nicolas. "We must not break the glass."

"Perenelle would love this," he whispered. "So much color. And some of these plants could be made into pigments and dyes." Nicolas removed a test tube from inside his jacket. Using a pair of tweezers, he removed a petal from a flower Dorian did not recognize.

Dorian much preferred Zoe's food-based garden to this feast for the eyes. Carnivorous plants made for a good conversation piece, but unlike the rainbow of vegetables, berries, and herbs in Zoe's garden, one could not eat them. Yes, the section of tea plants could be harvested and turned into tea leaves to brew, but personally, Dorian felt tea was over-rated. He would not express this outwardly to Max, as he wished to make a good impression when he finally met the man, yet give Dorian a shot of espresso made with freshly roasted coffee beans, and Dorian was a happy gargoyle.

"Nicolas?" Dorian whispered. Where had the blasted man wandered off to? It wouldn't do to have him caught on camera.

Dorian scampered from the carnivorous plants to the tea bushes.

"Dorian?" Nicolas blinked in quick succession. "How did you get over there?"

"I was looking at the carnivorous plants, which Zoe says should be more accurately called *insectivorous* plants."

"You were?" Nicolas frowned. "Then with whom was I speaking?"

Dorian gasped. "The monster! It speaks?"

The normally jocular Nicolas became gravely serious as he spoke. "I heard no voice, but I saw what I believed to be your eyes flash in the darkness, beyond this potted palm tree. Thinking I was addressing you, I conveyed my thoughts about these two plants that are stitched together.

They are dying, not merging." The old alchemist reached out to a drooping leaf, before remembering the gravity of the situation. Nicolas turned from the massacred leaf back to Dorian. "But if it was not you I saw..."

Dorian gasped once more, for his gaze fell to a spot behind the old alchemist. Dorian scampered to a pot a few meters beyond Nicolas—a pot large enough for a tree, which now stood empty. Inside, the only contents were disturbed dirt and a few scattered leaves. "A topiary has stepped off of its pedestal!"

"*Stepped*?"

"*Oui*. There is a footprint." Dorian bent to examine the clear outline of a boot left in the dirt.

A light clicked on in the house.

"We must go," Dorian whispered, grasping Nicolas's sleeve.

The old alchemists hurried back to the open window, wondering what exactly had once been inside that pot that stood up and walked away.

CHAPTER 24

I awoke at dawn, as I always do. The first rays of morning light were streaming in through the bedroom window. For the few seconds as I woke up, it felt as if the events of the previous day were only a dream. That nobody had been murdered, and that Max's dad wasn't the prime suspect.

As I shook off the remnants of sleep, I sensed an energy buzzing in the house I didn't usually feel. When I walked downstairs a few minutes later to fix myself a glass of lemon water, as I always did to start the day, I saw what it was. Dorian had spread out more than a dozen books on the dining room table. He had a mug of strong coffee at his elbow and a platter of fresh-baked pastries had been placed at the head of the table.

As a perfectionist, Dorian insisted that anything he baked that was sold at the Blue Sky Teas pastry counter look as perfect as it tasted. Anything that was misshapen was brought back to our house, rather than thrown away. Today, there were several blueberry muffins with tops that had cratered due to an abundance of blueberries, plus two lopsided oatmeal bars.

"Where did these books come from?" I picked up a heavy book on Hindu mythology.

"You have probably noticed that Nicolas has become a book hoarder."

"He's catching up on lost time. They adore him down at Powell's Books. I don't think he's ever left the bookshop without at least a dozen books. Have they already run out of room at their new house to store books?"

Dorian closed the book he was reading on mythological creatures of Cornwall. "This is important work, Zoe. Nicolas believes me that there is a plant who has been brought to life—a creature akin to Frankenstein's monster, if you will—roaming the halls of the Carpathian Conservatory. There is much precedent for such creatures—"

"In books on *mythology*."

Dorian sniffed. "It is not only in mythology. There are also books on folklore and witchcraft here."

"The authorities aren't going to believe a plant monster killed Frederick."

"This is not what I believe has taken place." Dorian steepled his clawed index fingers and tapped them together. "I have a theory."

I held up my own finger. "Give me two minutes."

Whatever Dorian was about to say, it would require energy. I slipped into the kitchen, poured myself a glass of water with a refreshing squeeze of lemon, and drank it while taking a peek at my backyard garden. The plants were just waking up like I was. It would be a warm day—perfect for making a solar infusion of herbal tea. I scooped half a cup of dried chamomile flowers into a mason jar and filled it with water, then set it on a spot on the back porch that would soon be bathed in sunlight. When I pushed through the swinging door back to the dining and living room, I was ready to face Dorian and his plant monster theories.

"What *do you* believe happened?" I asked.

"The existence of the plant creature does not mean that it is the killer. What if he is a *witness*?" Dorian beamed at me. "A witness, Zoe! Because of the cultural significance of Frankenstein, we were all so quick to assume a plant creature is a *monster* and one that has killed—"

"You're the one who insisted—"

"I have reassessed my own biases," Dorian said humbly. Or at least as humbly as was possible for the gargoyle who believed he was deserving of prestigious culinary awards.

"Do you not see?" he added impatiently. "This explains why *monsieur* Liu will not explain himself. He and the plant creature are secret allies in having witnessed a murder. Whatever he has witnessed, Andrew Liu knows nobody will believe him!"

I glanced at the book on Cornish mythological creatures Dorian had been reading. Had his imagination gotten the best of him, or had he really seen a plant creature? I had felt that I was being watched by someone hiding, but it was still a leap to assume it was a plant monster.

"Something strange happened at that house," I said, "and that's probably why Andrew can't explain himself, but I don't think it's a plant that was brought to life who killed Frederick. Definitely not a Cornish spriggan." I pronounced spriggan as it was pronounced in Cornwall, as *sprid-jan.* "Besides, they're not even made of plants. They simply like hanging out around trees because they're pixies."

"Evil, *malevolent* pixies," Dorian added. "Exactly the type of creature who would be hiding mischievously in the greenery and then come out of hiding to commit murder!"

I sighed. "I thought you said the plant creature was a witness, not the killer."

Dorian narrowed his black eyes at me. "I do not yet have all the answers. The plant creature as a witness is only one theory."

"Well, it wasn't a spriggan we saw in the conservatory. You don't actually believe a pixie killed Frederick Rasmussen, do you?"

Dorian shrugged his wings. "It is quite doubtful. A yakshi or yakshini would be more likely." He tapped a clawed hand on a book of Hindu mythology. "These nature-loving deities are well-recognized by Hindu and Buddhist cultural traditions. They are drawn to trees, especially—"

"Ashoka trees." I closed my eyes to better remember the details of the strange Carpathian Conservatory. "There was an Ashoka tree in the conservatory. And it was flowering out of season." Which of course would have to do with the carefully regulated temperature of a greenhouse, not the presence of a mythological being. A *peaceful* mythological being, if memory served.

I opened my eyes and scowled at the gargoyle. "We're not dealing with a mythological creature. It's possible to express alchemy in new ways, like Perenelle did with paint when she learned how to transform the essence of a person into and out of a painting, and like backward alchemists did when they harnessed the power of the death rotation. But those forms of alchemy aren't magic or mythology. These books are a distraction."

"*Oui*," Dorian agreed. "Alchemical transformations are fundamentally different from the stories of mythological beings. Yet I do not concur that these books are distractions. They are inspiration. I am feeding my little gray cells with these stories as inspiration."

"Because pieces of a larger truth can sometimes be found lurking in the shadows of folklore."

"*Exactement*. Folklore draws upon the hopes and fears of the people who create them, who build in their own curious experiences. It is a fascinating topic. Perhaps I will pursue a degree in this field of study one day. An online degree, of course." He wriggled his horns, something he would never be able to do in a university classroom.

"It's easier to audit courses without receiving a formal degree," I said from experience. "You can learn just as much, but without having a public record of the year you received a formal degree. But now we're *really* getting off track."

Dorian chuckled. "You transform plants by adding your intent to help them thrive. You have not brought them to life in a more transformative way, yet this does not mean such a transformation is impossible. What has been happening at the Carpathian Conservatory, and what plant creatures from lore are based in reality?"

My gaze fell to the pile of books. "When did Nicolas come over anyway?"

Dorian waved away the question. "You fall asleep so early, Zoe. Not all alchemists suffer this affliction. Nicolas needs sleep, yet since he deals with metals, his energy is not as affected by the sun as yours. Now that you are awake, may I tempt you with a pastry? Or are you walking to Max's home immediately?"

Max was going to try and see his dad first thing this morning, so I settled in to join Dorian for breakfast—a *second* breakfast for him—as we looked through the books for inspiration.

I enjoyed the nutty aroma of Dorian's coffee, but for myself I fixed an herbal tea blend with spicy ingredients to awaken my senses without caffeine: ginger root, cloves, and peppermint leaf. I lifted a misshapen oatmeal bar to my mouth and bit into a flavorful combination of toasted oats, cinnamon, coconut, and almond butter.

Dorian handed me a book held open to a page on mandrake root. "It is said that the mandrake screams when it is pulled from the earth. There have been many sightings—"

"There was no mandrake root in the conservatory," I said. "I would have noticed its rusty odor. Whatever living creature we might have seen, it wasn't a poisonous plant."

I was certain I was right about the poison. But I wasn't certain about much else. What secrets were hiding in the Carpathian Conservatory?

CHAPTER 25

I walked to Max's house with a basket of extra breakfast treats, my silver raincoat swaying behind me in the crisp, early morning breeze.

"Hey, darlin'." Max's mom opened his front door and gave me a hug. Her cowboy boots rested next to the front door, and she wore jeans and yellow socks that matched a white blouse dotted with a faint pattern of yellow daisies. "Perfect timing. Max is making tea in the kitchen."

I closed the door behind me and followed Mary through the living room to the kitchen, where a bouquet of purple irises in a simple glass vase adorned the countertop. The delicate petals looked like butterflies about to take flight. Iris flowers don't have a strong fragrance, so the aroma dominating the kitchen was the earthy scent of tea Max was preparing.

"Were you able to see him?" I asked as I set the muffin basket on the counter.

Max looked up from his cast iron teapot. "We were."

"But that man is as stubborn as a mule," said Mary. "He wouldn't tell us anything helpful."

"Do you think he's protecting someone?" I asked.

"I can't imagine who it would be." Mary shook her head. "He'd want to protect me and the kids, of course, but that doesn't make any sense. We don't need protecting. None of us hurt Max's shop or killed that poor man."

Max poured two cups of tea, but he hesitated before pouring a third. "I should go back and try him again. Alone this time. Just in case that makes a difference."

"Max." His mom took the teapot, poured the third cup, and handed it to Max. "You can't make that man do anything he doesn't want to do. When he's ready to talk with you, he'll get word to you."

"But we only have two more days—if that—until they decide whether they'll charge him with murder."

"Maximilian," Mary snapped. "You know that'll do more harm than good. Zoe, maybe you can talk some sense into him."

"I don't know that there's any sense in this situation." I closed my eyes and thought back to two days ago, when I'd first seen Max's dad looking in the window of The Alchemy of Tea. Andrew Liu didn't want Max to open the shop, but he was trying to use reason rather than force. I breathed in a woody scent, and when I opened my eyes, Mary was holding a cup of tea for me.

"I can make an herbal tea for you," said Max.

I took a sip. "This is perfect. I have a feeling I'll need the caffeine of this green tea to get through the day. Do you remember exactly what your father said to you when he asked you not to open your shop?"

"He said I was ruining my life. I'm an adult in my forties, I talk to the man twice a year, and he thinks he can talk to me like that?" Max's cheeks flushed.

"It's my fault," said Mary. "I talk with him regularly and keep him caught up on the kids."

"How regularly?" Max raised an eyebrow.

Mary shrugged. "I don't keep track. Whenever we feel like talking."

"Whenever you feel like talking with the man who left us?" Max gaped at his mom. "Why didn't you tell me you had an ongoing relationship?"

"It's not a relationship." Mary turned back to me. "Anyway, I told

Andrew about Max's shop. I had no idea he'd react so strongly. He already knew Max had retired from his job as a detective. That didn't bother him much. He was mainly concerned that Max have something else planned, which he did. It's not like he was simply quitting and would lose his house. Andrew wasn't concerned until I told him that the teashop you were setting up would include your grandmama's tea."

"When was that?" I asked.

"Just a week or so ago. I emailed him a link to the grand opening information. I wanted him to be proud of Max, like I am."

"He called me last week," said Max, "while I was putting the final touches on the shop. He asked me to reconsider what I was doing with my life, that I didn't want such a high-profile store. When I dismissed that ridiculous sentiment, he spouted a statistic about how most small businesses fail within the first year."

"He was never very good at pep talks when Max and Mina were kids," said Mary, "but that's especially awful, even for him."

"But I could tell there was something more to it," said Max. "Something he wasn't telling me."

"High profile?" I asked. "He said that?"

Max nodded. "He did. Like I said, he wasn't making any sense. If he was concerned about me failing, wouldn't it be *good* that it was getting attention?"

"Did he say why he thought it was high profile?" I asked. "Did you get any media coverage I don't know about?" I was careful not to be caught on film by anyone who would share the image publicly. I'd slipped up once after moving to Portland, featured in a weekly newspaper at Blue Sky Teas, back when I was keeping up the pretense that I was the pastry chef of the café, not Dorian.

"He's got a website set up." Mary held up her phone, showing the homepage of The Alchemy of Tea online. A big yellow banner under the header said, "Grand opening postponed." I was glad Max had thought of that.

"Even *I* have a website for Elixir," I said. "It's not like that means my online antiques are high profile just because I sell them online." I did my best to make them the exact opposite. I didn't include any photographs of myself on the site or use social media. I simply made sure to have unique items so people searching online for them would find them.

"I'm not set up to sell goods online like you are," said Max. "I wanted to create a cozy shop where people could browse in person. The website is to entice people to come in, not an e-commerce site."

"And your dad only got upset when Mary told him you'd be selling tea made from your grandmother's plants," I said.

"I suppose that's true," Mary agreed. "I'd already told him about the shop before that, but not the details."

"The devil is in the details," I murmured. "Would he be upset you were sharing something that had a personal connection to your family?"

Mary gasped, spilling half her tea onto the kitchen floor. "The tea plants!" she cried.

"What are you talking about?" Max asked. "Dad never had any sentimental attachment to those plants. They're only special to me."

"Because you planted them with your grandmother when you were little and Mina was a baby." Mary looked from Max back to me, her body tense and her energy unfocused.

"I know," said Max. "That's why the tea I'm working with now is so special to me."

I didn't know how much Max had explained to his mom about the alchemical principle of how a person can put their own energy and intent into the plants they work with. Her mother-in-law had been an apothecary, so she knew something about plant energy, but she didn't know I was over three hundred years old.

Mary ran into the living room. Max and I followed.

We found her pulling on her boots. "When your grandmama died and your granddad moved back to China," said Mary, "that's right around the time your father and I were splitting up." Mary wasn't a pacer, but a foot tapper. She tapped her boot as her body pulsed with nervous energy.

"I know," said Max. "That's why I was always over at my friends' houses after school, instead of being at home. Ma, what are you so excited about?"

"Andrew accepted a job as a professor at an East Coast university," Mary said to me, "and expected us to simply uproot our lives and move with him. Our marriage was already fractured, and that was the last straw." She turned back to Max. "You didn't express any interest in those tea plants, or nature in general, when you were a teenager, so I don't know if you even noticed when your father ripped them out."

Max drew his brow together. "I think I would have noticed that. I've been using those plants—"

"Ha. You didn't notice because I'm a good mama. When he left, he tore out those bushes, put them into trash bags that he threw away. But I couldn't let them go. You and your grandmama loved them so much. While he was busy packing up the rest of his things, I took those tea plants out of the bags and replaced the bulk with other yard waste. I hid the tea plants in the garage, and after he left, I put them back into the empty holes in the hillside. He never came to the house when he came to town to spend time with you and Mina."

"We always met him elsewhere," said Max. "You really did that with the plants?"

Mary shrugged. "It was easy. I didn't really do anything. When he took them out, he dug around the plants, taking all of their roots and huge amounts of dirt with them. His obsessive traits that I hated about his academic research came in handy here. It meant that the plants weren't even damaged."

"The roots," I whispered. "They could have grown back if he hadn't been so careful to remove every aspect of the plants. He had to be sure they wouldn't grow back."

Max and Mary stared at me.

"Don't you see?" I said. "Andrew wanted to destroy the plants *not* for a symbolic reason because of the divorce. He never wanted anyone making tea with those plants."

"But *why?*" Max asked as his mom grabbed her purse. Max swore. "You two think Dad dug up the tea plants again?"

"Only one way to find out." Mary pulled her car key from her bag. "We've gotta get back to Astoria."

"I can't." Max glanced at his phone. "I have to get back to the shop. I'm meeting the handyman who's helping me fix it up."

"Fancy a road trip with me, Zoe?" Mary asked me with a wink.

141

CHAPTER 26

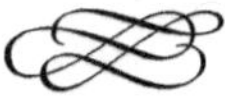

It was a two-hour drive from Portland to Astoria, where Max had grown up and where he'd planted tea plant cuttings with his grandmother.

"Tell me if I drive too fast for your comfort," Mary said as she pulled her pickup truck onto the road. "I learned to drive on a ranch and the open road around it, so I'm good at avoiding animals and hazards that come out of nowhere, but I'm sorry as homemade sin at sticking to the speed limit."

"You can drive as fast as you'd like with me as your passenger." I was over a hundred years old when the bicycle was invented, and I'd hated that thing since I'd first ridden one. But cars? It was love at first sight, and I remembered the days before speed limits. I knew they were necessary, but time was of the essence. "This qualifies as an emergency."

"I'll quote you on that if I get another ticket and Max finds out."

We headed west on Hawthorne Boulevard, cutting north before reaching the Willamette. Mary drove slowly on the side streets and came to a full stop at every stop sign. I was beginning to wonder if she thought of herself as more of a daredevil than she was, but all that changed when we merged on to Interstate 5. As soon as she eased onto the highway, I felt the force of her acceleration like we were on a racetrack.

"You're dying to ask me something," said Mary. "If you were waiting until we were on the open road, this is as open as it gets here, so fire away."

"I can't get a sense of Max's dad. It's like Andrew is a chimera. He's an illusion that's one thing in one context and something completely different in another."

"Oh, darlin', that's the nature of all of us." She grinned at me before turning her attention back to the road and overtaking a slow car —meaning it was only going a few miles over the speed limit. "Even you. I'm onto you, you know."

I tensed. "I don't know what you—"

"When Max brought you to meet me this year on my birthday, it was your gift that gave you away."

"The antique Victorian vampire hunting kit?" I had wanted to make a good impression, since it was the first time I was meeting Max's mom and sister, so I'd wrapped multiple birthday gifts. Once I'd spent a few hours with Mary, I could take an educated guess about which one she'd like, and that's the one I'd handed her. "I come across things like that for my shop, Elixir."

"You don't have to keep up the pretense with me. Those boots of yours are decades old as well. It's not just for your shop. It's *you*. You're a vintage junkie. I bet you attend steampunk and fantasy conventions dressed in costume."

I laughed. "I admit all of my clothes were vintage until a disaster wrecked most of my wardrobe. Then my and Max's friend Heather insisted on taking me shopping to buy some new clothes."

"I knew it!" Mary maneuvered around another car.

I wouldn't have been concerned about Mary knowing the secret of how old I was except for one thing. As Max's mom, she loved Max more than anything. But Max could never have a normal life with me. If Mary realized that, would she encourage Max to find someone more suitable? Would he listen?

"But I got us off track," said Mary. "You were interrogating me about Andrew."

"There has to be a reason for why he's behaving so strangely. Even though we've all got multiple sides to us, actions make sense if you know why someone is doing them. People behave differently depending on the setting. They might pretend to be nice when they're angry or lie to keep secrets. I know all that. But Andrew's actions make no sense here. Nothing he's done since arriving in Oregon makes sense." I looked out the window as the highway turned into a bridge and we sped over the Columbia River. I tried to think of the water as I would in alchemy, as one of the natural elements used to transform a problem, but the waterway didn't spur any brilliant realizations. "That's why I know I'm missing something. Something big."

"Andrew will always be the love of my life," said Mary, "but he chose his work over his family. He tried to teach the kids Mandarin when they were little, but since I don't speak it, it didn't work. My daddy was always supportive of us visiting my mom's family in China, but I wasn't raised with Chinese culture in the same way Andrew was. I don't think he meant to become obsessed with his research, but I wonder if it was an outlet for him that he didn't get from us. I don't know."

"Sometimes people can wake up one day and not recognize the person they've become." It had happened to me in the past, as it had for many an alchemist, and it felt almost too good to be true that I was content with every aspect of my life. Keeping Dorian a secret and making sure I wasn't photographed were small inconveniences I could happily live with to have this life here in Portland.

"Exactly," said Mary. "I don't think Andrew realized what he was doing. How far from our lives he'd strayed. And I wasn't about to uproot the kids from their lives in Astoria for a job he didn't even consult me about, when he already spent all his waking hours focusing on his research instead of me and the kids, not to mention all of his research trips when he wasn't home at all."

"I hate to make it sound like I'm disrespecting the social

sciences," I said, "but he's a historian putting together missing pieces of history, not a scientist who's on the brink of curing cancer."

"Ha. You wouldn't say that if you heard how he talked about it. I would have understood better if he was obsessed with inspiring students. He especially liked mentoring first generation grad students. I taught young kids, and I get it that seeing students blossom can be a kind of drug. But he talked about the history of tea and how it inspired different cultures like it was a life or death situation. Tell me, how does that make any sense?"

I looked out the window and watched the greenery speed by in a blur. We were in Washington state now, as we drove north, and would cut west back into Oregon to reach Astoria. There were two main routes to reach Astoria from Portland, and this was the largest highway and the fastest.

"Was he doing something like searching for war criminals who also traveled the Silk Road?" I asked.

"Touché. Maybe some aspects of history are life and death. Not his work, though Andrew would probably disagree. The way he talks about the overland trade route and bricks of fermented tea, you'd think it was a federal offense that you just called it the Silk Road rather than the Silk Roads, plural."

"But you two have stayed close, talking on the phone?"

Mary took a few moments before answering. "Not at first. I was angry for a long time. He sent money—more than he needed to, which was helpful on my elementary school teacher's salary. He even paid off the house for me, which meant he could only afford to rent a small apartment near the university that took him from us." She stole a glance at me. "That's residual bitterness you hear in my voice."

"But you got over the worst of the anger."

"I did. I still love the man, even though I want to throttle him. I've always kept him up to date on the kids. Mina is closer to him than Max. She was young enough when he left that she was hurt and sad, not angry, so she got past the worst of it. But Max was thirteen. Not a great age to have your daddy leave."

"I don't think there's ever a good age."

Mary winced. "I'm sorry, Zoe. I don't know the details of your own family background. Max has only told me that your parents aren't around and that you lost your brother when he was young. That can't have been easy."

"I still miss Thomas." I reached for the chain of my locket. "But it does get easier over time."

"That's how it feels with Andrew. Not that it's the same thing—losing him in my life to his work rather than having him truly gone from the world."

"You don't have any idea why Andrew would have torn up those tea plants?"

Mary shook her head. "If it wasn't him lashing out, then I wonder if it's something to do with his Silk Roads research?"

"Tea wasn't even an especially big export on the Silk Roads," I said.

"Ah, but it *was* in northern China. Andrew was obsessed with one route in particular: the Tea Horse Road. Mainly the early years of the trails, when tea and cultures were first being spread throughout Asia. But some of the last tea porters who carried tea out of China on foot are still alive today, though they're in their nineties. They're the last of what remains of an old era. Andrew has traveled there several times to interview them. He went earlier this year with one of the graduate students he mentors."

Mary's voice bristled as she spoke the last few words. She was jealous.

"You think Andrew is involved with one of his students?"

Mary barked a laugh and shook her head. "He's involved with Jonathan, for sure, but not romantically. He mentors that boy like he should have done with his own son. He co-authored a paper with his research assistant last year, something about using folklore as a historical source, and they're working on another paper now. I tried to read it. Really, I did. But my eyes glazed over as soon as a fairy tale about tea turned to a discussion of research methodology."

"So he cares about tea's role in history, but also wants to destroy tea?"

Mary shook her head once more, though I couldn't tell if it was directed at our conversation or a car driving slowly in the fast lane. "I suppose if we find he tore up those tea plants a second time, we'll know his obsession has turned dangerous."

"Maybe. But until we know what's going on, we can't know what his inexplicable behavior means."

Mary passed the slow car, and I once more felt the acceleration thrust me back into the seat of the car.

"Even with my driving," she said, "we've got at least half an hour more together. You've got your Max's mama as a captive audience, and I'm getting a headache talking about Andrew, when we don't even know what we're looking for. Feel free to ask me anything else. I'll use a mother's discretion if I reveal embarrassing details about Max's teenage years."

I smiled as I imagined a mischievous teenage Max. "Now you realize you have to tell me about his teenage years."

Mary laughed. "Maybe that was my gambit all along!"

Mary told me about Max's awkward phase (braces, unsurprisingly), his music obsessions (electronic music, which was somewhat surprising), and his favorite food he'd outgrown by the time he reached high school (he'd only eat peanut butter and banana sandwiches on soft bread with the crusts cut off for lunch in elementary school).

We made it to Astoria in half the time it took me in my old pickup truck. Once again, as soon as we were off the highway, Mary turned off the racecar driver part of her brain, and we made our way slowly through the small waterfront town.

Arriving at the house, the destruction at the side of the house was the first thing we saw. The sloped side of the yard, which had previously held thriving rows of mature tea plants next to newer ones, now lay in ruins.

I hopped out of the truck before Mary came to a full stop and ran to the disturbed earth.

This was a wasteland.

"Gone." I ran my hands through the displaced dirt. "They're all gone. Every last one of them. Both old ones and new." Max and I had planted rows of new tea plants from cuttings since Max had planned to harvest tea on a rolling basis and didn't want to overtax the earlier tea plants. Everything was gone.

Mary knelt beside me. "Bastard."

I pressed my hands further into the soil. "The roots are gone too. There's no evidence tea was ever here."

Mary ran to the trash bins, and returned less than a minute later. "He learned his lesson." She kicked the dirt. "He took the damn plants with him so I couldn't replant them."

"What's so special about these plants?"

"Maybe you can analyze them." Mary pointed. "He missed a couple of leaves. I don't suppose Max can grow new plants from leaves, but maybe you can at least learn something."

She was right that a couple of errant leaves were left in the soil— but these *weren't* tea leaves from the missing plants. "Those aren't fresh *camellia sinensis* tea leaves from your bushes," I said. "They're shriveled leaves from the *assamica* tea plant."

Assamica. Oh no … The last place I'd seen that variety of tea leaf was in the conservatory at Dante and Carla's mansion. *The dancing demons.* Those haunting topiary creations were made of *assamica* tea plants.

"Zoe, you don't look so good. Let me fetch some sweetened iced tea from the house."

I nodded as Mary ran to the house, but my thoughts were else-where. I lifted the two withered tea leaves into my hands. The earthy scent was strong, but something about the fragrance confused me. The tea leaves had been transformed by the presence of something else. Something I couldn't place.

I looked back at the expanse of dirt. Not a single root of the tea plants remained on Mary's land. Someone—or something—wanted to erase all traces of them. Had a tea monster traveled to Astoria to destroy these tea plants?

CHAPTER 27

Mayhem jumped from the parapet to the stone roof. The black cat rubbed her head against the legs of the walking plant, purring as she did so.

Frankenstein's plant monster did not have the power of speech, but he had learned language from the people who had nurtured him before he was ready to step from his earthen pedestal into the world.

The cat was a stray, and had no name, so he had named it Mayhem. Though he could not vocalize this name, he was certain she understood.

As for himself, his creator had not named him. Had they not believed he was truly alive? He had heard them refer to Franken-stein's monster, so this was the only name he knew to describe himself.

Though his creator had abandoned him, Mayhem had become his biggest protector, prowling the grounds for nitrogen-rich soil in which he could sleep and feed his stores of energy before step-ping from the earth to roam the world. He could—

The phone trilled, startling Dorian from his literary flow at the typewriter.

He was careful to observe his and Zoe's ring code—one ring, a pause, and then calling back—before scampering across the hardwood floor and grabbing the landline telephone.

"*Allô?*"

"I don't have long." Zoe's voice, as expected. "I'm in the bathroom at Max's mom's house."

"You are being held captive in a restroom in Astoria?" Dorian twisted a clawed finger around the telephone cord. "This is a most disturbing development. Should you not have called Tobias, who has an automobile?"

The older alchemist sighed. "I'm not being held captive." She spoke so softly he could barely hear her. "I don't want Mary to know I'm calling you. I need to know more about the monster you thought you saw in the conservatory."

"*Non!* Do not tell me the creature has escaped and hitchhiked up the Oregon coast?"

"No. At least I don't think so."

"Tell me everything."

Zoe explained, quite succinctly, that someone had uprooted and stolen the *camellia sinensis* plants that Max and his grandmother had planted at his childhood home. Only scattered leaves of an *assamica* tea plant remained.

"There are no *assamica* plants around here," Zoe concluded. "Whoever stole the tea plants brought these leaves with them."

"Or was made of leaves themselves," Dorian mused.

"Which is why I'm calling you. I need to rule that out as a possibility."

"Or be convinced that it is true."

"You're right," Zoe admitted. "I need to be open to wherever the evidence leads us. Even if it's to a plant that Carla brought to life."

"Or Dante," said Dorian. "Carla's eccentricities might be what he hides behind. On the surface, he looks to be the sane one, but we do not know—"

"I don't have long, so we can debate theories later. For now, I need to know what exactly you saw. Do you remember if the eyes you saw looked like they were coming from an *assamica* tea tree?"

"*Un moment.*" Dorian scampered past his typewriter to Zoe's laptop.

He typed in her password—which was far too simple to offer real security, he had learned from Veronica—and looked up this type of tea plant online. He had no interest in learning about plants that he could not eat or make into coffee, so he was not familiar with the differences between different varietals of tea.

With a few clicks, he found several images of this uninteresting specimen—modern technology was quite impressive, even when unfulfilling—then lifted the receiver back to his ear.

"This type of tea plant is ubiquitous at the conservatory and surrounding grounds," he told Zoe. "It is much taller than the other variety of tea plant, which I presume is why you referred to it as a tree, so it is quite possible that the eyes I saw came from this shrubbery."

Zoe did not seem pleased by his answer. She ended the conversation moments later, leaving the gargoyle alone in the attic to contemplate this interesting development.

Shaking his head, he hung up the phone. His creative flow was broken, and he was not sure what the cat called Mayhem and the monster would do next. Perhaps he should put his book away for the day. Yes, he would venture to the kitchen, where he had the ingredients to prepare a three-course dinner. He had not had a chance to ask Zoe if she would be home for dinner, but since she was in Astoria, he doubted she would return.

Perhaps he should invite the Flamels to dine with him this evening. Perenelle Flamel, in particular, was quite appreciative of his culinary feats. Zoe's backyard garden contained many colorful edible flowers, which would bring a burst of both color and flavor to the summer salad course. Perenelle would appreciate that. Yes, this is what he would do. He lifted the phone to ring the Flamels.

CHAPTER 28

Mary and I spent the next half hour searching the grounds of the Astoria house for any signs of the tea plants. As we'd first suspected, there was no trace of them anywhere. Whoever—or whatever—had taken them.

I couldn't believe I was seriously entertaining the notion that a plant monster had stolen the tea plants and murdered a man. Then again, two years ago I couldn't have imagined that a living gargoyle would be my housemate and closest friend.

I wished that Dorian had been able to rule out that it was a tea tree he'd seen peering at him in the conservatory, but I had to keep an open mind.

"What is it about this tea?" I ran my hands through the dirt once more, hoping for inspiration of any kind.

"I don't know," said Mary. "But let's get back on the road and call Max. Want another cup of iced tea before we leave?"

"I'd better not. I'm not great with too much caffeine. But I'd like to take one more look at the land before we go."

"You really are a plant whisperer if you think you can find any remnants that we've missed already."

"I've had a lot of practice."

I've been drawn to plants and the earth my entire life. Working with the earth was our way of life in Salem Village, growing oats and rye. I was the one who listened most closely to what the soil and plants needed. That first soil I experienced was hard and rocky, but I saw how to coax life into the grassy stalks. For my efforts, I was accused of witchcraft.

"Keep me company while I take a last look," I added. "Tell me more about this Tea Horse Trail you mentioned. Andrew's obsession."

"Andrew's research specialty," said Mary, "was tea and what it said about both historical townships and trade routes. He taught courses on the Silk Roads and that trade route's impact on world history, but—" She broke off as she steadied herself on a loose section of dirt. "But that's not what interested him about history initially."

"It wasn't?" I crouched in the dirt and surveyed the land. It didn't look like I'd missed anything, but I hated giving up. I sifted dirt as Mary spoke.

"He was interested in Chinese history and cultural traditions, like tea, when we first met. We met in college, in a Chinese history class. There was only one at our college. When I left home, I was just starting to get interested in my mom's cultural heritage. We fit in in my small town in Texas well enough, but that's because my mom made peanut butter and jelly sandwiches on white bread for my school lunches just like the other kids had. A couple of other immigrant parents made 'weird food' for their kids' lunches, and they were the ones who got bullied. My mom wanted to protect me from the discrimination she faced, so she went too far in not teaching me about her life back in China or any Chinese history.

"My dad loved her to pieces, and they were truly in love, but they both made compromises to be together. My dad lost out on some work from people who didn't want to work with him after he married my mom, but he said we were better off knowing what kind of people they were. And we weren't hurting for money, so it was fine. My mom kept her traditional clothing in the closet except for when the two of us visited family in China once a year.

"I rode horses, learned to shoot, and learned the secret sauce that made my daddy's barbecue the envy of our neighbors. My mom added her own secret ingredient—a pepper she knew from home that she found at the Asian market several towns over—and made it even better. She swore us to secrecy about the recipe after we won a contest at a county fair.

"They gave me a great childhood, but when I left for college, I realized how little I knew about the wider world beyond our ranch and small town. When I met Andrew in that Chinese history class, where half the students were Chinese American, I felt a shame that I never thought to ask my mom more about her life. Even when we went to China, I was a bratty kid. I never learned to speak Chinese, so I couldn't communicate well with my family, but I was accepted because I was a brave eater. I ate anything they put in front of me, even when cousins gave me things that I learned later even *they* didn't like eating.

"Andrew asked so many questions in class. I tell myself I fell for his mind. But he was also the cutest boy I'd ever seen." Mary winked at me. "I fell hard, and he did, too. He opened up to me about his interests. We were both freshmen, and he already knew he was going to attend grad school to get a PhD to study Chinese history."

"And he speaks Mandarin," I said as I moved over to one last section of dirt.

"That's right." Mary kicked a clump of dirt in frustration and followed me around the bend in the yard. "He speaks it but doesn't write it. He was born in Los Angeles shortly after his parents arrived. There was a lot of instability in China at the time they came in the 1940s, so they came to Los Angeles. Andrew had more Chinese friends than I did as a kid—which wasn't difficult, since I had zero— so his reasons for wanting to study Chinese history weren't the same as mine. It wasn't what it became later, once he was a professor. No, at first, Andrew really did want to know more about Chinese culture, and he had a particular fascination with tea. It was so interesting to me because he hated drinking tea!"

"Blasphemy!"

She laughed. "We were coffee drinkers. We thought we were so sophisticated because we'd buy specialty coffees long before it became popular like it is for your generation. Our friends were brewing drip coffee from the supermarket or ordering coffee at diners, but we bought beans and ground them ourselves and used imported brew pots, like a stovetop moka pot from Italy. It was so funny to me that Andrew cared so much about tea."

"But it makes sense," I said as I ran my hand through the rich soil, "if his interest came from *this* tea."

The tea that had vanished.

~

We called Max on our drive back from Astoria, putting him on speaker phone so Mary and I could both hear and talk to him.

"The plants are gone," said Mary. "Each and every one of them."

Max swore.

"I'm so sorry, Max." Mary gripped the steering wheel more tightly, and I expected she wished it was Andrew's neck.

"There's no longer any doubt that this is about the tea plants you and your grandmother planted," I said.

"Do you think you can arrange for me to see your father?" Mary asked. "Alone. Just me."

"I doubt it." A muffled sound came through the phone line. "Sorry, I'm here at the shop cleaning up. Let me step outside. Ma, I don't know if either of us will be able to see him again right now."

"Do you mean you don't trust me with him right now?" Mary's fingers tightened around the wheel.

"It's more the other way around."

Mary gasped. "You don't really think your father had a hand in that man's death—?"

"No. I don't. But I doubt we'll be able to talk to him to ask him."

"What if I turn him in for destruction of property?" Mary asked. "Don't I get to confront the perpetrator?"

"No!" Max snapped. "Don't report that theft. Not yet."

"He isn't the thief," I cut in.

Mary took her eyes off the road and stared at me. "But you were the one—"

"The timing," I said. "Mary. You didn't drive down from Astoria to Portland until *after* Andrew was taken into custody on suspicion of murder."

"That's right," Mary whispered. "I would have seen if anyone had torn up the yard while I was at home. Even if I slept through the destruction itself, I would have seen it in the light of day."

"So Dad didn't wreck my shop *or* steal the tea plants?" The confusion in Max's voice came through clearly.

"He's hiding something," I said, "but he's not a tea thief."

CHAPTER 29

Mary and I made good time once more, and we arrived at the Alchemy of Tea in the mid-afternoon.

Max said he'd have a late lunch waiting for us by the time we got there. Blue Sky Teas had run out of their limited selection of food by that time, so he picked up takeout food from a vegan restaurant around the corner.

Fragrant food and a transformed shop were waiting for us when we walked through the door. The smashed window was neatly boarded up, the foam from the fire extinguisher was gone, and the broken items had been swept up and discarded. The broken built-in shelving was still in place, and many shelves were bare, but it was possible to imagine the vision of a cozy shop once more.

In the center of the shop sat a table that had originally been used for a display of books related to tea, but now held a bag of food and a steaming pot of tea. Max set out three wooden folding chairs from the set of twelve he'd purchased with the idea of hosting small events at the shop.

"Moroccan mint?" I asked as Max poured tea into ceramic cups.

"Only a little bit of green tea is mixed in," said Max. "I think it's subtle enough that it shouldn't make you jittery."

I took a sip and felt Max's energy in the brew. "It's a blend you made. I'll be just fine."

We all savored a few more sips of tea before tackling the food. The aroma filling the shop was from roasted garlic cloves in a chunky heirloom tomato salsa and freshly ground cumin in the burritos we unwrapped.

"Let's take a step back," I said to Max after I'd inhaled half of a spicy black bean burrito. "We have two thefts and a murder. The connecting thread—"

"Is me." Max abandoned his burrito and stood up so quickly that his folding chair teetered and nearly toppled.

"I was going to say your *tea*, more specifically," I added as Max began to pace. "Can either of you think of anything about this tea Andrew or his parents told you? Maybe when you planted the tea bushes together?"

"Max was only three when he planted those tea bushes with my mother-in-law." Mary cast a glance at her restless son, but she didn't attempt to comfort him. "He wouldn't remember. Ling thought all plants with healing properties were special—and tea was right there at the top of the list of healing plants."

"I remember." Max came to a halt in front of a set of undamaged cast iron teapots. He ran his fingertips across the textured surface. "I remember that time well."

"You do?" Mary blinked at him.

"Of course I remember. How could I forget? Mina was a baby. It was the most amazing thing in the world to have a tiny, wrinkled alien at home—for about a day." He chuckled and shook his head at the memory. "But then you and Dad were totally focused on her, so when Grandma and Granddad came to stay with us, they made up activities for me, so I wouldn't tear down the house. Granddad made up treasure hunts and Grandma told me magical stories about plants, including teaching me about how plants grow from the earth."

"The magic?" I asked.

"The Alchemy of Tea." Max closed his eyes for a moment before speaking. "I don't remember her ever using the word alchemy, but the same intent was there in her work with plants. That's why The Alchemy of Tea felt like the perfect name for this shop. But I think the name had another influence."

I held Max's gaze. I wasn't worried about speaking freely in front of his mom. She knew both Max and I practiced alchemy. She just didn't know the full extent of what that meant. So many people today practice alchemy as the art and science of transformation that it can mean so many different things.

"Well," said Mary, "I didn't even know tea could grow in Oregon until Ling found those plants at a nursery."

Max frowned. "I thought she brought them with her when she and Granddad came."

"Really? I was so busy with the baby that if a troll from one of Oregon's many bridges had stomped its way through the house, I wouldn't have noticed."

"But you don't know where they came from?" I asked Max.

"I was three. I might not even be remembering properly that she brought them with her."

"Was your extended family involved in herbalism or tea production?"

"I didn't get to know any of my extended family until I was an adult," said Max. "If any of them had been apothecaries like my grandmother or grandad, they'd long since given it up."

"When my mother-in-law was alive," Mary added, "she kept some traditions alive in Oregon, like Chinese teas that Andrew was curious about, but we never traveled as a family."

"Did she harvest and dry tea from the tea bushes she grew herself?" I asked.

"She did," said Mary, "and she was kind enough not to object when I made it into sweet iced tea. Max does more with his tea than his grandmama ever did." She took Max's hand and pulled him back into his seat and handed him his abandoned burrito. "And remember I told you Andrew was never a big tea drinker. He always preferred coffee."

"His parents weren't involved with a broader Chinese American community?"

Max shook his head. "Not much."

"But at your house as a kid—"

"This was Astoria, Zoe. Not New York, Los Angeles, or even Portland. I had a good childhood and didn't feel excluded because my family was Chinese American. My community was my family and my school friends. Everything I knew about Chinese culture was from my grandparents, since they lived with us."

"For your whole childhood? I didn't realize they lived there for so long."

"Most of it."

"Mary, you're a saint to let your mother-in-law live with you for so long."

Mary barked out a laugh, and Max gave me a playful smile. "You've just spent several hours trapped in the car with her. Is that still your impression of her?" He looked fondly at his mom.

"Zoe and I had a grand ol' time. She can be honest if she disagrees."

"I like spending time with you precisely because you're *not* a saint," I said.

"Good answer," said Mary.

"If Ma doesn't care for someone," said Max, "they'll know it. I'm glad you two are getting along. You'll have more time to get to know each other. But we need to keep on track. This would be so much easier if he'd just talk to us."

I agreed with Max, but we had to deal with reality.

"Let me make sure I have the facts straight," I said. "Andrew got his interest in tea from his mom, but coffee was his drink of choice, and he took his parents and their cultural traditions for granted until he left for college—a pretty normal childhood. He invited his parents to move in with you after Mina was born, and his mom brought tea plants with her—their origins unknown. We don't know if she brought plants she was already growing, or where she got new ones."

"Sounds right to me." Max gave a frustrated sigh as his gaze fell to the once-pristine shelves that should have been filled with the items he'd selected so carefully. Maybe this hadn't been the best place to meet.

"I was closer to Andrew's parents than he was," said Mary. "Not closer in terms of their interests and culture—I'm a Texan more than anything—but because I truly liked them as people. I loved how much they doted on Max and Mina."

"But Dad?" Max's jaw tensed. "He was always getting frustrated with his parents and was interested in them more as academic subjects to be studied, not parents to be loved and respected."

"He wasn't always like that." Mary spun a chip in a compostable bowl of salsa, avoiding Max's gaze. "Academia got to him. The pressure to always be pursuing scholarly work and publishing more papers on esoteric topics. I'm not saying his choices were the right ones. Only that he's a good man."

"Esoteric?" My skin prickled with the implications of that word. "Was he interested in the history of Chinese alchemy?"

"Not that I know of," said Max. "Ma?"

Mary shook her head. "I don't think so. He did a lot of ethnographic research in addition to historical documents."

"Sounds like more of an anthropologist than a historian," I said.

"You're right. I teased him that he'd have been a better anthropologist than historian. Like that paper I mentioned he wrote with his research assistant. He and Jon traveled to northern China a couple of years ago to interview a few retired tea porters and record their stories before they died and their stories were lost. They documented the stories about their lives, and also the songs and stories the old porters sang and told each other to pass the time.

"He was interested in the history that people could tell him about, either through the memories of living people or the folklore that long-dead people recorded on paper. He was trying to convince the world that it was a valid research method to analyze how many facts were hidden in stories and songs. In that sense, he fit well into the discipline of history."

"Was that what you meant when you said his research was

esoteric?" I asked. "That some of the stories he heard were strange ones?"

"I guess it was more his mother I was thinking of," said Mary. "Her interest in the medicinal properties of tea and other herbs. Mina got interested in Traditional Chinese Medicine because of that."

"Dad tried to tell me about his research methods when I was a kid," said Max. "As a kid who loved going on treasure hunts with Grandad, I thought it was the most boring thing imaginable. The question of how historians can know what's the truth. How much of folklore can be trusted to have kernels of truth, and how do you pull out those nuggets? How much documentation do you need to compare to know if one written record is mostly true or completely fabricated by someone with an agenda? What can we truly know about history?"

Those were difficult questions to answer. I thought of the books of folklore and mythology Dorian and I had been looking at that morning. Andrew had it right. So many mysteries of history were recorded in plain sight, just wound up in the writing that average people had access to: stories.

Some of the events I've lived through that are now recorded as history are fairly accurate, but a large amount of the truth is obscured. Nicolas and Perenelle were born long before me, and while a fair bit of what is written about Nicolas is true, he looks absolutely nothing like the drawings of him that claim to document the man. As for Perenelle, she's been nearly written out of history even though she was every bit as powerful as her husband—more powerful, if you believe Nicolas. I'd seen what she could do, so I was inclined to believe him.

"But we're getting off track," Max added. "My dad's research sounds more interesting now that I'm an adult. But his historical research doesn't tell us—"

"It might," I said. I had the flicker of an idea, but I couldn't grasp it. "But let's move on to why your dad is all of a sudden interested in you opening The Alchemy of Tea."

"But we know for a fact that he *wasn't* the one who set fire to my shop or dug up the tea plants at my mom's house," said Max.

"Yet he *was* at the conservatory the morning of the murder, and he refuses to tell us why he was there or why he didn't want Max to open the shop."

"He *did* tell you why he doesn't want you to open the shop," said Mary. "He doesn't want you to throw away your money in a small business."

"He's lying, Ma. You said he didn't mind the idea of me changing careers when you first told him about my plans. This all started when you told him I was making the tea with the plants that grew from the cuttings I planted with my grandmother."

"That timing had to have been a coincidence," said Mary.

"How can it be?" asked Max. "Someone stole that tea from my shop and from your house."

"It wasn't Andrew," Mary insisted. "You know that. Zoe proved it with the timing."

The idea hovered at the edge of my consciousness once more. I was so close to making the connection, but I was missing something.

A knock on the door sounded, startling me and dissipating any figment of what I had been starting to realize.

"Uh, I'm sorry to interrupt." It was the handyman who'd been helping Max. "I've got the replacement window. Is now a bad time?"

We moved next door to Blue Sky Teas to let the window repairman swap the plywood for a proper window that Max was lucky was available without a custom order.

"You don't believe your dad," I said, "that he thinks you're throwing your life away for retiring from being a detective and starting a small business he thinks is doomed to fail?"

"He encouraged Mina to set up her own practice to do what she loved before integrative medicine was as mainstream as it is now. No, that's not what this is about. He's lying, but I don't know why. Yet." He ran a hand through his hair and looked down at the tree ring tabletop.

"Someone is going to a lot of effort to get their hands on your tea." I looked up to the shelving behind the counter. Blue kept her herbal teas in metal tins to keep out air and light. *Oh no…*

"Blue Sky Teas was vandalized a few days before your shop," I continued slowly, thinking it through. "*Were they after tea here, too?*"

"So it's *not* related to Max and Andrew?" Mary's face lit up.

Max shook his head. "That was only a bit of vandalism here at Blue's. Nobody took anything."

"Because they realized your tea wasn't here," I said. "They got the *wrong store.*"

Max shook his head again. "I talked with Blue. The perpetrator didn't even come inside. They only tossed something at the window, cracking the glass but not breaking through it. Even a gentle tap would have broken through the damaged glass, but they didn't go further—and before you ask, they weren't interrupted. Nobody chased them off. They only wanted to lash out and break the window, not to rob the café. I doubt it's connected. It's not uncommon for shops in our neighborhood to be vandalized."

"It's not that common either," I pointed out.

"I love that you're an optimist, Zoe. But it's a fact of life. I did tell the detective. But I still doubt it's connected."

"And you're sure the tea club are the only people who sampled your tea?" I asked. "Your mom or Mina didn't share it with anyone else? Or what about Blue?"

"I didn't give anyone extra samples," he said.

"It was very nice tea," said Mary, "and I felt such a swell of maternal pride when you shared it with me this spring."

Max blushed. "Because you know I made it."

"Fond feelings of a mother aside," I said, "there's also nothing that makes it believable that someone would steal it."

"There are lots of expensive teas coming out of China," said Mary. "Some of them are so rare that they sell for a lot of money."

"But Max is new to the tea business," I said. "He's not involved with the trade. It's not like his tea is immediately going to take off."

"Maybe one of the people in that tea club was a true connoisseur," suggested Mary. "A Supertaster who sees how special Max's tea is?"

"Maybe," Max agreed. "But how would the thief convince other people?"

"Maybe they wanted it for themselves," I suggested.

"Maybe," said Max. "The bigger question is *why is my tea so special*?"

"It's wonderful tea, darlin'," said Mary.

"You two know what I mean. Even if I'm a natural at making an elevated tea, how is it worth killing over?"

CHAPTER 30

Max and Mary decided it was worth seeing if they could talk with Andrew, to get answers, so I went to see the Flamels.

"May I tempt you with my home brew?" Nicolas wriggled his gray eyebrows and held up a pint of frothy beer.

I was unnaturally wired, so I accepted a small mug of the home-made beer. It wasn't bad. I'm not normally a beer drinker. It must have been the alchemy.

Beer in hand, we knocked on the doorframe of Perenelle's sunroom art studio. Shades of green paint were streaked across her hands, and there was even a spot on her nose.

"Good," she said. "I could use a distraction." She flung her brush aside and wiped her hands on a once-white cloth and strode away from her easel.

"Zoe has brought us a big distraction," Nicolas assured her. "The continued mystery of the apothecary from China who immigrated to the US and planted tea with her grandson, which has somehow led to robbery, murder, and *today*, yet another theft." He turned to me. "Did I get that right?"

I gaped at Nicolas. "How did you already know that?"

"Dorian telephoned earlier to invite us for dinner. He mentioned your excursion to Astoria."

"What was stolen today?" Perenelle's previous distress was gone, replaced by curiosity.

"She's been painting away," Nicolas explained. "I didn't have the heart to disturb her."

"You should have." She cast a wary glance at the unfinished painting on her easel. The scene of one corner of the garden outside her window was beautiful, but it lacked a certain spark that normally made her artwork so special.

"The rows of tea plants from Max's childhood home have been stolen," I said, pulling her attention from the canvas once more. "The tea plants Max has been using to learn alchemy, since they're the ones he planted with his grandmother nearly forty years ago."

"Such a short amount of time," Nicolas murmured. "He can easily replace them."

"I'm not worried about that right now." I didn't want to get into a discussion with Nicolas about how Max had no desire to find the Elixir of Life and that his alchemical interest was a personal journey to elevate aspects of a normal-length life. "This theft has to be related to the murder of Frederick Rasmussen, and Max's father is the prime suspect. Andrew is involved, but he's not the thief, and I don't think he's the killer. Either Andrew or one of the members from the Posh and Punk Rock Tea Club are responsible, since they're the only ones who were at the West's estate during the time of death. And I don't yet know *how*, but everything points back to the tea that originated with Max's apothecary grandmother."

"Who as far as we know had no connection to the suspects besides Andrew?" Nicolas asked.

I shook my head. "The police will be able to do a more thorough look into each of their pasts, but only if they choose to do so. For now, Max thinks they'll be focusing their energy on their main suspect."

"Apothecary was a safer word to use for our pursuits than alchemist," said Perenelle. "Are you sure Max's grandmother isn't an alchemist?"

"She died over thirty years ago, and Max doesn't know the answer. His dad might, but Andrew isn't talking."

"Perhaps I could bring him some of my beer?" Nicolas held up his half-empty pint glass. "It's quite potent and might loosen his tongue."

He wasn't kidding. The few sips I'd taken of the hoppy brew from his alchemy laboratory were already going to my head. I put down the mug on the windowsill. "I don't think you're allowed to bring him beer in his holding cell."

"Pity."

Perenelle took the pint glass from her husband's hand and took a sip. "Then we're left to our own devices to speculate about a possible alchemical connection."

Nicolas's expression transformed into that of an eager schoolboy. "Chinese alchemy is fascinating, since ending up with true gold was never the point. Creating *fake* gold was the ultimate goal. Through turning lead into a false gold, they believed immortality, or at the very least longevity, could be achieved. False gold *was* the Elixir of Life."

"Because natural gold didn't have an alchemist's intent and energy," I added.

"*Liànjīn shù*," said Nicolas. "The alchemy of forging gold."

"I always interpreted the term to refer to an energetic essence that could be extracted from plants," I said.

"Surely you know alchemy can mean more than one thing." Nicolas's eyes twinkled behind his thick glasses. "The golden Elixir of Life. Is it false gold made from metal, or a golden essence only an alchemist can extract from plants? Obviously, it is both, and it is the expertise and intent of the student of alchemy that brings it to life."

"Always a teacher." Perenelle smiled at her husband.

"I still think it applies mainly to plants," I said. "Especially since tea is so central to understanding Chinese alchemy. Tea itself was thought of as an alchemical process, since its properties could cure disease and expel toxins from the body."

Tea in China was originally thought of as a medicinal plant, not simply a beverage to be enjoyed. It gave monks essential nutrients that were lacking in their simple diets, and hundreds of years later it was thought to help people who smoked opium expel some of the most toxic elements of the drug.

"Far more women in China mastered alchemy than in Europe," said Perenelle with a raised eyebrow, and I knew she was thinking of her own challenges with both art and alchemy in her time.

A woman named Fang, who lived more than two thousand years ago, was possibly the first recorded alchemist in China. She discovered how to turn volatile mercury into pure silver. I learned of her when I first visited China, soon after my brother died and I left the Flamels. I was traveling to learn more about the world, but of course I was always drawn to plants and herbalism, which often led me back to alchemy. If I was being honest about what I was truly seeking during those aimless years, I was simply running away from my old life. The more different the places I visited, the further away my old life felt.

"Oh, I nearly forgot." Nicolas looked from side to side, as if he'd forgotten where he was. "It's time for me to check on my test results."

"On the fabric around that brick that set Max's shop on fire?" I asked.

"Indeed." He paused in the doorway. "With such a small amount of fabric, I had to think carefully about what I would do, so I preferred a slower chemical test, rather than a destructive one. Back in a jiffy." He frowned. "Is that the correct expression?"

"He learned it from watching a 1980s television show," said Perenelle. "I told him it was probably out of date, since I haven't heard it used by anyone we've spoken to here."

I pushed Nicolas through the doorway. "I don't care what words any of you use right now, as long as you come back with those test results in a jiffy."

"You used it!" Nicolas clapped. He kissed my cheek and disappeared into the alchemy lab he'd customized after they bought the house. His alchemy lab was the former den of the house, already equipped with a fireplace, and Perenelle's sunroom was used for both art and alchemy.

While we waited for Nicolas, Perenelle led me farther into her art and alchemy studio. One wall was lined with windows, making it feel similar to the conservatory at the Wests' mansion. But instead of plants, Perenelle's sunroom was filled with canvases, jars of paints and pigments in cabinets, tins holding paint brushes, two wooden worktables, one full length mirror, and an easel. There was no fireplace in this room. Perenelle didn't need an athanor furnace for the type of alchemy she practiced. Instead, one of the worktables held a small burner and various heat-proof glass vessels.

"I'm disappointed in this latest batch of pigments," she said. "It feels as if there's something lacking."

Moving past the easel holding the landscape painting I'd noticed earlier, she lifted a different canvas. The paint wasn't yet dry, and the earthy scents of ochre and madder root wafted up from the piece.

The canvas she held was an in-progress self-portrait. Her red hair was painted with rose madder and yellow ochre and looked every bit as vibrant as it was in real life. I was in awe of how it looked as if she'd painted each strand of hair, catching highlights from the light.

But she was right, there was a spark in her eyes that was lacking. They, too, held a highlight, but something was missing.

"I thought I'd find you two still in here." Nicolas's wild gray hair caught the light from the wall of windows and looked like Medusa's mane of snakes. In reality, it was mostly his animated gestures that gave me that impression, but with Nicolas and his experiments, you can't blame me for considering the possibility.

"Well?" Perenelle asked, putting her canvas back on its easel.

"That was certainly interesting. Interesting indeed."

"Do tell." Perenelle jabbed his side with her paint-stained fingertip.

"I knew there was something odd about the fabric, which is why I thought I could be of assistance."

"What was so strange about it?" I asked. I would have thought that Nicolas was being purposefully dramatic if it wasn't for the fact that I knew this was how his mind worked.

"It was no ordinary cloth." Nicolas's joviality fell away. "Well, that's not quite what I mean. The cloth itself was linen, nothing special. It's what was *on* the cloth."

"Which was?" I prompted.

"In addition to the unleaded gasoline that propelled the fire, there were traces of bamboo, silk, and mold."

Perenelle pursed her lips and caught my eye. "Now he's holding out on us simply to be dramatic."

"I'm not, dearest," he insisted. "I'm deciding the best way to tell Zoe that her paramour's father is mixed up in this murder business." Nicolas wore a look of regret. "There. I've said it. The spores and fibers on that cloth came from an old Chinese manuscript."

"The kind of document," I said, "that a professor of Chinese history would be working with."

I looked away from Nicolas's regretful face and walked to the window, where I could look out at Perenelle's pigment garden. It was thriving, but its energy was off. It felt like it was being stifled. Some things aren't meant to be contained.

I turned back to Nicolas. "You're certain?"

"I wish I could say I didn't take a large enough sample for it to be conclusive."

"Be honest," said Perenelle. "You don't actually wish that, dear."

"You are correct, as always, my love. What I do wish is that my tests had yielded different results. There is no doubt. The cloth itself is modern linen, but it had once been wrapped around something ancient from China."

What had Andrew Liu done?

CHAPTER 31

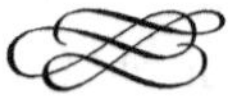

The Flamels informed me that Dorian had invited them over to dinner, so the three of us walked back to my house together.

Nicolas brought a large bottle of his homemade beer with him. He carried it in a satchel made of precariously loose stitches of yarn, which he explained he'd made himself in a local knitting circle.

Perenelle winced as the bag swung in his hand and the bottle dipped within inches of the sidewalk. "I told him he wasn't ready to move from knitting flat scarves to bags meant to carry anything heavier than those lopsided practice scarves."

Nicolas chuckled, but the levity didn't take. We were all too aware of the situation that was far more precarious than the possibility of a broken bottle of questionable beer.

"We need to figure out what Andrew Liu is hiding," I said as we gathered around the dining table ten minutes later.

The kitchen door swung open, and Dorian carried out a giant platter of arugula salad greens topped with crispy paprika-roasted chickpeas and roasted garlic cloves, with a creamy lemon dressing drizzled in a circular pattern that reminded me of an ouroboros serpent, and crunchy toasted sea palm scattered on top.

"A feast," Perenelle declared.

"The first course," Dorian said as he served us each a portion of the summer salad. "We have much to discuss, and we must bolster our energy. Do not take this the wrong way, *mes amis*, but I wish Max could be joining us this evening as well. Our investigation into *monsieur* Liu senior would be so much easier if I were to meet Max."

"Now doesn't seem like the best time," I said. "I don't want him getting distracted by processing your existence."

"I beg to differ, *mon amie*. Max needs as much assistance from his friends as he can get. I was about to meet him the other night—"

"Normally, I would agree with you, Dorian," said Nicolas, "but Zoe has a valid point."

Dorian flapped his wings once, then sat stiffly in his chair and raised his fork. "I can see when I am outnumbered." He stabbed a chickpea mercilessly.

"What do you think of this term *in a jiffy*?" Nicolas asked Dorian.

Dorian shrugged as he savored a bite of his creation. "As long as they do not start using it in France, I do not mind its usage in Oregon. Did you know that in modern France, the young people have begun to say *bye bye* in casual conversation in place of *au revoir*?"

"Language is always changing," Nicolas pointed out with a smile. He'd done his job in distracting Dorian from talking about meeting Max. I wanted them to meet as much as anyone, but Max's dad was our first priority.

The linguistic bickering continued as we finished our salads, but when Dorian brought out a main meal of a chanterelle mushroom risotto with toasted pistachios, Nicolas told Dorian about the fabric test that pointed to Andrew being connected to the damage to Max's shop.

"Andrew Liu is not the only person with access to Chinese manuscripts," Dorian pointed out. "Zoe has a few antique books from China in her Elixir collection."

"Mine aren't that old," I said, "but it's a good point. We know Andrew is connected because he was at the scene of the murder, but we don't know which of the other suspects could be working with old Chinese manuscripts."

"You look as if you have swallowed a bone," said Dorian. "Which is impossible, since there are no bones in this plant-based dish."

"She needs more beer." Nicolas attempted to refresh my glass, but I brushed him aside.

"I'm not choking. I'm frustrated that the more we learn, the less we seem to know. Antique Chinese manuscripts? What's next?"

"Crafter alchemists," Dorian said authoritatively. "I have been pondering the facts, and my little gray cells have led me here."

"Crafter alchemists, you say?" Nicolas turned his attention to the gargoyle, his eyes wide. "Do tell."

I pinched the bridge of my nose but let the conversation play out.

"The woman who stitches plants together," said Dorian. "Carla Carpathian. She is my leading suspect."

"She is?" I frowned at Dorian. "When did you arrive at that conclusion?"

"Just now. *Pardon*." He covered his mouth with a cloth napkin as a small burp escaped his lips. "I am convinced that she is the person who is bringing plants to life with the natural fibers of alchemical yarn, meaning she could command her creations to kill!"

That declaration killed the conversation. Or rather, it sent the four of us into so many directions that led nowhere that by the time we finished every last bite of the mushroom risotto, we were no further along with any ideas beyond wild speculation.

I helped Dorian clear dishes and fixed tea—the chamomile solar infusion that had been steeping in the backyard for me and Nicolas, black for Perenelle and Dorian—to go with Dorian's date and nut cake.

Perenelle moaned with culinary delight as she bit into the cake. "This cake goes so well with this black tea. I wish you could experience them together, Zoe."

My peppermint tea complimented the cake as well, but Perenelle was right that there were subtly distinct differences that could elevate transformations into more than the sum of their parts. We were drowning in so many pieces of information that we couldn't quite piece together which ones fit together to tell us what had really gone on in the conservatory.

CHAPTER 32

Mayhem curled herself around the plant monster's broad shoulders. She sensed his worry and was there to comfort him.

The pair had gathered all the supplies they needed—the supplies for the monster to bring his vocal cords to life.

The monster could not utter a sound, even a purr or a growl, yet the cat seemed to understand him when he pointed at items out of his reach that she should fetch for him.

Now, here in the abandoned tower, surrounded by crumbling limestone bricks and the lingering aura of death from the battles of a bygone era, when the lightning struck on this stormy night, he would speak!

Once again, Dorian's prose had taken a different direction than he had anticipated. He had read the writings of Freud, so he was aware he was unconsciously using his own history of being brought to life to fuel the story. However, his own father had cared for and protected him, which would not do for Gothic fiction.

Zoe had to deal with a large order for Elixir, so Dorian was left to his own devices before the memorial concert tonight. This meant he had much time to explore his blossoming Gothic novel. It was taxing mental work, and Dorian doubted he would be able to continue generating such exquisite prose for the entire day. Yet, he was not displeased to have the day on his own. Zoe was in a foul mood after calling Max to tell him what Nicolas had learned about the cloth used to burn down his shop.

Max claimed to be a man of science and rationality, yet he did not wish the evidence to lead to his father. Though they were estranged, Max clearly felt a familial pull towards his father. This was understandable. Dorian's own father, Jean Eugene Robert-Houdin, was a complicated man. The famous magician was far from perfect, yet he did his best to raise Dorian after he accidentally brought him to life by reading the words from a Latin book of alchemy he believed to be no more real than a stage prop.

This was no time to be sentimental! There was work to be done. A book to write. A mystery to solve. Food to prepare and enjoy.

Dorian did not usually succumb to such maudlin fancies, yet there was something about this case that disturbed him greatly. *Many elements.* The plant monster. The nonsensical behavior of Andrew Liu. The personal attacks on Max's shop and childhood home. The person creating this web of deception might have been his most formidable foe thus far. *Mon dieu.* Could Zoe be right that backward alchemists were involved?

And of course, they were neglecting the most important thread. *Why was Andrew Liu at the Carpathian Conservatory where the dead man was found?*

He lifted the receiver of the attic telephone and dialed the Flamels' number.

"Are you certain it is all right for us to borrow Zoe's automobile once more?" Nicolas asked. "She did not mind the minor damage to her front bumper?"

"It is rather late for you to be asking," said Dorian from where he was crouched in front of the front passenger seat of Zoe's old pickup truck. "Are we not nearly to the turnoff for the Carpathian Mountains?"

"My mind was elsewhere when you telephoned. Your argument was quite persuasive that the missing link was Andrew and Frederick's connection. You, Zoe, and Max have been focused on Andrew and the crimes affecting Max, not the man who was murdered. You are correct this was an omission."

Dorian did not correct Nicolas and tell him that Max and Zoe knew the police would be investigating the murdered man himself with more resources than an informal investigation. It was best not to disabuse Nicolas of the idea that Dorian's ideas were superior. It was, after all, quite true.

Today, Nicolas and Dorian would not be returning to the Carpathian Conservatory. The Wests would no doubt already be preparing for their memorial concert this eve. Instead, their objective was to investigate the home of Frederick Rasmussen.

"Remember," said Dorian. "Since the road only leads to the West estate and the Rasmussen house, if you meet anyone and are questioned—"

"I toss the plaid blanket on the seat over you, and say I'm a tourist looking for Pittock Mansion, and ask them which way it is. But that will not be necessary." Nicolas stopped the car. "We have already reached Frederick Rasmussen's home. There are no other cars here."

Dorian peeked out over the dashboard. They had indeed come farther than he imagined. He frowned. Poirot would have paid more attention to the twists and turns of the road. He would have known they had already reached their destination. This was all the plant creature's fault. The threat of a new foe had distracted him!

The pair exited the truck, and Dorian was dismayed to see more foliage stuck to the front bumper. His annoyance quickly fell away as he looked up at the house. It was not as grand as the Wests', but the three-story house had as much personality. This was a stone house, most likely the first of the two houses to have been built on this mountainous hillside. Multicolored stone walls dominated the structure, and a colorful stained glass window was above the oversize front door.

It was quick work to pick the lock of the front door. No alarm sounded, so they closed the door behind them and got to work.

They searched the house, starting with the kitchen, in search of tea that might be Max's. Zoe had done this at the Wests' home and had not found Max's stolen tea. Dorian was not sure he would recognize it, but he did not have to question himself. The only teas in this house were boxes of prepackaged tea bags. He recognized common name brands. Frederick Rasmussen drank tea, but he was not a tea connoisseur.

"What is that faint aroma?" Nicolas asked. "I cannot place it."

The old alchemist was correct. There was a lingering smell, not unpleasant but one Dorian could not place either.

"Ah." Dorian pointed at two empty dishes on the floor that indicated a pet had lived here.

They continued through the house. Dorian had expected the home to have a different energy, since it was Joyce Rasmussen who had lived here for half a century. Yet there was an unbalanced energy here. Next to well cared for antique wooden furniture along the walls, a modern leather armchair in the living room faced a wall-mounted television instead of the hearth. He was certain the chair and television were those of her son, Frederick.

"To the garden," said Dorian, leading the way. A large flower garden, boxed in by stones, was the only cultivated part of the garden. It looked as if it had been carefully maintained at one point, but now ran wild. In the summer heat, some of the flowers had grown tall and others had wilted.

While Nicolas investigated the plants themselves, looking for anything similar to what the Wests had in their conservatory, Dorian went back into the house.

He lifted a roll-top desk, but most of the hutch was empty. In years gone by, correspondence would have been kept here. But now, everything was electronic. Perhaps Zoe and Max were correct that the authorities would have an easier time looking into Frederick's finances and connections.

There was but one sheet of paper on the desk. A hand scrawled note that simply read, "boots."

Boots? Was he mistaken that it was Carla who had brought a plant to life? Had Frederick Rasmussen been shopping for boots for his plant monster?

CHAPTER 33

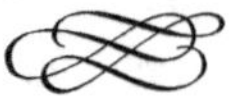

The memorial concert was to begin at sunset.

When Dorian and I arrived, the ruins of Dante's Inferno loomed even larger with lighting illuminating the stage that had been set up amongst the stones. Dorian's online research had unearthed the origins of Dante's Inferno. This had once been a barn, and after the wooden part of the structure burned, only the stone walls remained. Over the years, many of the stones were removed for other purposes, leaving it looking like the windswept ruins of a medieval castle.

More than fifty people were here, which was a large enough number that Dorian and I could mingle on the outskirts without anyone looking at Dorian too carefully. He wore his cape and a Venetian carnival mask. I had been skeptical of him blending in, but he was right that he fit in among this eclectic group.

There were no seats, only a sloping lawn. People who wished to see the stage could stand near the stage or sit on blankets on the one side of the hill that was higher than the stage. For now, only a few people were sitting down, and those who had done so had also brought blankets and picnic baskets.

Dorian and I were there to observe, and the plan was that I would both watch the people we knew and talk to them when I could, and Dorian would simply watch from the shadows.

Two bartenders were stationed at two separate drinks stations: one for alcoholic beverages and one for tea. In between the two was a table of bite-size appetizers and desserts.

Carla spotted me after I'd gotten a cup of steaming white tea with a light, floral scent, from the bartender.

"I'm glad you came." Carla clasped my free hand. Her black and white hair was plaited into two thick braids, made even thicker by strands of red yarn woven into the braids. She wore a black tunic dotted with glass beads that caught the fading sunlight.

I cast a downward glance and was relieved to see that Dorian had already slipped away. "I wasn't sure you'd want me here, but I wanted to pay my respects."

"Joyce would have loved you." *Joyce*. Frederick's mother, who the memorial concert would also be remembering. "I'm truly happy you're here. Max didn't come?"

I shook my head.

"I heard his father was arrested." Carla wound her index finger around one of her braids. "An intense man."

"You knew him?" I hadn't thought it would be this easy to find out why Andrew had a piece of Carla's stationery and a connection to the Wests.

"We met at Blue Sky Teas. When we heard that the café was now serving true teas, Dante and I visited. Andrew was there, asking lots of questions about tea. He wanted to know where Blue sourced her tea, and he talked with other customers as well, asking who grew tea locally. That's when we struck up a conversation."

"Because you grow tea here in your conservatory?"

Carla nodded. "We don't make tea from our own tea plants, but I still gave Andrew my card and wrote down the varieties of the tea plants we grow. I thought he was new in town and wanted to know how to cultivate plants here, but now I know otherwise... I don't know what his connection was to Frederick, though. Fred didn't grow tea plants. Neither did Joyce. I'm sorry I had to tell the police what I knew. I thought about keeping my mouth shut—"

"It's all right," I assured her.

"We can't control our families, Zoe." Carla grasped my hand so forcefully that I nearly lost my balance. "Joyce couldn't help that her son Frederick turned out like he did. I don't hold you accountable for what your father-in-law did."

"Oh, Andrew Liu is being held and questioned, but he hasn't been arrested. And he's not exactly my father-in-law. Max and I aren't married."

Carla tilted her head and studied me curiously, then leaned in close to my ear. "You will be."

The words were whispered so softly that I could almost believe I imagined them. Carla leaned back and let go of my hand as she gave a devilish grin. "I'm a little bit clairvoyant. Dante doesn't know whether or not to believe my premonitions. He says I'm simply intuitive. But really, when you think about it, what's the difference?"

The lights illuminating the ruins began to swirl across the stage. Carla's stance transformed with the light. Her whole body stiffened. Not with worry, but with purpose. I was watching the transformation of Carla West into her stage persona Carla Carpathian. She tugged on the yarn in her hair, and after flipping her head over, her hair was unleashed from the constraints of the braids. Her wild mane of frizzy black and white hair was free.

She grinned at me. "That's my cue."

As Carla jogged toward the stage, Dorian crept back to my side. The crowd had grown as Carla and I were talking, and I didn't see where he came from. I didn't have time to ask.

Dante and Carla both jumped onto the stage. Dante had a microphone in his hand and spoke to the crowd. "Thank you all for coming to honor the memory of our neighbors. All are welcome to share your memories—through music, of course. We don't want anyone to feel you need to line up and miss anything, so just give your name to Lena." He pointed to the side of the stage where Lena held up a clipboard. The young woman's prim attire stood out among the more punk, Goth, and theatrical clothes of most of the attendees.

"The first person who wishes to honor our departed friends is

Joyce's daughter, Farah. She's just arrived this afternoon from New York. Farah?"

A petite woman with an oversize stage presence gave Dante a hug and took the mic. She was dressed in a flowing black gown that touched the stage floor. Instead of speaking, Farah began singing a song I recognized as *Seasons of Love.*

"Ah!" Dorian said. "This is from *Rent.*"

"You saw the musical?"

I couldn't see Dorian's expression or hear his mumbled reply. The gargoyle I'd met just a couple of years ago would have held his nose at that type of popular entertainment, finding it beneath him, but he'd come a long way and now embraced more types of food and entertainment. I wondered if he snuck into a local performance and watched from the catwalk when a touring theater company had come to Portland or if he'd watched the filmed version on my laptop. I was afraid to ask.

I turned my attention back to the stage. Farah Rasmussen commanded the stage and made me feel as if I was attending a Broadway musical. She sang acapella, with no instruments accompanying her. But with each verse, someone new joined her on stage to add to the chorus. Carla first, then Dante, Lena, and then a man I didn't recognize. The audience clapped along to the bittersweet song, and the timed claps turned to applause as the voices brought the song to its conclusion.

"My mom had so many friends here," Farah said once the applause died down. "I wish she'd lived closer to me, but knowing how much she loved it here and was surrounded by friends who loved her so much, I know this is how she wanted to spend the last years of her life."

I assumed she was going to mention her brother next, or sing a song for him, but she simply handed the microphone to Carla.

"For this one, we need some instruments. Loud ones." Carla winked at the crowd.

Dante had an electric guitar in his hands, and a woman around their age took to the stage and sat down at a drum set I hadn't noticed earlier.

"This isn't our original lineup of Carla and the Carpathians," Carla continued, "but Dante and Agnes are the best backup a gal could ask for." She set the handheld mic onto a stand and adjusted it to the right height. "One, two. One, two, three, four!"

She sang a song about friendship I had never heard before, but true to her punk rock roots, *screamed* is probably a more appropriate word for her vocals. When the last chord rang out, tears ran down her cheeks, and the applause was deafening. People sitting on blankets stood, and I realized the crowd was now more than a hundred people strong.

"I've gone soft in my old age," said Carla through a sniffle. "Let's take five. Go refresh your drinks—the iced tea is sweetened with flowers from our own garden—and we'll be back shortly."

Through the packed crowd, I saw someone surprising.

I made my way through the crowd with Dorian sticking close to my side. If this had been a different crowd, people might have scolded me for bringing a child in a Halloween costume to a punk rock concert, but nobody paid us any attention.

"Tobias! I didn't expect to see you tonight."

"You didn't?" Tobias eyed Dorian. "This little fellow called me and told me I needed to get over here and be on the lookout for 'anything suspicious.'"

"We are most appreciative of your efforts, *monsieur* Freeman," said Dorian.

Tobias chuckled. "Glad to help." He looked back to me. "I take it you didn't know about his request."

"Excuse me." Dante West stepped up to us and addressed Tobias. "Sorry to interrupt, and this is going to sound really strange, but you're the doppelgänger of a musician I admire so much."

Tobias and I exchanged a glance. He had mixed feelings about publicly releasing "Accidental Life," especially once it had become a hit.

"If you mean the Philosopher," said Tobias, "he was my dad. I'm Tobias Jr."

That was his cover story. He wrote the song when he turned one hundred, as a way to cope with not aging when everyone he cared about grew old around him.

"That's amazing!" Dante shook his hand enthusiastically as he introduced himself. Dorian had disappeared into the crowd, though I doubt Dante noticed.

"He lived such a private life that I never had the opportunity to meet him even with my dad's connections," Dante continued. "I have his original album on vinyl. Gary, did you see who's here?" He motioned for Gary to join us.

The gardener was dressed in a suit and tie, looking decidedly uncomfortable.

"This," beamed Dante, "is the closest to the amazing Philosopher that I've ever gotten. Meet his son, Tobias Jr."

"*Accidental Life?*" Gary's discomfort fell away, and a boyish smile swept over his face.

"And did you meet Zoe the other day?" Dante asked.

"Briefly," I said.

"Gary manages the grounds here. The designs and execution of those topiary monsters are his creations."

Gary was also the person Lena had mysteriously referenced as having previously been a member of the tea club before something had happened. I wondered if I could bring it up naturally now, but I was all but forgotten next to the supposed son of the Philosopher.

"Have you considered rereleasing 'Accidental Life'?" Gary asked Tobias.

"I'm assuming you control the estate?" Dante added. "It's such a meaningful song to so many of us—I know a new generation would love it."

"I don't know." Tobias scratched the back of his neck. "Dad's music is still out there for folks to find."

"You've got his baritone voice, too. You sing?"

Tobias chuckled. "A bit."

Dante invited him to come on stage to sing "Accidental Life." He said he knew the guitar part by heart, so he offered to accompany Tobias. Before I knew it, Tobias was being ushered toward the stage by Dante and Gary, leaving me forgotten. Not that I minded. I needed to find Dorian.

Before I'd taken five steps, Dorian tugged on my silver raincoat. He really was quite good at hiding.

"We must follow Farah Rasmussen," he hissed. "She is slipping away."

An electric guitar chord sounded through the speakers. Carla and her backup musicians were back on stage.

I followed Dorian, who was following Farah. I caught up with him once we'd moved away from the crowd, and leaned close to his ear. "Farah didn't kill her brother. Not only was she not one of the people here at the house that day, she was in New York City performing on a Broadway stage at the time of the murder."

"*Oui*," said Dorian. "Her alibi is *too perfect* to be true, *mon amie*! She has hired someone, and her brother's murder was a hit!"

I fought the urge to roll my eyes. "That would mean one of the members of the tea club is an assassin. They were the only ones there that day, remember?"

"Why else is she running away?" Dorian pointed, letting his clawed hand show outside the cape.

A gasp sounded from behind us.

Someone had seen that clawed hand.

"I'll follow Farah," I said to appease him, kneeling and pulling his cape more closely around him. "Now go!"

But it was too late.

"Have we met?" Gary asked, back at my side.

I straightened and looked Gary in the eye. "Uh, just a minute ago and also two days ago—"

"No, I meant this fellow with you."

Dorian pulled his cape more tightly around himself.

"I recognize your voice," Gary continued. "Where have we met?"

"I do not believe I have had the pleasure," Dorian said in the worst approximation of an American accent I've ever heard. "I am sorry you are mistaken."

Before Gary could utter another word, Dorian slipped away through the crowd, who were now swaying along with Carla's song.

Gary pushed his way through the crowd, going after him. He'd seen that clawed hand, and I knew why he'd recognized his voice. Dorian had made a phone call from the house the night he'd snuck in.

In the midst of the crowd, I lost sight of them both.

"We're back!" Carla's voice called from the stage. "And with a special guest."

Dante brought Tobias up on stage. "'Accidental Life' by the Philosopher was one of Joyce's favorite songs," said Dante, "so it's my privilege to introduce the son of the Philosopher, Tobias Freeman, Jr."

I made my way around the stone ruins to the side of the stage, where I'd seen Dorian and Gary. My heart skipped a beat when I saw what was clenched in Gary's hand: Dorian's cape.

CHAPTER 34

Gary held up Dorian's black cloak—but Dorian *wasn't* inside it.

Gary's face contorted with frustration as he whipped his head around. "He was *right here,*" Gary muttered. "He can't have disappeared."

Dorian hadn't disappeared. I saw where he'd gone. He was standing on the stage itself—in stone form. He was now a background prop for the concert. If anyone had noticed him appear, they could easily assume it was a bit of stage lighting trickery.

I put a hand over my mouth to stop from laughing. Dorian would have to stand still in stone form until the songs and speeches ended, but at least he would be safe.

In another setting, I might have worried people would wonder why a stone gargoyle was on stage and inspect Dorian's stone form critically, perhaps even move him aside. But this was a punk rock memorial concert in the midst of stone ruins called Dante's Inferno. Nobody would question a gargoyle statue on the stage.

I had promised Dorian I'd go in search of Farah, so as "Accidental Life" transitioned from its intro to the first verse, I slipped toward the back of the crowd and toward a higher spot on the hillside, where I could get a better view of the crowd. The small amount of caffeine in the white tea had given my body a jolt of energy, so combined with the adrenaline of Dorian almost having been caught, I was on high alert. I didn't see Farah anywhere.

I didn't believe she had anything to do with her brother's murder. Still, I'd promised Dorian I'd follow her. And, I did admit it was rather strange that Farah hadn't mentioned anything about her brother who'd been murdered only days ago, only her elderly mom who'd passed away months ago. Then again, nobody at this memorial concert seemed to care a whit about Frederick. Only Joyce. Which meant everyone in the tea club who'd been here that day was a suspect in Frederick's murder.

I felt like I might pull out my hair with frustration, so I decided to give myself five minutes of peace. I climbed higher onto the hillside, away from the crowd, to a spot where I could still see the stage and hear the music, just not quite as loudly.

I had never seen Tobias sing "Accidental Life." He belted out the heartfelt song as if it was the day he had written it. Dante wasn't kidding about being a fan. He played the background part on an acoustic guitar not exactly as it sounded on the original recording, but the lifegiving spirit was the same. I felt a spot of moisture on my cheek as the song concluded.

"It's a beautiful song," said a deep voice next to me. The man stood close enough to me that I could smell the steam from the cup of tea in his hand. A nutty scent of black Nilgiri tea.

I turned and saw Elias Tamraz standing next to me, a cup of tea from the tea station in his hand.

"Usually, I like my music more hard edged," he continued, "but this one is every bit as rebellious—"

"If you listen to the lyrics," I finished for him.

"Accidental Life" was a song of raw realism written by an optimist working through a phase of pessimism. There's certainly a lot of confusion and anger that comes with the Elixir of Life when you realize you're probably going to outlive the people you love. Tobias and I had both made peace with our alchemical lives, but it had taken us both time to work through it. I cherish the time I have with the people I care about. One never knows what the future holds, even for an alchemist. We're not immortal. The Elixir of Life transforms certain cells and ceases aging—or in my case, aging of my body except for my hair.

The song finished, and we both applauded enthusiastically, as did the rest of the audience. Dante convinced Tobias to stay on stage for one more song, a lesser-known one from the single album Tobias had released as the Philosopher.

"I hope you take this as the compliment that it is," Elias said, "but I can't tell what look you're going for with your white hair."

"The Zoe Faust look."

He grinned and nodded in time with the music drifting up to us. "I love the short cut. When it's due for its next dye job, I think you'd look great with black hair."

"You're biased." I pointed at his own naturally black hair but did so with a smile.

"I know. But even though you're outwardly a lovely, friendly person, I get a sense that there's something darker beneath the surface. Something you'd love to let out." Elias extracted a half-size business card from the wallet he wore on a chain and tucked into his back pocket. "I have a chair at a hair salon. I specialize in finding peoples' true styles. And I only use nontoxic dyes. I don't believe in mass-produced corporate hair dye. You can't trust what's in that stuff."

I was about to say I already knew he worked as a hair stylist, and indeed already had the address, but it was probably best not to mention Dorian's murder board of research. The card was black with white type that read "find your style" in large type with the word "hair" in a barely visible size above "style." A white spiral design spun out behind the words, ending with a website and a street address in Portland.

"I might just take you up on that." I slipped the card into my bag. "Tell me something. What am I missing about the real purpose of tonight's concert?"

"What do you mean?" The area we were in was dark, so I couldn't see his expression well, but it struck me as genuine confusion on his face, not defensiveness.

"Everyone who's gone on stage has talked about Joyce, not Frederick."

"She was amazing. I wish you could have met her. I don't know if your grandparents are still around—"

"They're not."

"Mine either. I mean, they might be, somewhere. But I don't know them. But Joyce? She was like the grandmother I never had. When Dante invited me over and I shared a pot of tea with Joyce, I instantly understood why grandparents rock."

"But Fred wasn't a father figure?"

"*Frederick,*" Elias said sarcastically. "Don't ever let him hear you say—" He paused and took a sip of tea, his hand shaking as he did so. "Guess I'm still processing that he's dead. It's horrible, but only in the abstract sense. Nobody liked him. I wasn't surprised to hear that someone killed him."

"But you still invited him to be part of your tea club."

He shook his head. "That was Joyce. When he moved in with her, he tagged along. We thought he'd stop coming after she died, but he didn't. None of us could bring ourselves to kick him out. I mean, his mom had just died. We're not monsters."

Was it my imagination, or did his gaze fall to the two topiary monsters visible from where we stood?

"So, this concert…" I said, letting my sentence trail off.

"Dante floated the idea of a memorial concert to Frederick after Joyce died three months ago, but he didn't like the idea. But now?" Elias shrugged.

"It's a concert for both of them in name only, but really it's for Joyce."

The second song by the Philosopher concluded, and Elias shouted, "We miss you, Joyce!" and made his way back down to the rest of the crowd. As soon as I saw Tobias jump down from the stage, I followed.

Tobias spotted me and marched straight over to me and leaned close to my ear.

"Please tell me there's a good reason Dorian's on stage."

I hooked my elbow through his and led us away from the crowd.

We rounded the highest section of stone ruins and sat down on a fallen stone that was smooth enough to serve as a bench. "He was nearly spotted," I explained, "so he had to flee."

Tobias shook his head. "The little guy is behaving more recklessly than usual."

I laughed and put my head on his shoulder. "This is my daily life. For a guy your age, you can be surprisingly naïve."

"Hey, this is how I stay young. If I thought the worst of people—or gargoyles—I wouldn't do so well in the world."

"No. I don't suppose you would."

Tobias worked in emergency medical services serving an area with small towns outside Portland. Before that, he'd done the same type of work when he lived in Detroit with his wife, Rosa, and he'd moved out to Oregon after she died of old age. I knew he often tried to help people who couldn't be saved, but those weren't the ones he dwelled on.

"Looks like I'll be getting another workout tonight to carry the little guy down to my car after the concert." Tobias cleared his throat. "I'm off to the tea station. I haven't belted that loudly in quite some time. I hadn't warmed up properly. Where'd Nic get off to?"

I stared at my friend. "*Nicolas* is here?"

"He didn't tell you? Dorian invited him and Perenelle. Dorian invited them for the same reason as me—to be on the lookout for clues or anything suspicious. The more eyes the better, he said."

I put my head in my hands and laughed. I loved my friends dearly, even when they could be a bit much.

"Here she is!" cried Nicolas as he and Perenelle rounded the corner of the stone ruins.

Tobias excused himself to go in search of liquid to quench his parched throat.

Perenelle sat down next to me and took my hands in hers. "The land up here on this mountainous hillside is marvelous, Zoe. Do you have any idea how good this land would be for growing a pigment garden? Did you see any plants like madder or woad in that conservatory?"

"From what I've seen, their focus is more on carnivorous plants, tea varieties, tropical trees, and topiary shaped to resemble monsters."

"Shame," murmured Perenelle.

"The energy of this memorial gives me hope for the modern generations." Nicolas remained standing, where he could see above the top of the stone ruins. "This aesthetic called punk is quite refreshing. They're pushing the envelope—that is the expression, is it not?"

"It is."

"Modern idioms are so fascinating. Like the verse we're listening to now. Perhaps I will pursue an advanced degree in linguistics." He extracted a notebook from his inner pocket and scribbled a note with the stub of a pencil. He adjusted his glasses and smiled as if he knew the secrets of the world. Which, I suppose, he did.

The vocals drifting over to us from the stage that Nicolas referred to weren't music, but spoken word poetry accompanied by a tabla drum. I couldn't see the performers, but I didn't recognize the voice. As with the other performances, this one clearly was for Joyce, speaking of a living body of Mother Earth who had mothered the performer.

"I don't think Zoe is listening to you any longer, dear," said Perenelle.

"I'm listening," I said, but Perenelle was half right. "Perenelle, why did you say the land here would be good for a pigment garden?"

"Hmm." She considered the question.

"The soil here isn't especially suited to the plants you're thinking of." I stood from the stone where we were sitting and knelt on a patch of rough ground a few feet away. "Many of the plants that can be transformed into pigments aren't picky about their soil, so this would work, but no better than many other spots."

Perenelle joined me on the ground, pressing her hands to the earth and closing her eyes. "It's the energy of this place. As if many earthly materials have been transformed here."

"That's what I thought. Come on, you two. You can help me figure out what's really going on here."

CHAPTER 35

The storm was gathering strength.

Lightning crackled in the distance, lighting up the sky and sending a rumble more forceful than an earthquake through the creature's bones of bark.

So close, and yet so far...

No.

That last line Dorian imagined was a cliché. Some clichés belonged in Gothic fiction, of course. Heart-shaped faces, perhaps. Or chains rattling in dusty attics. Yet he did not think this one fit.

No matter. For all his strengths, Dorian did not possess a photographic memory. He would not be able to remember these imagined lines of prose when he returned to the Remington typewriter in his cozy attic home. He was simply distracting himself while forced to remain in stone form on this disagreeable stage.

He wished he could cover his ears, yet he was resigned to the fact he could not move from his stone form. He could not very well have posed in a form with his ears covered. He was not a carved monkey in a set of *"see no evil, hear no evil, speak no evil"* allegorical row of sculptures. There was no reason for a gargoyle to be carved with his hands covering his ears, and Dorian had not wished to draw attention to himself.

Dorian was not opposed to music, yet he did not have a great appreciation for the various styles being performed this evening. The sister of the dead man had held his interest the most, with her sonorous voice. He understood how she could command a crowd at a Broadway show. If only he had not been forced to flee from the suspicious Gary! He could have approached her and learned more of her. Where had the woman gone? He had lost sight of her when it took precedence to hide.

He tried to make the best of his embarrassing situation. From his vantage point, he could see the entire small crowd on the sloping hillside. Nobody was behaving suspiciously. These were people attending the memorial concert for what it was. A celebration of the life of Joyce Rasmussen.

What was Zoe up to? This, he could not see.

It was not easy being a gargoyle in the modern world.

CHAPTER 36

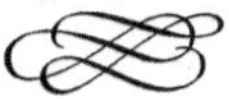

"How many more people are on the list?" I asked Lena, who was clutching her clipboard tightly as the next performer stepped onto the stage.

She frowned disapprovingly, looking older than her twenty-two years. "You didn't know Joyce. You'd still like to perform?"

"I'm not a night person, but I wanted to pay my respects. I was simply wondering how much longer the memorial performances would go on."

Her expression softened. "Six. Four songs and two speakers. It's Zoe, right?"

"It is."

"I was sorry to hear about Max's dad being the main suspect."

"He's not—" My words were cut off by an electric guitar chord.

Lena turned toward the stage, and I made my way back to the Flamels.

"We have at least half an hour to explore," I said to Nicolas and Perenelle. "Tobias knows what we're doing, so he's our lookout and will call my cell phone if anyone heads toward the conservatory, rather than the section of the house with the bathroom people can use. We need to be careful to avoid the cameras, in case they're on, so stick with me—"

"I remember where they are," said Nicolas.

I blinked at Nicolas, looking for any signs he was joking. "You've never been here," I said softly. I sometimes worried that Nicolas's imagination threatened to take over his rational mind, especially after the ordeal he and Perenelle had been through while being held captive, but I didn't realize how bad things had gotten.

"Don't be silly, my dear girl. Don't you remember I helped you two nights ago?"

My heart sank. "Two nights ago, I was with Max."

"Not with you," Nicolas said. "*For* you. When Dorian and I did reconnaissance for you."

I found myself unable to form words.

"You didn't tell me this, dear," Perenelle said. "I thought you were up late working on an experiment in your laboratory."

"Oh dear." Nicolas scratched his scruffy beard. "Perhaps I forgot that this was to remain between gentlemen alchemists. Dear me. Please forget my words. We found nothing of interest—well, except for the monster. Now, if you two will follow me, I remember the way to avoid the cameras."

Perenelle and I gaped after him.

Perenelle gave the loving, resigned sigh of a woman who'd done so thousands of times. "We'd better follow before he sees something interesting and forgets to wait for us."

I jogged to catch up with Nicolas. "What do you mean you found the monster?"

"We found his perch." Nicolas led us to the section of the conservatory with the dancing demon tea plants, where a large pot stood empty. Not *exactly* empty—it was filled with disturbed dirt, and a few leaves of an *assamica* tea plant.

Like the dried leaves I'd found in Astoria. Nicolas had the same theory I did, and even more evidence to back it up. All the evidence pointed toward a plant monster.

～

We didn't find an alchemy laboratory or any plant monsters. Only the suggestion of such creatures in pots of disturbed dirt.

When Tobias and I went to collect my gargoyle statue at the end of the night, I told Dante, Carla, Lena, and Elias that I thought a gargoyle would go well on their stage, and that I was sorry I hadn't thought to check with them ahead of time.

Carla handed me a woven crown of black and golden yarn. "You're a closet Goth. The stark dyed-white hair cut at an angle, ancient boots, and a gargoyle statue. If I'd been born ten years later, I'd have been a Goth instead of a punk. No question. But then I wouldn't have met Dante, my soulmate."

"You were ahead of your time." Dante reached our side and kissed his wife's cheek.

"I'm glad we'll be able to have our fortieth anniversary party here after all," said Carla.

Which they wouldn't have been able to do when their neighbor Frederick was alive, because he objected to the noise. Yet another reason they could have wanted Frederick out of the way. He was such an unpleasant man that motives were getting us nowhere.

CHAPTER 37

First thing in the morning, I met Max at his house to update him on what I'd learned at the memorial concert.

"We keep coming back to two things," I said. "All of the members of the Posh and Punk Rock Tea Cub hated Frederick—and this is connected to tea."

"And my dad." Max slunk down into his white couch.

I immediately pulled him up. "We can rest once this is over. I have an idea. Tell me everything you know about the tea you'll be sharing with customers at The Alchemy of Tea."

"You know nearly as much about tea as I do," said Max. "Far more if you count herbal teas."

"But this has something to do with your tea. What are you doing with it that's so special?"

"You know what I'm doing here at The Alchemy of Tea. Tea has always been a transformative element in my life. I wanted to share that with others. You know—"

"Humor me. Really. Just walk me through it. We're missing something, so I want you to treat me like a novice who's just walked into The Alchemy of Tea."

Max eyed me skeptically, but finally consented. "First, I need one more cup of tea and one of these pastries of Dorian's you brought over. Then I'll have the energy to go through this charade—"

"It's not a charade," I insisted. "It's a mental exercise that I hope will be a fact-finding mission."

"This calls for some of the last of my hand-prepared tea leaves. Green, so you can share the pot with me."

"You don't have much left, do you?"

He shrugged. "Not enough for the shop, but I'm trying to think positively. Even though the rows of tea from Mom's house are gone, we have those cuttings we made together that we planted in my backyard."

"Our shared garden." It might sound silly to those who aren't plant people, but the fact that we'd taken cuttings of those plants together, using our focus and intent, meant that we'd transformed those old plants into something new. Even though those little cuttings wouldn't turn into full-size bushes that could be harvested for years—at least a couple of years even with both of our skills—they were nurtured by our intent and would be something special one day.

We took the basket of misshapen pastries into the kitchen, and after the tea was brewed, Max took a sip of his tea and began his speech. I reminded him to treat me as if I was a customer who knew nothing about tea.

"When we talk about true tea, all the common varieties—white, green, black, and oolong—come from the_*camellia sinensis* plant native to Yunnan, China, or the *assamica* variety that originated in Assam, northern India. White tea is picked when the tea buds are inside new leaves, and the leaves are treated gingerly and quickly. They aren't rolled or crushed in any way, and they aren't allowed to oxidize. Therefore, it has barely any flavor. You have to taste carefully to determine its subtle flavors. It has hardly any caffeine—making it a great choice for you."

"You don't know me, remember?"

Max rolled his eyes but smiled and took another sip of tea. "Okay, green tea comes next. Green tea leaves also aren't oxidized, which is why they remain green. The leaves are heated as soon as they're plucked to prevent them from oxidizing or shriveling. The final dry leaf, which can be picked in the morning and enjoyed that same evening, is green. They have very little caffeine."

"How are they processed?"

"I'm glad you asked! Chinese and Japanese green teas are different. Chinese green teas are fried, but Japanese green teas are steamed. Oolong tea is semi-oxidized, so they can be thought of as in between green and black in both flavor and caffeine. This is a leaf that can be brewed multiple times. The dry leaves in a tea pot can be infused again and again in one sitting, though the caffeine decreases. This rebrewing isn't looked down on like it is for people used to tea bags; instead, it's a central part of the process for oolong and black teas."

"Your shop carries special tea you've processed yourself, right? Didn't I read that on your website?"

Max grinned, getting more into the role. "I pick and dry green and black tea from plants I grow myself. Black tea is fully oxidized, has a stronger flavor, and is darker in color from a red-brown to dark brown. It's the tea most people in the world think of when they think of tea. Lots of black tea is produced in India, not just China. And, of course, a lot of other parts of the world these days. After being plucked, leaves for black tea are left alone to wither, then rolled or crushed, depending on the final style desired. Once oxidized, the crushed or rolled leaves are baked in ovens to stop oxidation from continuing. Pu'erh tea is aged and naturally fermented, and it carries a great deal of health benefits."

"No chai?"

"Chai is simply the Hindi word for tea. The British popularized tea in India and stole some Chinese tea plants to form tea plantations in India, when it turned out India had its own variety already growing in the north. Some people get upset if someone says "chai tea" since it's like saying "tea tea," but again, you can call tea whatever you like. Teas can be named by the location and estate, or graded by the year plucked, and the quality of tea, which has a whole set of characteristics that are judged. And there are regional differences, so you might have heard of Darjeeling or Nilgiri tea. Both regions in India produce distinct tastes."

"What about Earl Grey?"

Max groaned. "That's a blended black tea that's flavored with bergamot, a type of citrus fruit from Europe that has a distinctive flavor."

"Herbal tea?"

"Not technically tea, as you know—"

"I don't know who you think I am, but I've never met you before, kind sir."

"Of course you have, Zoe! You're the love of my life. I can't pretend otherwise."

I took in Max's frazzled appearance, there in his kitchen baring his soul to me. He had shaved this morning, as usual, but had a small nick on his jaw line, which wasn't like him. I took his empty mug and set it on the counter, then cupped his face in my hands and kissed him.

A few minutes later—or perhaps longer, as I'd lost all concept of time—I knew we needed to get back to the matter at hand.

I pulled away and cleared my throat. "Herbal teas?"

Max kept hold of my hands. "I can't talk about herbal tea. I can't do this anymore, Zoe. I'm terrified that if we get to the bottom of this, I'll find out my dad is a murderer, and I'll be the one sending him to prison."

"You didn't tell me that."

He shrugged. "What was I supposed to say? I'm a detective—I know I'm not employed as one any longer, but it's what I do. The thing I was always good at. If I was more rigorous in exploring all aspects I thought might lead to the truth, then I'd be the one to put him away."

"That's why you weren't investigating as much as me and Dorian!"

He reddened.

I thought he'd been overly focused on wanting to see his dad, but now I understood why. It wasn't that he thought it was his best lead. It was the *safest*.

"I guess I should get back to this game." He lifted the teapot to pour the last of the tea into our cups. I'd barely touched mine, so I insisted he have the rest.

"Teas that aren't really teas? Is that where I was?"

I nodded, unsure if I should let him continue, but he carried on.

"Herbal infusions and decoctions, like Blue makes at Blue Sky Teas, aren't technically tea, because they don't come from the *camellia sinensis* plant. But I'm not a purist. If you want to call a lemon balm tea *tea*, go for it. My shop doesn't specialize in the wide range of herbal teas, but there are a lot of shops and resources around this neighborhood to explore that world of tea. Almost as important as the tea leaves are the other pieces that go into making tea. Good water, a good brewing vessel, and if you can swing it, something that makes you slow down and enjoy the cup you're drinking. Which we are *not* a good example of right now." He swept his arm across the uncharacteristically messy kitchen where we were standing.

"Tea has a long history in China. Though I have Chinese ancestry, I was raised in Oregon. My mom is half Chinese and half Texan, and my dad's parents were Chinese immigrants. I know a lot more about the properties of tea itself than the culture of tea. That's why a large section of my shop is dedicated to various types of tea to brew, and the tea accessories you'll see aren't just Chinese but from all over the world, as are the books for sale.

"That said, I do have a fondness for tea pets—yes *pets*, not pots— those are the little clay figures used in Chinese tea services. My grandmother left me her teapot when she passed away and my grandfather left me one of his tea pets—my sister got the other one. Tea pets are placed on a tea tray when you're brewing tea, and the hot water from the initial rinse of tea is poured over the tea pet. It's not a sacrifice; but that's the quick rinse of tea leaves that prepares the loose-leaf tea for a brew. The clay absorbs the flavor of tea, so the tea pet will change color over time and also start to smell like tea. Popular tea pet animals are ones with good fortune, like a toad with three legs. My grandfather had a dragon, which my sister got, and a turtle, which I got. I was always envious of Mina for getting that dragon. I was horribly angry for the longest time." He shook his head.

"You never told me that," I said. "I thought you loved that ugly turtle figurine in your collection."

Max gave a start. "I can't believe I said that out loud. I must be exhausted from everything going on this week."

"Max." The white hairs on my arms prickled as I realized what was happening. I couldn't be right, could I? No, I knew I was right. All the pieces fit. But how could I be sure? "Tell me what you think of Nicolas Flamel's hair."

"What? Why are you asking such a random—"

"Please. Just tell me."

"Because it looks like he hasn't washed it since you rescued him —" Max clasped his free hand to his mouth. "Jeez, I don't know why I said that. I'm fond of Nicolas. I really am. There's nothing wrong with his hair. He likes it wild and long. That's fine. Please don't tell him I said anything about it."

"I wouldn't. And I don't think you'd normally voice it aloud."

"How did you know I would say that? Please don't tell me alchemy goes along with clairvoyance. That would be too much for me."

"No. Not clairvoyance. But I don't think you're going to like what I have to say any better."

Max winced. "Is it about my dad?"

"In a sense, yes. We've been speaking so openly while drinking your tea. *Your* brew, made from the plants you planted with your grandmother. Max, don't you see? You've created a truth serum. This is a Tea of Honesty."

CHAPTER 38

Max dropped his teacup. The clay piece shattered, and tea splashed across the kitchen floor. "I didn't mean to turn this into a truth serum!"

"You didn't." I took his hand. "You enhanced a quality that was *already there*. That's why the tea plants are special *and* why your dad is so afraid of them."

"*He knows*." Max's face was pale.

I nodded. "But what I don't understand is why it's such a big deal. It's not *exactly* a truth serum. I'd say it feels like a subtle nudge to be a bit more open and honest."

"Like alcohol."

"Except alcohol affects people differently. Some people get angry when they drink. Only some people get happy and open up. We didn't realize the subtle secrets of the tea earlier, because we *are* close, so when we drank your tea together, we didn't realize the gentle nudges it gave us. But think about it. We've always had our most open conversations while sitting and drinking your tea, even though we've had a lot to work through, what with me being a three-hundred-fifty-year-old alchemist."

Max groaned. "That's why my father chugged the cup of tea and then *lied* to us that night, when he said he was guilty of vandalizing my shop. He wanted to see how far I'd perfected the tea. He wanted to see if he'd be able to lie. And he *could*. That's why he was happy, even though it meant he was temporarily arrested."

"Because he didn't know the tea he was drinking wasn't *your* tea. He made the wrong assumption." I thought back to that night. It all fit. Andrew's worry, followed by his relief that he could confess.

"But why," said Max, "was he so worried about the tea, if he knew so little about it?"

I took Max's hand. "It's the things we don't fully understand that frighten us most."

Max broke free and picked up the fragments of the teacup, avoiding my gaze. "I don't understand what the hell my father is up to, but I'm not frightened. I'm angry." A line of red appeared on his palm as he squeezed the jagged edges of clay.

Instinctively, I went to the first aid kit in the junk drawer. Max didn't object as I silently cleaned and dressed the small wound.

I leaned back on my heels and inspected the clean bandage. I'd given him a bigger one than necessary so it wouldn't come off if he balled his hand into a fist, as I expected he'd be reflexively doing until we figured out what was going on.

"Nobody in your family ever said anything about the tea plants you and your grandmother planted being special?" I asked.

"Not to me. I was a kid. I didn't know my dad had ripped out the tea plants when my parents split up, so I don't know what else they were keeping from me." Max's voice broke. "I've been making tea for people for years. Everything I thought I knew about my life has been a lie. And my career."

"Max. Your life and career aren't a lie."

"I've given up my old life for The Alchemy of Tea… Don't you see what this means? I was never a good detective—at least not because of my own efforts."

"That's not true, for so many reasons."

"But I've always made my own tea, and that's the tea I kept at the station. What if it was always my tea that made people confess? Not me?"

"It's *intent* in preparation that elevates any plant preparation. You've always put your intent into your tea harvesting and drying, even before you were practicing alchemy more seriously this year. Your alchemical preparations this year have elevated the tea even further. Before that, it wasn't as strong, but it was still there."

"Still—"

"It's not a truth serum. It only makes people suggestive and makes them want to speak the truth."

"But confessions—"

"Max. How many of your cases were built on confessions?"

"Not many," he admitted.

"And even those that were confessions were only people who confessed because you had already done the legwork and conducted a thorough investigation that showed the suspect that you would be able to prove your case."

"Maybe…"

"And how many suspects even accepted a cup of tea?"

He gave me a chagrined smile. "Fine. You win. A few of them, but not many." He leaned in as if he was going to kiss me, but abruptly pulled back. "Dammit, I don't have much of the tea left. How are we going to prove any of this? And how am I supposed to find out what my dad is up to and save my shop? We need to talk to him again."

"I don't know how to help with your dad—yet. But for your shop, remember only a small number of customers would have bought that high-end product. It's everything else you've gathered together for people to share your love of tea. You've got your curated selection of some of your favorite teas from around the world, with your personal descriptions of each one. Plus, all the books—"

"I don't see how you can be so calm right now. With my grandmother, my dad, my livelihood—*us*!" Max fidgeted with his bandage. "Would you have told me about you being an alchemist if it hadn't been for—?"

"First of all, before this summer when you began to process the leaves with alchemical techniques, your Tea of Honesty wouldn't have been nearly as strong. Second, I *always* wanted to tell you the truth. From the moment I first met you. That had nothing to do with tea."

It was true. From that first moment he'd knocked on my front door, just moments after I'd found Dorian hiding in my moving crates, I was struck by the fact that he felt like a kindred spirit who was balancing caution and candor. Max Liu was someone who understood plant magic but didn't openly admit it, even to himself.

"But I told you the truth before you were ready," I added, "and you thought I needed psychological help."

He winced. "Can you forgive me?"

"Only if you trust me that this is going to turn out okay."

"I don't know—" We were interrupted by his phone ringing.

"JJ?" said Max. "Is everything all right at the shop? Wait, what?" Max put the phone on speakerphone.

"A huge crate of mail was just delivered," the handyman said. "It looks like someone set up an online campaign to save your shop, and physical cards are coming in as well."

"Really?" Max looked from the phone to me, incredulous.

"I'll bring them inside," JJ said, "but I just wanted you to know why it's going to look so messy when you get here."

"Thanks, JJ," said Max, "I have something to do, so I can't be there for a little while. You okay to keep going on your own?"

"Of course. It'll take me at least another few hours to finish these cabinets."

After hanging up with JJ, Max looked it up on his phone and found out that our teenage friend Veronica had set up a crowdfunding campaign that included a photo of the front window display before it was destroyed. The original display included poetry on a sheet of paper sticking out of a typewriter, so people knew Max valued paper over electronic communication. That's why so many people were writing physical cards of support as well.

"See?" I said. "The Alchemy of Tea is going to be a neighborhood hit."

"Maybe," Max agreed. "But first, let's go find my dad."

CHAPTER 39

Max was planning to call in any number of favors so we could talk to Andrew again—but it wasn't necessary, because he was released without being charged. It had been seventy-two hours, and they didn't have any solid evidence that implicated Andrew above the other possible suspects.

But by the time we got there, Andrew was gone—and he wasn't answering his phone.

"This is bad, Zoe." Max pocketed his phone and gripped the steering wheel of his parked jeep.

"I bet his phone isn't charged," I said. "We need to think where he'd go. Who does he want to—"

"Me. He'll be at my house."

We peeled out of the parking lot and were back at Max's house within minutes. But Andrew wasn't there.

"The Alchemy of Tea?" I suggested.

But as we opened the front door of the shop and stepped inside a few minutes later, we didn't see anyone. Not even JJ.

The bell from above the front door had fallen during the destruction, so we hadn't made a sound when we walked inside. I didn't hear or see anyone—but I sensed another presence. "Hello?" I called out.

A man emerged from behind the counter. Andrew Liu. He gave us both an awkward wave and held up a piece of porcelain he'd bent over to retrieve.

"How did you get inside?" Max asked.

"It's good to see you," I said with a smile, trying to make up for Max's terse question.

"The door was unlocked." Andrew motioned toward the front door.

Following his gaze, I spotted where the bell had fallen. I stood on my tiptoes to hang it back in place. I'd had enough surprises for the day.

"Where did JJ go?" asked Max.

"JJ?"

"The handyman helping me fix the place." Max scratched the back of his neck. "He was here working on my shelves this morning. When did you get here?"

"Max, I really don't think you need to interrogate—" I began.

"JJ wouldn't have just left," said Max. "Dad, why were you hiding, and when did you—"

"I only got here a minute ago. And I wasn't hiding. I was back here because this is a fragment of a pattern I remember we had when you were a kid." Andrew held up a shard of porcelain and gave a sad smile. "I'm so sorry this was done to your shop. It wasn't my doing. Please know that—"

"I know." Max stepped past both of us, toward the small back room. "Wait out here. Both of you."

"You think something's happened to JJ?" I whispered.

"Just wait here for a minute."

We obliged, and I kept my hand on my cell phone if I needed to call an emergency operator. But Max emerged a few seconds later, shaking his head. "Looks like he just left. No sign of foul play."

I'd have said "young people today" had no work ethic, except for the young people of today take on more responsibility than those of many previous generations I'd encountered. Even though each genera-tion has its stereotypes, which can also exert influence, most people are their own unique people, regardless of when they were born.

"Maybe JJ left a note, and it was blown to the ground when the door opened," I suggested. "There's certainly enough paper around here from these letters of support."

Max locked both the front and back doors, then crossed his arms. "I know about the tea, Dad." said Max. "We both do. We know it's a Tea of Honesty."

Andrew tensed. He looked to me, and I nodded.

"I was trying to protect you," Andrew whispered. As he spoke the words, his body deflated, and he looked at least a decade older.

"Protect me from what?" Max snapped. "Why are you so worried about the world being a slightly more honest place? It's not like it's a full-on truth serum."

"It's not about the tea itself," said Andrew. "I don't care what it does. It's *how you came to have it.*"

"You mean because you tried to destroy it when you and Mom split up?" Max glared at his dad.

Andrew winced. "I was trying to protect you. All of you."

"From what?" Max was nearly shouting.

"From the truth. Your grandmother stole the tea plant. She smuggled it out of China. That's why she could never go back—and why I think she was murdered."

CHAPTER 40

As Max and I gaped at Andrew, the shop's front door rattled. Someone was trying to get inside.

We all turned to see Max's mom waving at us through the glass door. The smile on her face instantly fell away when she saw our faces. Max unlocked the door for her.

"I leave you alone for five minutes to park the car," said Mary, "and you've already alienated your son again? You both look madder than a box of frogs. Even Zoe looks pale. Do you need to sit down, darlin'?"

"I think we should all sit down." I locked the door behind Mary, then pulled out four folding chairs. Mary helped me open them.

"Sit." She grabbed her ex-husband and son by their collars and pushed them into the chairs.

Max obliged, but he continued to glare at his father. "Dad was telling me some nonsense about my grandmother being—"

Andrew cut him off before Max could finish his sentence. "Your mother doesn't know."

"What don't I know?" Mary looked from her son to Andrew. "I'm the person you called when you were being released, and now you're keeping even more secrets from me?"

"I never wanted to tell Max either," said Andrew, "But things have gotten out of control."

"It's time," said Mary. "Whatever you've kept from us all these years, it's time to come clean."

"I—" Andrew croaked, but he couldn't go further.

"I'll make tea," I said. "An herbal infusion of chamomile to calm our nerves, nothing else. Then you can start at the beginning."

Andrew silently nodded his assent. Nobody spoke as I made tea. The cozy shop filled with the scent of earthy flowers as the herbal blend infused with the hot water. I found a box of cookies behind the counter as well. Dorian would have been horrified to see me opening a box of mass-produced cookies, but Max and his family needed sugar.

"When I first met your mother in a Chinese history class," Andrew began after two sips of the calming tea, "I had never been to China. As a kid, I didn't question this much, but as I grew older, I wondered why. We weren't poor. We could afford to travel."

"You told me the family was unhappy with their marriage," said Mary. "That they'd had a falling out."

"That's what I'd been told myself. Once I was an adult, I started to wonder what the full story was. Because my mother was *afraid*."

"Not of grandfather," Max said. "That's not possible."

Andrew shook his head. "She wasn't afraid of her husband. They loved each other so much. I could always see that. She was afraid of strangers. Of anyone coming to the house who was unexpected. Remember that time we surprised them, Mary—"

"I thought I'd given your darlin' mama a heart attack! Ling was so mad at us for what we thought was going to be a lovely surprise visit."

"Like a criminal who's been waiting for the law to catch up with them," Max said softly.

"I still didn't put the pieces together," said Andrew. "Her being frightened of the unexpected was just part of her, like her knowing how to work with plants. It wasn't until I was in graduate school doing ethnographic research that I learned about the legend of a tea plant—a tea that compelled the truth."

"You always loved your legends," said Mary. "I told you more than once you should have been a folklorist."

Andrew bristled. "I was always looking for the truth in those legends. *And I found it.* A dangerous truth serum that lured people to their deaths. Historical records of Chinese alchemists talked of it."

Max and I exchanged a glance.

"A special tea tree from a mountainous region could be used to compel the truth from one's enemies—but it always resulted in death. I'd heard my mother talking about the special properties of her own tea plants."

Mary, finished with her herbal tea, set down her cup and crossed her arms. The folding chair squeaked as she leaned back and scrutinized Andrew. "Folklore about alchemists? And the fact that your mama was good with plants like your son and Zoe? This is what led you to an obsession? I suppose the region you're referring to from the legends is at least where your parents were from."

Andrew reddened. "Accounts are contradictory. But that's true with all history. That's why people like me are needed to interpret it."

"At the expense of your own family," Max snapped.

Andrew looked at the floor. "I deserve that," he said softly. "When you and your sister were young, I only had vague theories about your grandmother's fears. I couldn't let it go, even though rationally I should have—but I was proven right." His head snapped up, and there was a feverish look in his eyes as he looked from Mary to Max. "Shortly before she died, I found a source in an archive that kept newspapers and signage. There was both a news story and an old flyer. It was several decades old, and it hadn't yet been digitized."

"That trip you took that summer that lasted for a whole month." Mary shook her head. "That trip was the end of us."

"I couldn't tell you what I was doing." Andrew's voice shook. "The newspaper article. It recounted news of a horrible theft of a dangerous plant, and the flyer was a sketch of a fugitive. A woman."

Mary gasped. "Your mama?"

Andrew nodded. "She stole a truth serum tea plant and fled China with my father. She was a fugitive."

"This can't be true," Max whispered. "She was a thief?"

"That summer," said Andrew, "shortly after I got home from China … she died."

"But she wasn't murdered," said Mary. "She had a heart condition."

"She was so afraid of something," Andrew insisted. "And then I came back—"

"Dad's right," said Max. "I remember that. And grandfather went back to China. I didn't realize it at the time, because I was a stupid teenager wrapped up in myself, but it was as if he'd been freed from exile."

"Your granddad loved you and your sister more than anything," said Mary. "He wasn't running away from you."

"I know," Max assured her. "I knew that at the time, too. It wasn't like with Dad."

"I'm sorry," Andrew whispered. "Don't you see? I'm terrified that they found my mom because of me. That something in my research might have tipped them off. That's why I dug up the tea plants she'd propagated at the Astoria house and threw them away. I needed to get rid of them so no harm would come to any of the rest of you."

All the pieces fell into place about his research obsession. He wasn't simply obsessed with abstract academic research. He believed his mom was hiding a dangerous secret, and he wanted to keep his family safe.

"Did you confront your mother?" I asked Andrew.

"I didn't have time. I was thinking about how best to do it when she died. I asked my father, but he said I was mistaken. He joked that I was so American that I couldn't tell my mom apart from other Chinese women. I was hurt by his words at the time, but I now know he was simply trying to protect me."

"Do you have a copy of the wanted poster we can see?" Max asked.

"Only a hard copy that's not with me. I deleted electronic files after she was killed, so it couldn't be traced to me."

"None of this makes sense," said Mary. "Why would a mysterious 'they' come and kill your mama and make it look like a heart attack? If she was a fugitive for a terrible crime—which stealin' a little tea plant doesn't sound like—wouldn't they simply extradite her and make her stand trial? Why kill her?"

"The ancient texts say that misusing this tea tree was punishable by death—"

"Oh, Andrew!" Mary leapt out of her chair and toward Andrew.

At first, I thought she was going to slap him, but instead she pulled him up and embraced him.

"Foolish man," Mary whispered. "I understand more about your obsession now, but you didn't have to keep this from me."

"I didn't know you'd saved the plants, or I would have come back again. To make sure you were safe."

"Then you *did* steal the plants?" I asked. "How could you have—"

"No!" Andrew let go of Mary and faced me. "I didn't uproot the plants from Mary's house—not this time. And I didn't hurt Max's shop either. Neither of those thefts were me—I didn't kill that man either."

"Why were you at the Wests' conservatory that day?" Max asked.

"I was worried you'd given them a cutting of the tea plants. You're a generous man, Max, and they grow tea. I met Carla at Blue Sky Teas and learned that you'd been to their tea club. I thought I could convince you not to sell the tea, but if you'd already started to give it away?" Andrew shrugged. "Things were getting out of control. I needed to stop the tea from getting out into the world until I figured out the truth about the tea."

"But instead of your mother's tea plants," I said, "you found a dead body that day."

Andrew swallowed hard and nodded. "I saw him lying there… With those bizarre plants draped over his body. I panicked and ran."

"Who," growled Max, "are you protecting?"

"I didn't see the killer. I'm not protecting them. I'm doing the same thing I've always done: protecting you from the truth. I didn't want it to get out into the world that you possessed these special tea plants—tea that got your grandmother killed."

"Stop staying that," said Mary. "Did you ever see evidence that anyone had killed her?"

"I didn't, which is why I knew they must have been very skilled—"

"You sound like a conspiracy theorist," Max groaned.

"That's why I accepted the job at a university with more resources. I needed to find out what had really happened, to be sure you'd all be safe."

His mother never revealed the truth before she died, so it made sense that Andrew became even more obsessed with finding the truth after that. Even if he couldn't be with his family, at least he could keep them safe.

"Your academic research," I said, remembering the cloth Nicolas had tested. "You work with old Chinese manuscripts."

"Of course. That's what I've been telling you about my research."

"The cloth," said Max. "That's what Zoe is talking about. The cloth dipped in an accelerant used to destroy my shop had traces of spores from an old Chinese manuscript."

Andrew grew pale. "They must know about you working with the tea. I'm so sorry, Max. I tried to protect you—"

"Stop," said Max. "Stop right there. I refuse to admit there's a secret group so committed to destroying my grandmother's tea plants that they're randomly killing people who've sampled the tea I made from those plants."

"But—"

"I can settle the matter," I cut in. "The members of the Posh and Punk Rock Tea Club are the only people who were at the conservatory that day. We have a closed circle of suspects. Unless this group has the resources to skydive onto the Wests' estate and have a helicopter pick them up after their senseless murder—and I'm being sarcastic, in case that wasn't crystal clear—we're not looking for a secret society protecting this unique tea."

"One of them is after the plants?" Mary asked.

"Andrew showing up in Portland confused things," I said. "But he didn't wreck Max's shop, steal the tea plants from Astoria, or kill

Frederick. That means someone in the tea club knows what's special about the tea."

"Andrew must be right that it's dangerous." Mary squeezed his hand.

"But for a different reason," I said. "The members of the tea club couldn't have known about Andrew's research into this legendary tea. One of them must have realized what was going on *after Max served them the tea.*"

"I don't suppose you could invite them all to another tea party?" Mary suggested. "Gathering all the suspects together."

Max grunted a laugh.

"I know," said Mary. "Don't mind a foolish old woman."

"You're sixty-seven, Ma. That's hardly old—"

"Maximilian, stop trying to make your mama feel better. We need to figure out what the hell is goin' on."

"I was actually thinking that you sound just like Zoe's friend Dorian," said Max.

"Dorian is exactly who we need right now." I lifted up my cell phone. "Anyone object to me calling a friend who's read just about every classic closed-circle detective novel ever written?"

CHAPTER 41

"Mayhem," said the monster. The brittle, olive-green leaves that formed his lips parted into a smile.

The powerful jolt of electricity from the lightning had worked its magic. He could now speak the name of his best friend.

The trilling of the telephone interrupted the tapping of the Remington typewriter's keys. Dorian answered the telephone after assuring himself it was Zoe's special sequence of rings.

"*Allô?*"

"Andrew Liu has been released," she said. "And we need your help."

Dorian grinned at the sound of his friend's voice. He would be prepared for whatever she needed. Scaling the stone walls of one of the suspect's homes. Baking a sleeping draught into a pastry that would lull a suspect to sleep while he searched their home. Breaking into a bank vault with valuable information. No. Perhaps breaking into a bank vault would be too much. He could only pick locks in which he could use his claws. Combination locks of high-end safes eluded him. He could, of course, watch online tutorials, but even those could only take one so far.

But as Zoe spoke, he realized that what she needed was none of those active pursuits.

"You need me to listen to Max and his father's story and help you think of a good plan?" he repeated. "This is all you require of me?"

"I thought you'd enjoy putting your little gray cells to work."

Dorian smiled once more. It was not as broad a smile as when he had imagined a bolder activity, but it would do.

His eyes grew wide as Zoe recounted the broad strokes of Max's criminal family. *Mon dieu!* How must Max be feeling, learning his grandmother was a stealthy thief who might have been murdered?

"I've got you caught up to everything we know," said Zoe, "so I'm putting you on speaker phone."

"Max must enter his Mind Palace," Dorian said after Zoe had introduced Max's parents. "In order for him to remember the events of that day, he must close his eyes and think back to everything he observed that day where he shared his special tea with the Posh and Punk Rock Tea Club."

Though he could not see his friends' expressions, he imagined the stoic Max balking at his suggestion. When the former detective spoke, it was indeed to rebut the suggestion.

"Frederick Rasmussen wasn't a nice man," Max said. "He was terrible to everyone that day, which doesn't narrow things down. I don't know what else I can tell you from that day."

"You must try," Dorian said.

With the phone tucked between his chin and shoulder, Dorian took notes on the typewriter. He absorbed Max's words and imagined he was in the Carpathian Conservatory, surrounded by carnivorous plants and a hidden plant monster, not in his attic.

"My first impression of them was the following," Max began. "I already knew Dante, who behaves like a Zen monk when drinking tea, but the punk rock days of his youth come through whenever there's music playing. I can't get a handle on Carla, to know if she really believes she's stitching plants together, or if it's an affectation that goes with her sense of self."

"From her glory days in Carla and the Carpathians," Max's mother added. Dorian wondered if she had a wistful look in her eyes, as it sounded like from her tone. Perhaps she had been in a band in her youth.

Dorian had not met Mary, and it was most likely never possible for him to do so.

"Elias and his sister Lena are an odd pair," Max continued. "I could tell they were very close within minutes of meeting them, but they're polar opposites. Elias is in the punk world of Dante and Carla, and Lena looks like a hospitality server even when she's not at work."

"She's young," added Zoe, "so she might not be able to afford clothes beyond her work attire."

"Fast fashion," Dorian cut in, "would allow her to buy stylish youthful clothing for the cost of a cup of coffee. Max is correct. She must prefer her conservative attire."

"Good call, Dorian," said Max. "She definitely seems at ease being different from other people her age. Outwardly, she was the most similar to Frederick. But I could tell he was the outcast of the group pretty quickly. Not because he was dressed formally, like Lena, but because he didn't have a kind word to say about any of them."

"Because of your tea," Mary murmured.

"After small talk," said Max, "we turned to discussing the tea, and how its flavor profile was—"

"*Non,*" Dorian cut in.

"I think I remember what we talked about," Max said tersely.

"I think Dorian means you glossed over some things," Zoe said. "If we're going to figure out what happened that day, we need the details. All of them."

Max blew out a breath so loudly that Dorian heard it clearly through the phone line. "I'm an eyewitness. And eyewitness testimony is horribly unreliable."

"This isn't for a court of law," Zoe scolded. "We're trying to pinpoint what you might not have thought was relevant that day, but we now know is important if they were under the influence of your Tea of Honesty."

"All right." Max continued his story, this time with more details. Their introductory pleasantries included much discussion of the weather—Americans were so predictable! And then Carla told Max about her plants.

"I commented on the rare plants in the conservatory," Max said, "and

Carla explained that although her interest in carnivorous plants had initially come from that campy movie with a big, people-eating Venus flytrap, as soon as she began cultivating them, she realized they were so much more interesting than that pop culture reference. They thrive in inhospitable environments, and Charles Darwin was a fellow fan who wrote a book about them. Dante got annoyed with her when she admitted to stabbing a guest with a knitting needle when they stuck their finger into one of the traps of her largest Venus flytrap."

"Aha!" Dorian cried. "Why have you hidden this fact until now! Carla admitted to being a murderer—"

"She stabbed them in the back of the hand," Max explained. "She's not even an attempted murderer. Only someone who overreacts. But you're right, now that I understand more about my tea, I doubt she would have admitted as much to someone who she barely knew if it hadn't been for the effects of my tea."

"This was a good idea," said Mary. "Go on, Max."

"Apparently, it's bad for carnivorous plants when people mishandle them like that as a party trick, so Carla makes sure guests know not to touch the plants. What else... The microclimates in the conservatory are quite expensive to maintain. Lena seemed to bristle at how much money the Wests throw around."

"Aha!" Dorian cried once more. "Jealousy is a strong motive."

"But Carla and Dante West weren't the ones who were killed," said Max. "And she didn't even seem angry at them, only frustrated that they didn't recognize how big a deal their money was to someone like her. Someone who's just starting out who doesn't come from money or have much. Elias didn't seem bothered by it; he doesn't seem to care about money."

"What about Frederick?" Dorian asked. "You said he insulted them."

"Frederick Rasmussen. Shortly after I arrived, he pointedly insulted all of them for one reason or another: Carla for a faux persona, Dante for keeping a secret from his wife—"

"A secret?" Zoe asked.

"Dante sneaks an occasional cigarette," Max said. "Not something worth killing over. Frederick faulted Elias for ruining his clients' hair, and

Lena acting like a prude. He also pointed out how petty all of them were with their concerns, compared to his own problems. He was looking after his mom when she died, even though she was a meddler who'd ruined his life, but it was still painful to watch her have a heart attack. It was strange … almost as if the tea's effects made him a better person, since after he said such bad things about her, he admitted to the pain he felt seeing her die."

As Max continued with his story, Dorian extracted the full sheet of typed notes and hurriedly added a fresh piece of paper.

"My shop was broken into not long after that tea club meeting," Max concluded.

"The killer must have realized what was going on with the tea," Andrew said. "You really didn't realize what you had?"

"Mom raised me to be honest," Max snapped. "For honest people, the tea is simply excellent tea."

"You two aren't helping anything." Mary growled like he imagined his fictional plant monster would sound. "Yell at each other later, once there's no longer a killer running around out there."

Andrew groaned. Dorian imagined Max's father cradling his head in his hands, and he was once again frustrated that he could not be there in person.

"A killer," said Andrew, "who's now got their hands on the secret my mom uprooted her life for and one that has consumed my own."

"I don't think so." Zoe spoke so softly that Dorian could barely hear her. "Under the influence of the Tea of Honesty that first day, everyone was more suggestible to being honest. We know Frederick was a terrible guy, hated by his sister and neighbors, so there's a strong probability he was also a dishonest one."

"He hated being honest," Dorian cut in, "so he stole the tea so he would never again be forced to drink tea that would force him to tell the truth!"

"No," said Zoe. "I was thinking the opposite. From Max's retelling of what people talked about that day he visited the Posh and Punk Rock Tea Club, Frederick said some awful things about his mom, who everyone loved. Frederick accused her of ruining his life. What kind of person would say that about a beloved person who just died? What if that made the killer hate him even more? They snapped."

Dorian considered her theory. Max and his parents were likely doing the same, as nobody spoke for several seconds.

"My theory fits the facts as well," Dorian said.

"It doesn't, actually," said Zoe.

Dorian scowled at the phone, though his friend could not see him.

"Remember," she said, "the tea plants in Astoria were only stolen *after* Frederick was dead."

"Ah. This is a fair point," said Dorian. "I stand corrected."

Dorian was a gracious gargoyle. He was aware that his friends considered him stubborn. This was an unfair stance. Dorian was unfairly maligned. Surely this would prove to Zoe that he was not stubborn. When the facts pointed a different direction, he graciously accepted a differing opinion to his own.

It was Max who spoke next, yet the man did not address Dorian's gracious admission! No, Max's words were clearly directed at Zoe. "You think one of them killed Frederick because he was an even bigger jerk than usual? I don't know. That's a stretch."

"But it is *not* a stretch," said Dorian, "if we consider one additional fact." A brilliant idea formed in his mind. He wriggled his horns and smiled. His little gray cells had solved the case!

"What's that?" Zoe asked.

"People acting *individually* are more likely to behave rationally, yet when they are caught up in a group, the dynamic shifts." Dorian stood from the typewriter and paced as he spoke into the receiver. The telephone cord was beginning to tangle, but this was only a minor inconvenience. "Recall, if you will, the people in attendance at the tea club meeting. Dante and Carla West, the neighbors who loved their elderly neighbor, Joyce, yet hated her son who made them give up their nighttime concerts. Lena and Elias Tamraz, the youngsters with no extended family of their own who thought of Joyce as a grandmother. Four people consumed by grief. Even the gardener has admitted to loving Joyce. Five people who wished it was Frederick who had suffered a heart attack rather than Joyce. Five people who heard Frederick speak venomous words against his departed mother!"

"You think they did it together!" It was Max's mother, Mary, who spoke. Though Dorian could not see her expression, her intonation made it clear she was impressed.

"*Oui.* Think of the crime scene that Andrew, Zoe, and Max all discovered: a man with multiple carnivorous plants over his face. This is a symbolic gesture. Yes, *mes amis.* This was not a rational crime." Though there was nobody to see the gesticulation, Dorian raised a pointed claw as he concluded his brilliant deduction. "Group hysteria took hold of these friends brought together by tea. They all killed Frederick Rasmussen. Together."

CHAPTER 42

Mary and Andrew looked impressed by Dorian's wild theory, but Max and I shared a glance that assured me he was as skeptical as I was.

"That theory of a group of good people acting together to kill a bad man worked for Agatha Christie," I said. "But in real life, it's really hard for a group of decent people to agree to commit murder."

"Especially because they're angry at a jerk," added Max.

"I was open to abandoning my earlier theory when the facts did not fit," said Dorian. "You could at least do me the courtesy of doing the same now that I have presented a plausible theory."

"You're right," I admitted. "Implausible doesn't mean impossible."

Max's phone buzzed, and he looked at a text message. "I need to make a call." He stood up and stepped outside.

I took my phone off speaker phone and told Dorian I'd call him back soon.

"I really hope they aren't going to bring me in again," Andrew said as Max walked outside. "With that expression, he has to be talking to a detective."

"They wouldn't have taken you in in the first place," said Mary, "if you hadn't confessed to something you didn't do."

Andrew reddened. "I know I muddled things. So many things."

"You certainly did." Mary brushed a lock of hair from his forehead, then leaned in and kissed it. "Foolish man." She leaned back quickly as the bell above the door jingled.

Max pocketed his phone. "An old friend is keeping me in the loop. Forensic evidence connects Elias to the crime scene. I think that's why they released Dad. They had Elias in for questioning this morning, but he's got an alibi, so they let him go."

"An alibi?" I asked. "I thought they were all there at the time of the murder."

Max shook his head. "Remember the cameras showed *cars*, not people. Elias and Lena's car was there, but it was Lena who was there. Turns out Elias was at work."

"And then there were five." Lena, Carla, Dante, Gary, and Max's dad.

Max nodded. "And since all five of them where there that day, they all left fingerprints and other traces in the conservatory."

Now that the police were actively investigating suspects aside from Andrew, Mary and Andrew left to get reacquainted.

"I'm surprised you're leaving things to the police," I told Max.

"I'm not. This is connected to alchemy and my tea. They're not going to get that. But they're good at what they do, so they'll get us part of the way there. I'm not sure what else I can do right now."

"There's something I can do, though." I unlocked my phone.

"What are you up to?"

"It was suggested to me recently that I was a closet goth. What do you think of me changing my hair style?"

Elias's hair salon was tucked into a cozy alley on the west side of downtown Portland, not far from Powell's Books, where the streets ran at odd angles and trees were given as much land as parking spaces.

If I hadn't had such a bad experience with bicycles when they first were invented, I would have been a bicycle person. I prefer slacks to dresses, my hair is short enough that it doesn't get in my way in the wind, and at just under three miles from my house, it was the perfect distance to ride a bike in this city of plenty of bike lanes. But we can't always escape our pasts. I took my old pickup truck.

"I was surprised to hear from you," Elias said as I stepped through the door.

"Why? I'm ready for a change with my hair." I swept my gaze around the high-ceilinged salon, with natural light from the front windows catching on the shiny metal of mirrors, tables, chair arms. A row of mannequin heads with different styles of wigs adorned high shelves of one wall, and photos of people enjoying the Pacific Northwest wilderness filled the opposite wall—all the people in the photos had stylish haircuts, often in interesting colors.

Besides Elias, two other stylists were there, plus two patrons, both of whom were currently sitting underneath the domes of hair dryers, the hum of the hot air creating background music that melded with the trance music that played in the background.

Next to the unattended desk, a small tea and coffee station was nestled on a shelf between two spider plants.

The two stylists were talking with each other and nodded at me while I walked back to Elias's chair.

He flapped a black smock, but instead of draping it over me, he pulled back and held it in his fist. He met my gaze in the mirror we both faced. "I might as well tell you, since you'll know soon enough anyway. The police aren't so sure it was Andrew Liu, even though he was seen running away from the crime scene. They questioned me in Frederick's death."

I spun the chair around and faced him. He hadn't lowered his voice.

"Elias was here working when that man was killed," said a hair stylist with bright blue hair. "The police already questioned us."

"Don't worry about them," said the stylist with an auburn afro, tilting her head toward the two people under the hair dryers. One was scrolling on their phone, and the other looked to be taking a nap. Their ears were covered by the hair dryers, so they couldn't hear a thing we were saying. "And don't worry about Elias. He's good people."

"Plus, he was here with us," the first stylist added. "You don't need to worry about having your hair dyed by a murderer."

I turned back to Elias. "I know the police found something of yours at the crime scene."

Elias's fist tightened around the smock. "I go there all the time. It's not surprising they found my Swiss army knife." His grip relaxed. "But they know I was here—"

"We're his alibi," the second stylist cut in. With her hands on her hips, there was something defiant in her posture, as if she was daring me to question the truth of her statement.

"—so they didn't arrest me," Elias finished.

"I never thought you were guilty." I held up a packet of tea from my bag. "I'm stressed out by this whole situation, though. I need a change with my hair, but I thought the tea would relax us. And I guessed right—" I nodded toward the tea station. "I thought you might have something like that set up."

He smiled and started an electric kettle of hot water.

Twenty minutes later, my hair was cut at a sharp angle that was surprisingly flattering, and Elias was preparing the natural hair dye he used.

"What do you think happened?" I asked as he sectioned off my hair for the dye. "You have to have a theory."

"I know that's why you came today. Because you're worried about your boyfriend's dad."

"He wasn't charged." I watched his reaction in the mirror.

"Simone and Ida would totally lie to give me an alibi and protect me."

I forced myself to remain calm. The tea had worked. He was opening up in ways he never otherwise would have.

"But they didn't," he added. "I really was here. I hated Frederick, but I didn't kill him." He tightened his grip around a section of my hair.

I tilted my head and saw something I hadn't counted on: the other patrons' hair was done, so the other stylists had left for lunch together.

I was alone in the salon with Elias.

CHAPTER 43

Mayhem carried a carnivorous pitcher plant in her teeth, dropping the plant at the monster's feet.

"Why did you bring this to me?" the monster asked.

Mayhem nudged the roots with her nose.

"The dirt?" the monster asked. "Are you trying to tell me something about the dirt?"

Dorian narrowed his eyes at the page. He was straying far from his own Gothic novel. This prose was clearly his own subconscious working out Max's mystery on the page. *Bof!* This would not do.

Dorian ripped the paper from the typewriter and crumpled it into a ball. Abandoning his manuscript, he gave up all pretense of pretending he could think of something else beyond the murder.

He flipped through the well-worn paperback detective novels Zoe owned. Most of his reading had been of library books, since Zoe was terrible at transmuting lead into gold.

Dorian was certain he would have been a powerful metallurgic alchemist if he turned his attention toward working with metals. It was culinary alchemy he was more interested in. If only he were not a gargoyle, he would most certainly have received multiple James Beard awards and Michelin stars to recognize his excellence as a chef. He was both traditional and innovative in his culinary creations, so he was certain he was worthy of both.

If he were not a gargoyle, he would also have been able to accompany Zoe on her dangerous missions. She had insisted on questioning Elias under the pretense of wishing to dye her white hair black. Her research into the salon indicated several other people would be there, so he knew she would be safe. Still, he did not trust any of the members of the Posh and Punk Rock Tea Club. Any one of them could be the person controlling the plant monster and using it to do their bidding!

Dorian tossed *Daughter of Time* over his shoulder, ridding himself of its mocking cover. Armchair detecting was all well and good in a detective novel, yet it would not solve their problem now!

He clasped his hands behind his back and paced the length of the shelves in the attic. Her antique wares on the attic shelves were dwindling. She attended estate sales to look for new antiques to sell through Elixir, but she had not done much of this lately. Their needs were modest, yet Dorian feared she would soon need to be supporting Max as well. Once the novelty of donating to a sabotaged shop wore off, people would stop donating to the fundraising page Veronica had set up to help Max fix up the damaged shop. And without Max's tea to make the shop special, would The Alchemy of Tea survive?

Bon! The front door was opening. He heard Zoe's steps on the stairs. But when the attic door opened, a stranger stood before him.

"Zoe?" croaked Dorian. "Is that you?"

"You don't like my black hair?" The woman who he had only previously seen with white hair tucked a lock of her short black hair behind her ear. It was quite amazing how much a haircut and color could alter the appearance of a person.

"You look," Dorian said, "as if you have stepped out of a photograph of the crowd from an Andy Warhol art show. This hairstyle accentuates your lips and gives you a pout I never knew you had."

"I *am* pouting. Or at least I'm guessing that's what my frustration looks like. I don't think Elias is guilty, but we don't have enough tea for me to question everyone individually."

"It would not be safe for you to do so regardless."

"But I was thinking," she said, "if we brewed one big teapot with the remaining tea, it would be enough for everyone."

Dorian blinked. Could it really be true? Did black-haired Zoe agree with Dorian's ingenious methods she had previously dismissed? "You mean it is time to gather the suspects together!"

"It is," Zoe said. "We need to bring the suspects together in the Carpathian Conservatory of carnivorous plants and tea monster topiary to get to the bottom of this mystery."

CHAPTER 44

I couldn't quite believe I was *suggesting* a plan Dorian had previously forced upon me. He'd gone around my back to arrange for such gatherings of suspects in the past, and it hadn't turned out as he'd hoped. Now, I was hoping by taking charge, I could retain some control of the situation.

I explained my idea to Dorian. "The members of the Posh and Punk Rock Tea Club loved Frederick's mother Joyce, so we can get them together under the pretense of honoring Joyce once more. The believable way I think we can suggest it is that Max has one last batch of his home-prepared tea—"

"*C'est vrai?* Only enough for one brew?"

"It might not be quite that small an amount. But yes, there's hardly any left. So we can tell them Max wants to use it to honor Joyce. Everyone except the killer will think it's normal tea, and the killer can't very well say what they know, so we'll have to watch who doesn't drink it—"

"Or for the scoundrel who attempts to sabotage the whole affair."

"Good point," I said. "We'll need to plan this carefully."

"*Oui,*" said Dorian. "Meaning I must meet Max."

Well, apparently, I was to have no such control of the situation.

"I was to meet him this past week," Dorian continued. "I know you did not wish him to become distracted after his shop was destroyed, but he is ready. You saw how awkward it was when I was on the telephone when Max was describing the actions of the tea club members. If we are to execute this plan properly, we two detectives must meet face to face."

I took a breath and was about to object, but he was right. I'd attempted to tell Max about Dorian's true self. It hadn't worked, since how can one explain Dorian to someone who hasn't met him?

"You're right," I said. "I hate keeping secrets from Max, and if you'll be there in the conservatory with us when we gather everyone together, we might need to change plans quickly if the plant monster makes an appearance."

"Even if the monster turns out to be a person hiding in a plant costume."

"*Especially* then," I said. "Max will need to help me cover up for you if anyone sees you."

Mary was still catching up with Andrew, so it gave us the perfect opening to invite Max over tonight—alone. It was time. The two most important guys in my life would finally meet each other in person.

I told Max that Dorian was cooking dinner over at my house, so we could discuss next steps to figure out what was really going on with the tea his fugitive grandmother had smuggled from China and discuss the idea of gathering the suspects together at the conservatory.

Dorian took it upon himself to make the dinner a feast, approximating the celebratory summer solstice dinner. I tried to tell him the focus wouldn't be the food tonight, but he held up a clawed hand and said, "Zoe, one must eat well to fuel the mind!"

With that, I stayed out of the kitchen and crept up to the attic to review Dorian's MURDER BOARD. We had a closed circle of suspects. However, the evidence was cars, not people, that were shown to be at the West estate during the window of time when Frederick was killed. As Elias had proved, he was at work, and it was his sister who'd taken the car to visit the Wests. Or *Frederick*, if she was our killer.

Dorian had saved the cake he'd cooked earlier in the week in the freezer. "It will not be as perfect as fresh," Dorian mumbled, "but most people do not know how well many foods freeze. This cake will be ninety percent as good as new. Max will no doubt be somewhat distracted, so I hope he does not notice."

As Dorian was pulling a nut roast out of the oven to rest, the doorbell rang. We looked at each other and nodded silently.

While Dorian removed his apron and washed his hands, I went to open the door, feeling every bit as anxious as I had the first time I'd opened the door for Max Liu, when he'd come looking for Brixton, who'd broken into my house on a dare. That had been the first day at my new house. So much had happened since then, and I was so ready for Max to know the last of my secrets.

My heart thudded as I opened the door. Max stood on my doorstep, a bouquet of colorful poppies in one hand, a bottle of white wine in the other, and a broad smile on his face. The smile was accompanied by a crinkle on his forehead, telling me he was every bit as anxious as I was.

"Your hair!"

I tucked a lock of my newly black hair around my ear. It was too short, so it immediately fell back into my face. "You like it?"

"I love any way you look, Zoe Faust." He leaned forward and kissed my cheek, where my strange new hair had fallen. He lingered for a moment before straightening, and I breathed in the earthy summer scents of his garden. He must've been in his back garden immediately before walking over here.

"Flowers for you, and wine for the chef." Max held out both.

"Come on in." I ushered Max inside and closed the door, taking both the wine and flowers. As I touched the red and orange flowers, I knew that these flowers were from his own yard.

As soon as I'd locked the front door, the kitchen door swung open.

"This," I said, my voice not quite as steady as it had been a moment ago, "is Dorian." I stepped aside, letting Max see the gargoyle.

CHAPTER 45

Max stood in my living room, unblinking, as still as if he was a statue himself.

Finally, he blinked and took a breath. At least it appeared I hadn't given him a heart attack.

His knees began to sway. In retrospect, I should have stayed closer to him, but I'd walked straight to the dining table to deposit the flowers and bottle of wine. I was too far away to catch him as he fell to his knees.

"It must have been my dad who did this." Max squeezed his eyes shut and rubbed his temples.

"Did what?" I rushed to his side.

"Drugged me, of course." He rubbed his eyes, as if willing his view to change. "It must have taken a while to take effect. I don't know what he's up to—"

"You're not drugged, Max."

Max rubbed his eyes even harder. "I'm hallucinating. I had tea with my dad. Why would he have drugged me?"

"It wasn't your dad," I said. "You're not—"

"I've never experienced a drug like this." Max staggered toward Dorian. "It's so real! It's exactly like your gargoyle statue came to life. I always knew your statue looked a bit like one of the gargoyles at

Notre Dame Cathedral in Paris, but wow… now that I'm on whatever drug this is—"

"Max." I stepped between him and Dorian as Dorian's eyes grew wide with horror.

"Did I ever tell you about the summer I backpacked through Europe during college?" Max asked. "I know I told you about the summer I backpacked through Asia with a friend, when we ran out of money, which makes for a good story afterward but was miserable at the time… but I can't remember if I told you about my impressions of Notre Dame. I climbed the steps. All those circular steps. At the top, those gargoyles were so much bigger than I'd imagined from the ground. Your statue isn't as big… but it looks like the one called *Thinker*. I've told you that before. But did I tell you about that trip?"

"You didn't, but this isn't the time—"

"You're right. I need to wait until this drug is out of my system. But really." Max stepped around me and reached out toward Dorian's face. He grabbed the gargoyle's snout.

Dorian cried out as Max's fingers gripped his snout. "*Mon dieu*! Max has lost his mind!"

Max let go of Dorian's nose and stumbled backward and fell to the floor. "This hallucinogenic…. It's really taking hold now. I *heard* your statue. The auditory hallucination sounded just like Dorian."

"It is I, Max." Dorian scowled at Max's prone form. "Dorian Robert-Houdin."

"Dorian? It's really you?" Max winced. "I'm so sorry. My mind is more scrambled than I thought. My brain must be mixing up visuals. I'm hallucinating that Zoe's gargoyle statue and your body are one in the same. I didn't know that was a neurological possibility from the drug." Max took two deep breaths.

Dorian scowled at me as he rubbed his nose. "This is not how I imagined this meeting would go. I was not expecting this incomprehensible rant. He accepted you. You are far, far older than I am."

"Even that took a while," I reminded Dorian. "He thought I suffered from a delusion."

"It is true," said Dorian. "I imagined he might take time to adjust to my true visage. This is why I called Tobias to join us. He is most skilled with smelling salts. But the man is late."

Max took his hands from his eyes. "Tobias? Tobias knows you … the statue … as Dorian? I'm *not* drugged? It's really you? You're a—a gargoyle?"

"*Oui.*" Dorian bowed, giving one flap of his gray wings before folding them at his side once more.

Max proceeded to faint.

It looked like Dorian was right. We'd need those smelling salts after all.

CHAPTER 46

Tobias shone a narrow light into Max's eyes. "He'll be fine."

"I'm sorry." Max pushed himself up. "I've been running myself ragged. I knew I was tired, but I didn't know I'd reached a level of hallucinating. I'm so—" He broke off as his gaze went from Tobias to Dorian.

He remained seated, slumped against the wall of the dining room, and stared up at Dorian.

Tobias, Nicolas, Perenelle, and I all stood by. Tobias had stopped by the Flamels' house on the way over, thinking it would be easier for Max to adjust if he could see more people accepting Dorian.

"This," Nicolas said, "is truly Dorian Robert-Houdin, our French chef friend who we know through his baking for Blue Sky Teas, and for his friendship by telephone."

"But he…" Max looked from Nicolas back to the gargoyle.

"I understand it takes expanded thinking to accept this." Nicolas adjusted his glasses. "I, myself, was under the mistaken impression that Dorian had transformed himself from man to gargoyle in an alchemy lab. Yet when you hear his story, you will understand it is far more interesting than an alchemical experiment gone awry."

"*Bonjour, monsieur* Liu." Dorian smiled and bowed his head, keeping his wings at his side this time. "I am pleased to finally meet you in person."

"Brandy," said Perenelle. "This is what he needs."

Nicolas rummaged through my sparse liquor cabinet. "It does not appear that she has any brandy, dear."

"Whisky," I said, grabbing a barely touched bottle of single malt Scotch that had been a gift. I splashed a generous amount of the amber liquid into a glass tumbler and handed it to Max. He drank it without taking his eyes off Dorian.

Max coughed, then stood up. "I'm sorry. I didn't expect… But that was incredibly rude of me… I should have… Zoe even tried to tell me … but how could I have…?"

"There is no need to apologize," said Dorian. "You understand now, *mon ami*, why I must stay in the shadows. If even someone such as yourself has this reaction."

Max reddened. "You have my humblest apology. I didn't realize this was possible. That alchemy … that it could…"

"This isn't normally how alchemy works," I said.

"So there aren't more living gargoyles running around out in the world?" Max gave a nervous laugh.

I couldn't lie to Max. "Only one more living gargoyle that we know of."

"Another one?" Max croaked.

"It's only because of the alchemical connection to Notre Dame Cathedral in Paris," I said. I hadn't seen Leopold in quite some time, so didn't know if the drunken gargoyle had turned to stone once more. At least he hadn't turned up in any headlines. "But that's a story for another time. Maybe you should sit down at the dining table."

"These are not the circumstances under which I wished to meet." Dorian frowned. "Yet it was imperative that we speak of a plan to absolve your father—"

"Notre Dame," Max murmured, nearly missing the seat of the chair as his gaze remained transfixed on Dorian. "You really do look so much like one of the gargoyles. Is that how you refer to yourself?"

"A gargoyle," Dorian said. "This term is perfectly appropriate. As is chimera or grotesque. I prefer gargoyle."

"Zoe's statue," Max said. "You look nearly identical to Zoe's statue."

"*Oui*. You have seen me in my stone form."

"Stone form…" Max repeated. "You… You're *actually* Zoe's statue?"

Dorian wriggled his horns. "You will notice that I am smaller than *Le Penseur* stone figure perched on the gallery of gargoyles at Notre Dame de Paris. I was the original carving—the prototype, as it were—yet I am too small to be seen from the street. Jean Eugene Viollet-le-duc realized the creatures filling the gallery of gargoyles needed to be larger. Thus, I was given to his friend, Jean Eugene Robert-Houdin."

"The French stage magician?" Max looked like he might fall down once more.

"You have heard of him!" Dorian gave Max a gleeful grin.

"I hate to interrupt," said Perenelle, "but I was under the impression that there was some urgency in these two meeting tonight. Max's father is still connected to a serious crime—"

"Right." Max set his shaking hands on the table.

"Perhaps another drink?" Dorian took Max's glass.

The sensation of Dorian's very real gray fingers brushing against Max's hand must have been what snapped Max out of his funk. A look of clarity came over Max's face, replacing the glassy-eyed confusion that had been there a moment ago.

"I don't need another drink." Max's voice was forceful now, too. He reached not for his glass, but for a teacup on the hutch within reach of the table, against the wall. "Perenelle is right. We need to get to work. To do so, I need a clear head. There will be time later for me to get to know Dorian properly. But we have work to do now. I know Zoe has a plan she wants to discuss. Whatever it takes, I want to clear my dad for good and figure out what's really going on with those tea plants my grandmother took, and we need to figure out how to make the plan work."

"I'll make tea." Tobias took the teacup from Max's hand. "What's your poison?"

"Oolong," said Max. "That's what Zoe said my dad was drinking the day she met him outside The Alchemy of Tea."

Tobias disappeared through the kitchen's swinging door.

"*What's your poison,*" Nicolas repeated to himself. "Such strange and splendid idioms. What a fascinating world we live in. I must surely study more about linguistics…"

Max laughed. Not a polite laugh, but a full-bodied roar that released the stress he'd been holding. "Thank you, Nicolas, for that reality check." He clasped the old alchemist's shoulder. "I'm ready to get to work. Wait, one more question first."

"Yes?" We all said as one.

"Where exactly does Dorian live?"

Dorian steepled his clawed fingertips together. "Can you not guess? As a gargoyle, I do not need sleep, and I prefer a high perch. I live in the attic."

"*Zoe's* attic?"

Dorian frowned. "Only one half of the attic contains her wares for Elixir."

"Right. The attic. Of course." He ran his hands across his face.

"Your hands have continued to shake." Dorian pointed at Max's unsteady hands.

"Not helpful," I pointed out.

"I'm all right. Truly." Max hid both hands under the table. "I'm sorry it took me a few minutes to get accustomed to this. Zoe tells me you two have a plan?"

"*Oui.*" Dorian grinned and wriggled his horns. "Between Zoe's intelligent mind and my little gray cells, we have formed a perfect plan. With your assistance, we will be sure to catch the killer."

CHAPTER 47

All of the members of the tea club were eager to take us up on the invitation to meet at the Carpathian Conservatory the next morning.

We decided against the idea of honoring Joyce with Max's tea. Max had an even better idea. As a former detective, Max claimed to have the latest details about the case. He said he wanted to give them an update on the case.

With Andrew released from police custody and Elias being questioned but having an alibi, everyone claimed to be curious to know what was really going on.

As planned, we used Max's Tea of Honesty. It was nearly gone, and this would use up most of it. Dorian expertly parceled the tea into tea bags that made it look as if it was packaged tea. We didn't know if the killer had realized the true properties of the tea, but if so, this would be a way to still get them to drink the tea.

Dorian would creep into the conservatory as he'd done before and hide in the shrubbery. If he was about to be found out, he'd turn to stone like he did at the concert.

Everything was in place for our four remaining suspects. Dante and Carla West, Lena Tamraz, and Gary the groundskeeper.

"Love the hair," Carla said to me as I stepped underneath a new pot of pothos ivy tendrils into the conservatory.

"Elias convinced me to give it a try." I was too absorbed in the multilayered mystery causing Max grief to remember to be self-conscious about my hair. I've had the same hair style for three hundred years. I'd process the change another time.

"You said you had an update for us?" Dante asked as Max, Carla, and I passed the section of carnivorous plants and reached the clearing where the tea table sat.

All five people we expected were already there. Elias and his sister Lena sat near each other at the table. Dante stood next to a hutch where a kettle had recently boiled. Even Gary was there, though he stood off to one side, inspecting the loamy soil of one of the plants.

"I brought tea." Max held up the satchel Dorian had created, which looked very much like a packaged tea you'd find at a high-end tea shop. "My update might take a little while, so I thought it would be nice to have some refreshment. This is a rare black tea I'm thinking of ordering for my shop, so I'd love to get your opinion."

"I love a man who shows up with gifts." Carla leaned close to the satchel and inhaled. "This'll be good."

"I take it your answer means you still don't know who did it?" said Dante. He poured a splash of hot water into a teapot, swished it around, then dumped it out. He then let Max add the satchel of tea and filled it with the nearly boiling water.

"Is that true?" Elias asked from the spot where he was sitting next to his sister. "What kind of an update is it if you don't know who did it?"

"I'll let Zoe give the explanation."

Lena tilted her serene face, as if his answer didn't compute. "But she's not the detective."

"It's true that I'm the one who has an update on the facts of the case because of my connections on the police force," said Max. "But Zoe is the one who understands plants. And plants are key to what happened. Zoe?"

"Something happened the day Max visited your tea club," I began.

We didn't actually know what had happened that day that had set off the chain of events leading to Max's teashop theft, Frederick's murder, and the theft of the tea plants from Astoria that Max's fugitive grandmother had stolen, but me going over what we knew would serve two purposes. First, we could gauge reactions to what I said. And second, most importantly, we could stall for enough time for the tea to take effect.

"He knew Dante and Carla were tea enthusiasts, so he shared with you all a special tea that he'd produced for The Alchemy of Tea, which wouldn't be for sale until his shop opened a week later. Frederick was an unpleasant man, but you all kept him part of your tea club out of respect for his mother, Joyce, who you all had loved."

At Max's indication that the tea was ready to serve, Dante poured the steaming, fragrant liquid into our cups. For a few moments we all sat in silence and sipped the Tea of Honesty. As far as I could tell, nobody abstained from drinking the tea.

"Everyone enjoyed Max's tea that day," I continued. "Perhaps *too much*. Because the night before the Alchemy of Tea was supposed to open, the very tea he shared with all of you was stolen. His own father was arrested for the crime, only it was impossible for him to have been the thief. Why would Andrew Liu lie? For several days, he refused to tell us. However, Andrew drove his rental car to this house. That was the day Frederick Rasmussen was found dead with carnivorous plants placed on his body."

My audience was transfixed. Which wasn't a good thing. I needed them to drink their tea. I paused and took a very small sip of my own tea. The power of suggestion worked, and they each raised a cup to their lips.

"While Max's father was being held by the police on suspicion of murder, more tea was stolen. This time it was tea plants from Max's childhood home."

"How bizarre!" cried Carla.

Lena's hand shook as she placed her teacup back onto the table.

"I did it," blurted out Elias. "You don't need to go through a whole speech to the truth."

"You have an alibi," I said. I glanced at his cup. He'd barely touched his tea. He could still be lying.

"My coworkers are covering up for me," Elias insisted.

"Or you're protecting someone." Just like Andrew … was he was protecting his family? "Lena," I whispered. She'd gone pale. "You're covering for your sister."

"She had nothing to do with this." Elias stood so quickly that he toppled his teacup from the edge of the table. The liquid splashed over the floor as the porcelain shattered.

The screech of a frightened animal sounded.

"What the hell was that?" Dante whipped around, splashing the remainder of his tea onto the ground.

"Nothing, dear." Carla stroked his long hair, her knitting needles barely avoiding his ear. "Must have been the wind."

The plant monster. I was about to run in the direction of the sound when Lena's words stopped me.

"Elias," Lena snapped. "Shut. Up."

"Letting your brother take the fall for your crime?" I asked. "That's classy."

"I didn't kill Frederick," Lena said, but she wasn't speaking to me. She faced her brother. "If you're confessing for my sake, there's no need for you to be a martyr. I didn't strike the blow that killed him."

Her teacup was nearly empty, which suggested she was telling the truth.

"You didn't?" Elias stared at his sister. "Really? But I heard what Frederick said that day. I didn't realize at the time what it meant, but you did, didn't you?"

Lena bit her lip but didn't speak.

"That day." It was Dante who spoke. "That day Max brought over his homemade tea, Frederick was especially chatty—probably because he had a new person to berate. He was rambling on about how disturbing it was to be with his mom when she died. But Joyce died alone. She had a heart attack. She was alone. That's what the paramedics said. There was a 911 call from her phone, but they found her alone. My God. He *killed her*? He killed his own mother?"

Lena nodded. "I think so. I was gathering evidence to take to the police...."

"You shouldn't be saying this," said Elias. "They'll think you—"

"I have an alibi, too, Eli."

"The police know you brought our car here. You're the only other person who can drive that hunk of junk up this road with that sticking clutch."

Her cheeks reddened. She caught Gary's gaze. "I was here meeting Gary. We meet in the garden shed."

"They don't deserve an explanation about our private lives," Gary snapped.

"Why didn't you tell me you were seeing Gary?" Elias sounded more hurt than angry.

"You always get overly excited about people I'm dating. I didn't want to say anything before I knew where it was going."

"But if you didn't..." Elias turned toward Carla and Dante.

"Max heard Frederick's slip-up that day as well," I said, "but he didn't realize what it meant. That means *all of you* who knew Joyce supposedly died alone could have realized the discrepancy."

I should have paid more attention to Dorian's murder board. He had read about her dying alone in the paper and the information had been on that cork board. But every single one of the people in the Posh and Punk Rock Tea Club heard Frederick admit otherwise.

Carla shook her head. "I didn't notice what he said. I tried my best not to listen to anything that man said."

"Like I said a minute ago, it didn't register with me at the time either." Dante shrugged. "But it doesn't matter. Carla and I have alibis."

"You were here when Frederick was killed," Max said. "All four of you were."

"Sure," Dante agreed. "That doesn't mean I don't have an alibi.

Carla and I were on a video conference call with one of the bands I used to manage, catching up. The detective already verified it. I'm surprised you didn't know that, Max."

"Then there's nobody left," I murmured. Except a plant monster. I eyed the empty pot where a tea tree topiary had once stood.

"We didn't come out of the main house all morning," added Carla. "Gary wanted to spray a couple of the dying topiary plants with that natural insecticide that's supposed to be good for the environment but that still makes Dante's allergies act up."

"We wanted to save the plants that are dying from the same fate as that one." Dante pointed at the empty pot where it looked as if a plant had walked away.

Of course. The plant *hadn't* walked away. It had died, and the groundskeeper had removed it. An innocent explanation that didn't require a plant monster.

"Dante is allergic to everything," said Carla. "But he still thought it was worth it to save our beloved plants."

Gary rubbed his neck and fidgeted. Did he feel guilty about using a product Dante was allergic to? No… That wasn't it. I caught Max's eye.

"Gary," I whispered. "If Gary was spraying an insecticide that morning, he wasn't having a romantic tryst with Lena. And Gary thought of Joyce like a mom. Just like how Carla and Dante did, and Elias and Lena thought of her as a grandmother. You all are suspects, but you all have alibis—Elias from his salon coworkers, Carla and Dante from a whole band, but only Lena and Gary alibi each other, with no other witnesses."

I turned to the supposed lovebirds. "You both loved Joyce. Gary loved her so much that he couldn't continue attending the tea club gatherings without her." As I spoke, grief transformed his face. "You and Lena aren't romantically involved, are you?"

A tear rolled down Lena's cheek. "We were, briefly. We comforted each other in our grief. Once. We loved her so much. And Frederick killed her. He—" Her voice broke.

Gary took her hand. "That monster couldn't wait for Joyce to die, so he had to steal whatever time she had left on earth. Time she should've had to spend with us."

Lena leaned into Gary's chest, and we all watched in stunned silence as she cried in his arms.

"But why did you steal my tea?" Max asked softly. "If you wanted to compel him to confess, you could have waited and simply bought a portion when my shop opened."

Lena shook her head as she stifled her sobs. "What are you talking about? We didn't steal anything. What does your stupid, amazingly delicious tea have to do with anything?"

The Tea of Honesty was certainly working. She was angry, grieving, and terrified, but she couldn't stop herself from saying it was excellent tea.

As Max reached for his phone to call the authorities, Gary tensed. Seeing what Max was doing, he grabbed Lena's hand and bolted.

As they ran past us, Carla stuck one of her knitting needles into Gary's arm. He cried out but kept running, orange yarn trailing after him. The yarn wouldn't stop him, so I lifted my foot and tripped him with my boot. He let go of Lena's hand as he crashed to the ground.

Max was on top of him a second later. He put a knee on Gary's back and secured his hands with a zip-tie from his pocket. Lena gave a frightened glance behind her as Max did so, then kept running.

But before she'd gone more than a few paces, that loud animal shriek sounded once more. A creature jumped out of the tea trees and onto her shoulders. Lena screamed as its claws dug into her skin.

For a horrifying moment, I was afraid Dorian had decided to come out into the open to stop Lena, but it wasn't a gargoyle. Nor was it a plant monster.

It was a *hairless cat.*

"Boots?" said Dante. "What's Joyce's old cat doing here?"

"Frederick hated her and wasn't going to keep her." Carla looked forlornly between the hissing cat on Lena's shoulders and her ruined knitting needle in Gary's arm. "But I couldn't bear to think of Boots losing her freedom while she waited to be adopted. You were afraid to give her a chance even though she's hairless, so I thought I'd leave food out for her to see if she liked it here, and to see if your allergies would be all right since she doesn't have fur. Boots, honey. Come to mama and stop trying to kill the bad murderer."

Dorian hadn't been right about a monster, but he'd been right about the murder itself. This *was* a case of murder perpetrated by multiple people who hated the victim, working together.

CHAPTER 48

Lena and Gary had committed the murder together, and we knew the Tea of Honesty was responsible for Frederick slipping up and admitting a fact that revealed he'd murdered Joyce, who was beloved by all. But we still didn't know who had stolen Max's tea.

Max secured both Gary and Lena, and made sure Elias wasn't close enough to his sister to be tempted to cut the zip-ties off her wrists and help her escape. The police would be arriving soon, so we were in an awkward phase with our adrenaline still surging but nowhere to direct it. The Tea of Honesty would still be working for Carla and Dante, who'd drunk most of their tea, so I took advantage of the situation to get answers to our remaining questions.

"I have a confession," I said to Carla, who was carrying the cat Boots in her arms in place of her knitting that she'd used to help catch Gary. "When I was here earlier this week, I felt like someone was watching me through the trees. The cat is good at hiding, so I had the silly thought that one of your topiary tea plants had come to life."

Carla laughed. "They're so lifelike, aren't they?" Her laughter died as she glared at Gary. "I'll need to find another skilled plant artist now. It's only my knitted plants that I created to come to life."

I couldn't contain a gasp. Could it be true?

Dante scratched the back of his neck and caught my eye. "Yeah …

that's me. Carla was inspired by yarn bombing, that political act of street art to cover sterile public spaces with colorful artwork made of yarn. She loved her creations so much that I replaced her dying plants with new ones." He was standing a few feet away from Carla, still wary of the cat, but turned to his wife. "Sorry, babe. I wanted to keep it a secret, so you'd think you really were transforming your plants with love."

Carla blew him a kiss. "I've always known it was you, Dante. I'm eccentric, not mad. Since yarn bombing gives new life to dying public spaces, I thought I'd knit together some of my carnivorous plants that were dying, to give them new life as art. I knew it was only an art project, not something I thought would really come back to life."

"Luckily you got bored with that art project," said Dante. "It's really hard to source some of the carnivorous plants you like."

Carla cocked her head. "What are you talking about? You replaced my sundews just yesterday."

Dante stared at her. "I did no such thing."

"In the sun and moon planter box," I cut in. "There's a new, healthy sundew flypaper trap plant."

As Carla and Dante exchanged a confused glance, the police arrived and took charge, leaving me to wonder: Was Max's Tea of Honesty strong enough to be certain they were telling the truth to each other? Had Carla truly transformed those plants with yarn?

After we'd given our statements, Max and I found a scowling Dorian hiding in the back of my truck. He was covered in cat scratches.

"I was correct there was a monster in the conservatory." Dorian glared at us with one eye. The other was swollen shut from the gash of a claw. "I found the creature, but I could not verbally convince her to detain Lena, so I had no choice but to lift the furious feline and toss her onto Lena's shoulders. I am pleased you do not wish to share our home with a cat, Zoe. They are most disagreeable creatures."

"That was really heroic," said Max. "And smart for you not to have done it yourself."

Dorian sniffed. "I know how to live in the shadows yet also get the job done, as they say."

I handed Dorian a healing salve I kept in my bag. "This should help for the stinging sensation of your cuts as we drive home, and I've got plenty more herbal remedies for these cat scratches at the house."

Back home, I focused my energy on patching up Dorian. Only then did the reality sink in that we hadn't solved the mystery of who was after Max's grandmother's tea.

Andrew Liu was no longer a murder suspect, which was a relief, but I didn't believe there was a whole shadowy organization willing to kill over these tea plants that we'd seen no evidence of outside of Andrew's academic research. When I'd battled backward alchemists, the clues had been hiding in plain sight the whole time. I saw no such evidence here. Had Max's grandmother truly been murdered? What were we missing?

Dorian paced the length of the living room with his clawed hands clasped behind his back. He swore as he tripped over the arm of the couch. His depth perception was out of whack because of the eye patch I'd given him to wear over his scratched eyelid until the injury healed.

"We have less than thirty minutes until Andrew and Mary arrive and I must depart for the attic," he said as he steadied himself and glowered at the offending sofa. "What do we three alchemists need to discuss before the mortals arrive?"

"We're all mortals," I pointed out.

"And I'm only a tea alchemist," Max added.

Dorian crossed his gray arms and looked up at us. "It is helpful to have a healthy ego to solve crimes. Do not be so modest."

"Being mortal is helpful," I insisted. "As is humility. Alchemists who think themselves invincible lose their humanity."

Dorian waved away my protest. "We are three highly intelligent alchemists. How is it that we cannot see the truth?"

The doorbell rang.

"Dad prides himself on his punctuality," Max said. "He always shows up to his classes at least fifteen minutes early to set a good example for his students. I should have thought it might extend to the rest of his life."

Dorian sighed. "I will be in the attic. Call the land line before you answer the door, Zoe, so I can listen in." He scampered up the stairs, stumbling over a step and grumbling about pirates making eye patches look easier to deal with than in reality.

As soon as I opened the front door, Mary threw herself into her son's arms. "You did it. You cleared your father. I knew you would!"

"Thank you," said Andrew. "Thank you both."

"Don't thank us yet," I said. "The killers didn't realize that it was the tea that made Frederick slip up and inadvertently reveal that he'd killed his mother. There's still a tea thief out there."

"And a tea shop for me to finish repairing," added Max.

"It's not safe," Andrew began. "You can't—"

"Dad, I'm truly thankful that you're not in prison, but I'm not going to uproot my entire life because of a legend you read about that has a kernel of truth. Grandmother died of a heart attack far younger than she should have from the stress of having committed a theft that made her flee her family."

"But—"

"She understood there was something special about those tea plants," Max continued. "I don't know what made her decide it was worth committing a crime to steal them, and with Granddad gone now, too, I doubt we'll ever know. But what we do know is that there's a subtle characteristic inherent in those plants, and that using her skills as an apothecary, she enhanced the properties that make it a Tea of Honesty, which I'm learning about now as well."

"But you can't—" his father tried again.

"I'm not going to sell the Tea of Honesty in my shop," Max continued. "I'm nearly out anyway. As Zoe helped me see, The

Alchemy of Tea is about so much more than that one special variety of tea plant. I hope you can understand that and honor my wishes."

Andrew stood in silence for a moment, then embraced his son.

While father and son stood hugging in my living room, their arms entwined like tea leaves, I understood the thread we'd overlooked.

"The vandalism of Blue Sky Teas," I said, becoming more certain as I spoke the words. "That was the first clue."

The men broke apart as Max shook his head. "That's not related. You said it yourself. It was a vandal, not a thief. They didn't even try to get inside—"

"But they *did*," I said. "They got something even more valuable."

"Zoe, darlin'," said Mary, "you're going to have to spell it out for some of us."

"Max," I said. "We need to go back to The Alchemy of Tea. *Right now.*"

CHAPTER 49

Ten minutes later, the four of us burst through the door of The Alchemy of Tea. JJ, who was finishing the cabinets, was so surprised that he nearly smashed his thumb with his hammer.

"Jon?" Andrew gaped at the young man. "What are you doing here?"

The handyman froze.

"Why don't you put down the hammer," Max said calmly.

The handyman gave a start. He blinked at the hammer, as if he'd forgotten he was holding it. "What? *This*? I wouldn't.… You think I'd *hurt* someone?"

"If you're not going to hurt anyone," Max continued in the same soothing voice, "why don't you put it down."

The young man swallowed hard and set the hammer down.

"You know this man, Dad?" Max kicked the hammer out of reach.

"He's my graduate research assistant. Jon, what's going on?"

Jon's shoulders sagged. "I knew I shouldn't have stuck around to finish the cabinetry. But I had to meet with the agents this morning anyway. I thought it couldn't do any harm to finish up before flying back home. My dad always taught me to take pride in my work."

"Agents?" asked Max.

"Will someone please explain what's going on?" said Mary.

"Max's handyman," I said, "who introduced himself as JJ to Blue and Max, is Andrew's research assistant and co-author, Jonathan Jin. He's one of the few people who understands the special nature of this tea, because *that's what he's been researching with Andrew*. Andrew was obsessed with this quest, and his obsession influenced impressionable young Jon, who thinks this tea is terribly important—and dangerous."

"It is!" Jon cried.

"I know you think so," I said. "But you don't really understand what you're dealing with. You were too concerned with your own cleverness. You followed Andrew to Portland, and when you learned the tea was about to be released into the world, you came up with a plan to stop it. One that would also ingratiate yourself to the man working with the tea, so you could get close to him and make sure there wasn't more out there. To set your plan in motion, you smashed the front window of Blue Sky Teas. You made sure you were the first customer of the day the next day, and as a skilled handyman and carpenter, you were happy to help. You made sure you were so helpful that Blue would be sure to recommend you to Max when his own shop window was broken later that week."

Max groaned. "It was connected after all."

"Mary told us that Andrew likes to mentor first generation graduate students," I said. "Are you from a family of carpenters and the first to attend graduate school, Jon?"

After a stunned pause, Jon nodded.

"You really did this?" Andrew said. "*Why?*"

Jon's attention snapped to Andrew. "For the same reason as you. This tea is too dangerous to be unleashed on the world. You understood that, once. But when your son became involved, I saw that you'd gone soft. You weren't going to take it away from him—so I had to do it."

"You're the person who stole the tea plants." I laughed at the absurdity of having thought it was a tea tree topiary that had traveled to Astoria. "We found *assamica* tea leaves in the dirt, because those tea leaves were in the treads of your work boots, *from Max's shop*."

When The Alchemy of Tea was vandalized, I had noticed the loose-leaf tea on the floor, which Jon helped clean up. If I hadn't been thinking of plant monsters that day in Astoria, I would have realized they were dried tea leaves that had been partially reconstituted from the moist soil. Not fresh leaves from the West's conservatory.

"But who are these agents Jon mentioned?" Andrew asked.

Jon smirked. "You're too late. I've already shared our research findings with the government, and I handed over the tea plants. They'll make sure to study the plants properly and keep them out of the public's hands. Professor Liu didn't have the courage to do what needed to be done, but I did."

"The government?" Andrew laughed. "You trust them to know what to do with the tea?"

Jon's smile faltered. "I couldn't bring myself to destroy it. Even though it's dangerous, it needs to be studied."

Andrew swept his ex-wife and son into his arms, shaking with laughter. "I can't believe my cocky, immature student caused so much grief."

"I'm not—" Jon began.

"Just leave them be," I said. He wasn't a bad kid. Not entirely. I suspected his academic career was over, but I doubted Mary would press charges over the tea plants, so he wouldn't go to jail. He was a skilled carpenter, so he'd land on his feet.

"Get over here, Zoe," said Mary, inviting me into the group hug.

It was a warm and wonderful feeling, and I wasn't the only one who felt that way. None of us moved when the bell above the door jangled, indicating that Jon had left.

"This is a very X-Files moment," said Max.

"Or Indiana Jones," I added. "They won't be able to turn the tea plants into truth serum. Not like they imagine. Government scientists won't add their own alchemical energy and intent into every step of the process. They'll simply look for the chemical properties, which will only tell them a small part of the story about what makes those plants special. After laboratory tests fail, specimens from the plants that they've killed will end up in the depths of a warehouse somewhere."

"It's over," said Andrew. "It's finally over."

It wasn't *exactly* over, though. There was still a lingering doubt about what had really happened to Max's grandmother, and Jon and Andrew didn't know about the tea plant cuttings Max and I had taken this summer and planted in Max's backyard. They wouldn't be ready to harvest soon, but one day they would.

CHAPTER 50

In the weeks that followed, Max, his mom, and his sister all forgave Andrew, and it looked like Mary and Andrew might be giving their failed marriage another chance. Andrew couldn't stay in Portland for the long term, because he had to go back to his university teaching job at the end of the summer. But there was plenty of summer left. It would be interesting to see what happened.

Frederick's sister inherited the Rasmussen house, but she didn't want to move into it, so she immediately listed it for sale. The day it listed, Perenelle Flamel put in an offer for it.

Perenelle had fallen in love with the land on the hillside, which would allow her to grow the wild and free pigment garden she wanted, as well as have a huge art studio with plenty of natural light.

I loved this idea, because as much as I loved having my stand-in parents back in my life and living in the same city, I wasn't sure I loved having them *quite* as close as they were. I also thought she'd get along great with Carla, who just might have invented crafter alchemy with her carnivorous plants.

Dante asked me if I could share the name of the stone carver who carved my gargoyle statue. I told him the truth: the stone carver had retired long ago. But I'd recently seen an art show by a young sculptor named Gideon Torres, so I recommended he look him up.

Lena and Gary confessed to their crime. An autopsy showed that Frederick had indeed killed Joyce, so Lena and Gary's attorneys were arguing that there were extenuating circumstances. I expected they would likely receive lighter sentences considering the truth about Frederick.

A few weeks after the originally planned summer solstice grand opening, we got to celebrate a real grand opening of The Alchemy of Tea. By that time, my white roots were starting to show.

"I like your real white hair best," Max confided in my kitchen. We were sharing a pot of herbal tea before walking over to the shop. Max was anxious, and he wanted to get there a couple of hours before he'd turn the sign from "closed" to "open" for the first time.

"Even though my white hair is a reminder of how abnormal I am?" I asked.

"Special," Max corrected. "I love it because that's the real you. We're the moon and the sun, just like in alchemy and in life. We complement each other, rather than being mirror images of each other. I don't want to be the type of alchemist you are, but I love you for being exactly who you are."

He saw another question on my lips, but he stopped it with a kiss.

"Do you regret learning about alchemy through tea this year?" I asked when I came up for air.

Max shook his head. "It got me closer to you, made Dorian trust me enough that I finally got to meet him, and my dad is back in my life."

Andrew and Mary would be meeting us at the shop shortly. Dorian couldn't attend the public opening, of course, but I knew he had a gift to give Max before Max and I walked over to The Alchemy of Tea.

"Speaking of Dorian," I said, "I wonder where he is. He has a present he wants to give you."

"I'm too nervous to eat, so I hope it's not a culinary creation."

I left the kitchen and climbed the stairs to the attic. I found Dorian seated at the table that held his typewriter, staring at his gift for Max that he'd unwrapped.

"Unhappy with the wrapping paper?" I spotted crumpled wrapping paper in the trash bin. He'd used a vintage map of Paris to wrap the gift, which had seemed fitting to me.

Dorian's snout twitched. "After everything that had transpired this week, I fear that my gift is no longer miraculous enough."

"Max isn't expecting a gift at all."

"*Alors,* you admit it is not miraculous?"

I grinned. Life was back to normal. "Come, on Dorian. Max and I need to get to the shop. Do you want him to have it on his opening day or not?"

Dorian followed me down the stairs, mumbling about draconian alchemists, and presented Max with the gift that had been sitting on my kitchen counter all week: a small stone.

"Is this what I think it is?" Max's eyes filled with wonder as he accepted the small, smooth stone.

"It is not the Philosopher's Stone," said Dorian, "for such a thing does not exist as a physical reality as some amateurs posit."

"I know," said Max. "It's warm … but it feels as if it's warm from *within.*"

Dorian wriggled his horns with delight. "If I have succeeded, it will remain eternally warm."

"This is amazing. I can use it to keep tea warm in the teapot I'll be using for samples at my shop."

"Did Zoe tell you this was my intent?" Dorian asked.

I shook my head. "I wanted it to be a surprise."

"It's perfect," said Max. "Thank you, Dorian."

When Max and I rounded the corner of Hawthorne Boulevard a few minutes later, we came to an abrupt stop. At least fifty people were waiting outside Max's shop already, even though it was more than an hour until it was due to open. In addition to Mary and Andrew, we spotted the Flamels, Tobias, Mina, Heather, and even Brixton and Veronica were there.

But it wasn't only our friends. There were so many people neither of us knew. The community had come together around The Alchemy of Tea. I took Max's hand and led him to this next transformation.

THE END

The Accidental Alchemist Mysteries will continue with **The Alchemist of Brushstrokes and Brimstone.** *Get your copy now!*

Never miss a release. Keep up with all Gigi's latest books and get a free novelette and more recipes by joining Gigi's newsletter. *Scan the code below, or go to www.gigipandian.com.*

Read on for recipes and more goodies!

Scan to subscribe to Gigi's newsletter

RECIPES

ZOE'S SUMMER SALAD (AND THE BASICS OF HOW TO BUILD A SUMMER SALAD)

The theory of building a simple yet flavorful summer salad: Take heaping handfuls of any salad green you like, chop one or two additional raw vegetables you like, and mix in a favorite grain and bean. Here are the two steps that elevate this salad: toss it with a homemade vinaigrette dressing (recipe below) and add crunchy toppings.

The quantities below are for a single serving of one version of this salad, so scale up as needed.

Ingredients:

- 3 cups lettuce of choice, ripped into bite-size pieces
- 1/2 cup cucumber, chopped
- 1/3 cup cooked and cooled wild rice
- 1/3 cup cooked and cooled chickpeas
- 1/2 medium avocado, sliced
- 1 Tbsp dried cranberries
- 1 Tbsp slivered almonds

Directions:

Toss all the ingredients together in a bowl, along with salad dressing (recipe below).

Variations:

Don't like almonds? Add another nut or seed for crunch, such as shelled pistachios.

Want to elevate the flavor even more? Add the wild rice, chickpeas, and almonds to a baking sheet, toss with 1 tsp oil and a dash of salt, and broil for approx. 3 minutes (the time will vary depending on your oven and how close the pan is to the flame, so watch closely the first time you make it). Let cool for a few minutes before adding to the salad.

For an added pop of flavor, sprinkle a tablespoon of nutritional yeast on top, right before eating.

Once the salad is dressed, add homemade croutons (see www.gigi pandian.com/recipes for a simple crouton recipe).

DORIAN'S AUTUMN SALAD (AND THE BASICS OF HOW TO BUILD AN AUTUMN SALAD)

The theory of building an autumn salad: Once the weather cools, adding a few warm, roasted ingredients can turn a summer salad into a cozy autumn treat. Use a hearty salad green that won't wilt when hot food is added, take a few minutes to lightly roast additional vegetables, warm your grains and beans while you're cooking your vegetables, use a homemade salad dressing, and add a crunchy topping.

The quantities below are for a single serving, but scale up well.

Ingredients:

- 2 cups arugula
- 1 tsp olive oil
- Dash (approx. 1/8 tsp) sea salt
- Dash (approx. 1/8 tsp) freshly ground black pepper
- 2/3 cup chopped red cabbage
- 2 cremini mushrooms or button mushrooms, quartered
- 1/3 cup cooked farro
- 1/3 cup cooked chickpeas
- 4 kalamata olives
- 1 Tbsp pepitas/pumpkin seeds

Directions:

Spread the chopped red cabbage, quartered mushrooms, cooked farro, and cooked chickpeas on a baking sheet. Toss with 1 tsp oil and a dash of salt and pepper. Put under a broiler on low heat for approx. 5 minutes (the time will vary depending on your oven and how close the pan is to the flame, so watch closely the first time you make it), tossing once in the middle of broiling.

Once the items are warmed through and beginning to crips, add them to a bowl with the remaining ingredients, except for the pepitas.

Arugula is a hearty green, so it won't wilt too much, but it will be slightly warmed.

Toss with salad dressing (recipe below). Sprinkle the pepitas on top.

Variations:

Don't have pepitas? Add another nut or seed for crunch, such as slivered almonds, walnut pieces, or sunflower seeds.

Don't have red cabbage or mushrooms? Other lightly roasted vegetables that work well are red bell peppers and fennel, each sliced finely.

For an added pop of flavor, toss the vegetables going under the broiler with a dash one of your favorite spices, such as turmeric. One note of warning is that spices burn easily, so be careful to check your baking sheet often.

Once the salad is dressed, add homemade croutons (see www.gigi pandian.com/recipes for a simple crouton recipe).

HOMEMADE VINAIGRETTE SALAD DRESSING (AND THE BASICS OF HOW TO BUILD A SALAD DRESSING FROM SCRATCH)

The building blocks of making a simple salad dressing at home are 2 parts oil, 1 part acid, plus *at least* one more ingredient to enhance the flavor.

The quantities below are for a single serving, but easily scale up, and leftovers will keep in the fridge in a mason jar for a week.

Basic ingredients:

- 2 Tbsp olive oil
- 1 Tbsp balsamic vinegar <u>or</u> fresh-squeezed lemon juice
- Dash (approx. 1/8 tsp) freshly ground black pepper
- Dash (approx. 1/8 tsp) sea salt

Optional add-ons to the basics above, for even more flavor:

- 1 tsp Dijon mustard
- 1 small clove of garlic, finely diced, <u>or</u> garlic powder

Directions:

Put all the ingredients in a small mason jar with a lid, and shake. No jar? Whisk the dressing ingredients a bowl. Don't skip this step, as it's important to blend the flavors together before tossing the salad.

Customize this salad dressing by using oils, vinegars, and spices you enjoy.

AUTHOR'S NOTE

The Alchemist of Monsters and Mayhem is a work of fiction, but many of the ideas are based on fact.

Chinese alchemy has a long-documented history, but the historical details are obscure and can be contradictory. Some sources mention a connection between tea and alchemy, though there's no evidence of tea being used quite as my characters do. Because Chinese alchemy was primarily concerned with an elixir of longevity and immortality rather than creating gold for monetary wealth, tea's association with alchemy might have been for its transformative healing properties—like an elixir of life for nutrient-deprived monks. But beyond the nutrients in tea, there's also a long history of tea culture that involves slowing down when brewing and enjoying a cup of tea. Max's teashop The Alchemy of Tea was inspired by a mix of many of these ideas. Daniel Reid's book *The Art and Alchemy of Chinese Tea* does a deep dive into esoteric ideas about tea and alchemy.

The mansion high in the Portland hills is fictional, but it was inspired by Pittock mansion, a historic home in the West Hills of Portland, not far from the Witch's Castle in Forest Park (which you may remember from *The Alchemist of Fire and Fortune*). Like the drive described in the book, the road to Pittock Mansion is a narrow, winding road covered by a canopy of lush trees. Unfortunately, the real Pittock Mansion isn't surrounded by monster-shaped topiary, nor does it house a conservatory of carnivorous plants.

Charles Darwin was fascinated by carnivorous plants. He was especially interested in them because various species had evolved to be carnivorous in order to survive in inhospitable conditions. In 1875, he published the book *Insectivorous Plants,* and thought the term "insectivorous" was more appropriate than "carnivorous," because during his years observing their behavior, he noticed they got their nutrients only from insects. Molly Williams' *Killer Plants* was probably my favorite research book I read while researching this novel; it has a beautiful layout and includes fascinating details such as the historical use of sundews that Zoe references as being used as a medicinal plant.

When I first created my Accidental Alchemist characters, I didn't know how they would evolve. I didn't even know if they would exist beyond the book I was writing at the time while going through chemotherapy. I'll share a secret: While I loved the idea of writing famous mythical alchemist Nicolas Flamel into *The Accidental Alchemist* as Zoe's long-lost mentor, I didn't realize at the time that Zoe would find Nicolas and Perenelle Flamel once more (in *The Alchemist's Illusion*). Nor did I realize how big a role they would each come to play, or how much the ever-curious Nicolas would enable Dorian!

I'm now working on *The Alchemist of Brushstrokes and Brimstone*, in which Perenelle Flamel is front and center. Because so little is known about the real Nicolas and Perenelle, and so much about them is shrouded in mystery, they're such fun characters to write. All we know for certain is that they lived in 14th and 15th century Paris, Nicolas was a scribe and bookseller, Perenelle brought wealth to their union from an earlier marriage, and they gave much of that money to charity. Did Nicolas truly encounter a book of alchemy and discover the Elixir of Life? Were there graves really found to be empty when exhumed? Isn't it fun to wonder… *what if?*

Sign up for my email newsletter at https://www.gigipandian.com/

subscribe for more fun facts relating to history and mystery. And recipes. I can't forget the recipes. Now it's time for me to get back to researching and writing the next book.

275

In the spellbinding 8th installment of the Accidental Alchemist Mysteries, centuries-old alchemist Zoe Faust and her gargoyle sidekick Dorian face their most colorful case yet!

A stolen masterpiece. A brilliant woman written out of history. And a recipe for a lost color worth killing for.

Buy it now!

THE ALCHEMIST OF BRUSHSTROKES AND BRIMSTONE: CHAPTER 1

A haunting shade of white illuminated the faces of the two people in the portrait. It wasn't the usual lead white pigment you'd expect from a painting from 1700. The artist had used quicksilver and brimstone to create this paint, and the color in the oil painting was as vibrant as it had been 300 years ago.

The *Brother and Sister* portrait is the most prized possession I own. That doesn't mean it's worth much, as old paintings go. It's only priceless to me because it's a portrait of me and my brother, Thomas, who died of the plague shortly after it was painted.

As far as the world knows, this humble painting is by an unknown artist. It isn't. I know exactly who painted it. But if I were to reveal the truth, nobody would believe me.

There was no reason for the *Brother and Sister* painting to be of much value to anyone besides me. Why, then, was an art collector desperate to get his hands on it? There was no way for him to know the truth. *Was there?*

The emails began two weeks ago. Friendly, at first. Then more aggressive.

English art collector Arthur Finder contacted my mentor, who had bought the painting for me last year from where it was gathering dust in a dark corner of a small family museum in France. The purchase wasn't a secret, and the painting wasn't famous or worth much. We never thought it would attract attention. Why, then, was a wealthy

English lawyer willing to pay far more than the painting was worth, and angry when his offer was refused? Why *now*?

I stepped back and took in the framed work of art, trying to understand why the collector was pursuing this humble painting. Thankfully, he believed the painting was still somewhere in France, not across the world in my house in Portland, Oregon.

I looked more closely at the scene. Thomas and I were bathed in light from a side window of the French farmhouse. I loved the green dress I wore, and Thomas adored his simple wool waistcoat, though I always suspected that was because of the young woman who'd mended it for him. Familiar books and bottles lined a smooth wooden shelf behind us. I didn't recognize a thin parchment notebook that was tucked between thick glass jars of cinnabar and saltpeter. The smaller jar of rough, red cinnabar had a jagged crack from when a raging storm had blown open the window and toppled the inventory logbook from a high shelf, knocking over two hand-blown jars as it fell. Strange, the details one remembered. I wondered why I'd forgotten the beautiful little notebook nestled between those jars.

The portrait was a beautiful work of art. But beauty alone isn't enough to create value.

Perhaps the collector was an art forger. Not that art forgers are nearly as common as pop culture would have you believe. But if an old canvas was his goal, an earlier Renaissance era canvas would be more enticing.

Or maybe it was because the unusual pigments hadn't lost their vibrancy over the centuries. Not even the greens—a color family notorious for turning a muddy brown when exposed to light—had faded. But that couldn't be it. There were plenty of paintings kept out of sunlight that hadn't deteriorated much.

Brother and Sister, artist unknown, France, circa 1700. That's what the small family museum in France had written on a placard, because nobody knew the truth about who painted it.

Well, as I mentioned, I shouldn't say *nobody.*

"Zoe," my boyfriend Max called from upstairs, interrupting my thoughts. "I need some moral support here."

"He is attempting to cheat," a second voice called, this one with a French accent.

"You know that's not true." Max's voice was barely audible now, as he was no longer attempting to be heard halfway across the house.

After one last glance at Thomas's mischievous face, I stepped into the hallway and climbed the stairs to the attic, smiling to myself as I did so.

The art collector didn't know I existed. My mentor was careful not to mention me in his correspondence. I didn't need to worry. I could enjoy this life I'd fought hard to create, surrounded by loved ones. A life I'd never had before. Why did I always try to ruin it by worrying unnecessarily? I knew the answer, of course. I've survived for centuries by being cautious. Alchemists always have to be on guard.

I stepped into my high-ceilinged attic, a fully finished room stuffed to the gills with the antiques I sell to make a modest living.

In the cozy far corner of the attic, Max Liu and a gargoyle stared at each other across a chessboard. The pieces of this antique set were mechanical, so when you pushed a wooden knight's arm, its horse stood on its hind legs. But the queen was my favorite. She tipped her crown when you pressed the stone she stood upon. I didn't think it was just my imagination that the craftsman who'd carved the set had given her a mysterious Mona Lisa smile.

"It is Max's move," the gargoyle said to me in his thick French accent, never lifting his gaze from the board. He gave a salute-like flap of his wings and crossed his gray arms. "He picked up his queen, then claimed it was a mistake."

Max, for his part, was doing rather well for only having learned a few months ago that my friend Dorian is a gargoyle. Dorian tells people he's shy of being seen because of a deformity. But in truth, he was carved in limestone for Notre Dame Cathedral in Paris. That was, of course, before he was accidentally brought to life through alchemy.

The sight of Dorian's wings flapping still startled Max, but I'd say that for a man who'd reached his forties without knowing alchemy was more than a child's fantasy, he was handling the truth about me and Dorian remarkably well.

Max isn't a gargoyle. Or an alchemist. He's sexy, smart, and has exquisite taste in tea. He's a magnificent man all around. I still can't quite believe my luck that he loves me as passionately as I love him.

I'm Zoe Faust. Alchemist, herbalist, and small business owner of Elixir, an online antique shop. I used to run Elixir out of my Airstream trailer, and it's now based in the attic of this fixer-upper in Portland, Oregon's Hawthorne neighborhood that I bought almost two years ago. Even though I'm an alchemist, that doesn't mean I excel at making gold. I'm a plant alchemist, which is great for creating healing tinctures, but not so great for buying a house without a hole in its roof.

I discovered the Elixir of Life in 1704, when I was twenty-eight. Young, for an alchemical discovery, but I was obsessed with saving the life of my younger brother after he'd fallen ill. Desperate to believe my own efforts could save Thomas, I ignored the advice of my mentor who told me the unvarnished truth that I couldn't transfer the Elixir to someone else. Only dangerous backward alchemy could transfer the energy of life to another, but at a cost far too great. The corrupted form of alchemy involved dangerous shortcuts that took the energy of others instead of using their own purity of intent.

Max shook his head, but he was grinning at me as he did so. "You didn't warn me that Dorian was a chess master or that he would insist on the rules of a chess competition."

Dorian wriggled his horns. "I did not create the rules, *monsieur* Liu. If you lift a piece, it means you have selected—"

"I'm the arbiter," I cut in. "You two are having a cup of tea and breakfast muffins in my attic, so my rules. Until a player sets a piece down in a new square, they can change their mind. Fair?"

"It is my attic as well," Dorian grumbled, "and I baked the carrot muffins." But after an audible sigh and a glance at the chessboard they'd been sitting in front of for half an hour, he gave Max a congenial nod.

Before they could decide what to disagree about next, the landline phone rang. I picked up the hefty black receiver of the antique phone in the attic.

"Good. You're still home."

The voice was that of my mentor, Nicolas Flamel. The man who bought the *Brother and Sister* painting for me. You might have heard of him, though I promise you he's nothing like historical references would have you believe. It's true that he's forgetful when it comes to shaving, but he's never had a long, bushy beard like the dowdy man in the most famous illustration of Nicolas Flamel in recorded history— which, I might add, someone sketched a century after he first faked his death.

"I'll be on my way in a few minutes," I answered. Nicolas and his wife Perenelle were expecting me to stop by with some marigolds harvested from my garden for Perenelle to turn into a natural dye, but I wanted to see how the chess game played out. Max and Dorian needed to wrap up shortly, since Max had to get to his shop, The Alchemy of Tea.

"I'm calling," said Nicolas, "so you *don't* leave."

"If you slept in and haven't eaten," I said, "I have plenty of extra carrot muffins I can bring—"

"No!" He uttered the word so forcefully that I was sure Max and Dorian would hear it.

Dorian's black eyes widened. He jumped up and scampered to my side, where he grabbed the receiver from me with his clawed, gray hand.

"You do me a disservice," Dorian huffed. "If you do not appreciate my muffin recipe, which I do believe is one of my finest creations, you have had ample opportunity to mention it."

I snatched the receiver back. "What's going on?"

"I fear it's best we do not communicate for a while."

I stared at the phone. "I'm coming over."

Nicolas sighed. "Perenelle was right that you'd insist. In that case, I only ask one small favor of you. Whatever you do, *make sure you aren't followed.*"

Of all the things I thought he might say, that wasn't one of them. I grabbed my silver raincoat and headed out the door.

Buy it now!

BOOKS BY GIGI PANDIAN

The Accidental Alchemist Mysteries

The Accidental Alchemist (Book 1)

The Masquerading Magician (Book 2)

The Elusive Elixir (Book 3)

The Alchemist's Illusion (Book 4)

The Lost Gargoyle of Paris (Book 4.5, a novella)

The Alchemist of Fire and Fortune (Book 5)

The Alchemist of Riddle and Ruin (Book 6)

The Alchemist of Monsters and Mayhem (Book 7)

The Alchemist of Brushstrokes and Brimstone (Book 8)

Jaya Jones Treasure Hunt Mysteries

Artifact (Book 1)

Pirate Vishnu (Book 2)

Quicksand (Book 3)

Michelangelo's Ghost (Book 4)

The Ninja's Illusion (Book 5)

The Glass Thief (Book 6)

The Cambodian Curse & Other Stories (Locked Room Mystery Collection)

The Secret Staircase Mysteries

Under Lock & Skeleton Key (Book 1)

The Raven Thief (Book 2)

A Midnight Puzzle (Book 3)

The Library Game (Book 4) - coming in March 2025

NEW SERIES FROM GIGI: THE SECRET STAIRCASE MYSTERIES

An ode to classic locked-room mysteries, this series blends traditional and cozy, with a dash of romance and gothic undertones: *Impossible crimes. A family legacy. The intrigue of hidden rooms and secret staircases.* **Learn more at www.gigipandian.com.**

Under Lock & Skeleton Key (Book 1)
The Raven Thief (Book 2)
A Midnight Puzzle (Book 3)
The Library Game (Book 4) - coming in March 2025

PRAISE FOR THE SECRET STAIRCASE MYSTERIES

"Wildly entertaining." —*The New York Times Book Review*

"An enchanting new series . . . **a must-read**." —Deanna Raybourn

"Pandian is **this generation's queen of the locked-room mystery!** A whimsical confection." —Naomi Hirahara

"Excellent... a fresh and magical locked-room mystery filled with fascinating and likable characters, incredible settings, and Tempest's grandfather's home-cooked Indian meals." —*Library Journal*

"Pandian is in top form in this thoroughly enjoyable series launch. . . Lovers of traditional mysteries with quirky characters will be well rewarded." —*Publishers Weekly* (starred review)

ABOUT THE AUTHOR

Gigi Pandian is a *USA Today* bestselling and award-winning mystery author, breast cancer survivor, and accidental almost-vegan. The child of cultural anthropologists from New Mexico and the southern tip of India, she spent her childhood traveling around the world on their research trips. She now lives in the San Francisco Bay Area with her husband and a gargoyle who watches over the backyard vegetable garden. A cancer diagnosis in her thirties taught her that life's too short to waste a single moment, so she's having fun writing quirky novels and cooking recipes from around the world. Her debut novel, *Artifact*, was awarded the Malice Domestic Grant, and she's won Anthony, Agatha, Lefty, and Derringer awards, and was a finalist for the Edgar Award. Her books include the Accidental Alchemist Mysteries, the Jaya Jones Treasure Hunt Mysteries, and the Secret Staircase Mysteries. Read more and sign up for Gigi's email news-letter at www.gigipandian.com.

bookbub.com/profile/gigi-pandian

facebook.com/GigiPandian

instagram.com/GigiPandian